The Crawfords
Series

MORE THAN A Rogue

SOPHIE BARNES

Cover Design and Interior Format

© **KILLION**
THE
GROUP INC.

ALSO BY SOPHIE BARNES

NOVELS
More Than A Rogue
The Infamous Duchess
No Ordinary Duke
The Illegitimate Duke
The Girl Who Stepped Into The Past
The Duke of Her Desire
Christmas at Thorncliff Manor
A Most Unlikely Duke
His Scandalous Kiss
The Earl's Complete Surrender
Lady Sarah's Sinful Desires
The Danger in Tempting an Earl
The Scandal in Kissing an Heir
The Trouble with Being a Duke
The Secret Life of Lady Lucinda
There's Something About Lady Mary
Lady Alexandra's Excellent Adventure
How Miss Rutherford Got Her Groove Back

NOVELLAS
When Love Leads To Scandal
Miss Compton's Christmas Romance
The Duke Who Came To Town
The Earl Who Loved Her
The Governess Who Captured His Heart
Mistletoe Magic
(from Five Golden Rings: A Christmas Collection)

CHAPTER ONE

CAMBERLY HOUSE WAS FILLED TO capacity with guests who'd come to attend the first ball of the Season, their boisterous chatter akin to the twittering of birds. The downstairs rooms had been opened up to facilitate movement between them and to let the air circulate. Only the library and the Duke of Camberly's study had been closed off for the evening. Emily had found the doors securely locked when she'd checked, which was why she'd chosen to escape the stuffy ballroom and her overbearing mother by seeking refuge in the parlor.

It wasn't ideal, but she could at least have a seat on the sofa and rest her feet for a moment. A wistful smile tugged at her lips. During the six years she'd spent tucked away in the countryside with her friends, Lady Cassandra Moore and Mary Clemens, who was now the Duchess of Camberly, she'd never believed she would ever return to Society. And certainly not like this, with no short supply of gentlemen eager to dance with her.

There was no question in her mind that her altered appearance was to blame for her new-found popularity, a superficiality that seemed more important than her age at this point. At six and twenty, she knew she was not the young debutante most gentlemen would consider when seeking a bride. Clearly, the only thing that held their interest was her transformation from a podgy girl whose mother had always insisted on an over-abundance of frills and lace in bright shades of orange and yellow, to a woman with curves in just the right places.

"There you are," Cassandra said as she entered the room and came to sit beside Emily. She'd brought Mary with her, and she claimed the arm-chair adjacent to the sofa.

"I just need a brief reprieve," Emily said.

"You're not the only one," Mary told her as she flopped back most inelegantly against her chair. Emily knew Mary had never wanted to be a duchess, but when she'd fallen in love with Caleb Crawford, she'd had to accept the position in order to marry him. "Had I been able to avoid this circus I would have, but Caleb's mother has been so eager to entertain, and well…she is a lovely woman and now that a year has passed since her husband and oldest son died, I could not deny her the pleasure of bringing Camberly House back to life."

"You are a good daughter-in-law," Emily said, "and you must not misunderstand me. I am glad to be here this evening, though I do wish my mother would stop chasing me around the room and inquiring about every man I happen to speak with."

Cassandra smirked. "She probably sees a new opportunity to get you settled."

"Which is understandable," Mary said with a

mischievous smile. "You've managed to take attention away from some very unhappy young ladies."

Emily sighed. "I had forgotten how tiring her eagerness can be. She is once again pushing me toward a goal I have no hope of achieving." She glanced at each of her friends. "These men might like what they see when they glance my way, but they will not court a spinster whose dowry has been redistributed to her sister."

Mary frowned. "You always claimed you had no interest in courtship and yet—"

"So did you," Cassandra murmured.

"Well, yes, but then I met Caleb and all of that changed." Mary's eyes took on the faraway look of complete contentment that filled her gaze when she thought of her husband.

"It is not so much the courtship I care about," Emily confided. "It is the romance."

"The romance?" both her friends asked in wonder.

Emily drew a deep breath. "I don't even know what it's like to be kissed by a man."

Cassandra and Mary both stared at her for a long drawn-out moment. Then Cassandra said, "We should try to find a way in which to change that."

The statement and what it suggested would have been shocking if it had been uttered by anyone else. But this was Cassandra, a woman who'd loved her fiancé so much she'd chosen to bed him before their wedding. But then he'd died on the way to the church in a terrible carriage accident, leaving Cassandra heartbroken, pregnant, and ruined. She'd left London almost immediately, assisted by her brother, Viscount Aldridge, who'd set her up in a large country house named Clearview. Mary and Emily had eventually joined her, and together they'd found a new purpose by offering orphaned children a home filled with love and happiness. "How?" Emily asked. "By luring some poor unsuspecting man into a dark corner?" She shook her head. "I've no desire to trap anyone."

Mary's lips twisted in thought. "Perhaps there's a man out there," she nodded in the direction of the ballroom, "who's willing to oblige without having to be lured."

"What if we start by considering the men you would like to share the experience with," Cassandra suggested as if they were simply speaking of trying an ice for the very first time. "There must be someone to whom you are drawn?"

Emily pretended to consider, even though Cass was right. There was one particular gentleman who made her heart flutter — a man she dreamed of in those quiet moments before sleep claimed her. She just didn't want to share the fact with anyone, for she feared that if she kissed *him*, she might never recover once he left England. And he *would* leave. She'd heard him discussing the matter with his family and friends. Indeed, she recalled him saying quite clearly that nothing would keep him from returning to Vienna as soon as possible.

Determined to keep her secret close to her heart, Emily shook her head. "Even if there were, if someone caught me kissing a man to whom I am unattached, Laura's chance of finding a husband would be even more ruined than it already is," she said in reference to her youngest sister who'd made her debut the previous year. It pained Emily more than anything, knowing that her hasty choice to leave home in the wake of her broken attachment to Lord Langdon remained a blemish on Laura's reputation. No respectable gentleman would consider marrying a woman whose sister was rumored to live in sin, no matter her sizeable dowry. The risk of scandal was simply too great. "If anything, it will only make things worse."

"So then we will simply have to ensure that you're not discovered," Mary said.

Emily gaped at her friend. "Are we really having this conversation, or have I taken a hit to the head?"

Both women stared back at her, unblinking.

"This is a serious matter," Cassandra eventually said. "It is important for us to discuss it and to take every option into consideration. Or would you rather go to your grave without ever knowing what it's like to be kissed?"

"My intention to perish from this earth is far from imminent," Emily grumbled. "I daresay I have a few decades in which to accomplish the feat."

Mary looked at her as if she'd just said that she meant to go off and join the circus. "Better sooner rather than later," she told Emily dryly. "The older you get, the more difficult it will be to find a man who's willing to accommodate you."

"She's right," Cassandra said gravely. "But I understand the concern you have for your sister's wellbeing."

"We both do," Mary added. "Which is why this kissing business would likely be best accomplished somewhere else. Away from London society."

"Like at Clearview..." Cassandra let the idea hang in the air.

Emily snorted. "The trouble with that suggestion is having an agreeable gentleman stop by and offer his...ahem...services."

Mary's eyes sparkled. "Caleb did."

Emily and Cassandra were forced to smother their laughter when other guests entered the room at that moment. The newcomers glanced their way briefly before claiming the seating arrangement in the opposite corner.

"Yes, but what are the chances of that ever happening again?" Emily whispered. She shook her head. "I know you're both trying to help and I thank you for it." Their willingness to facilitate an illicit kiss between her and some unknown man for the sole purpose of satisfying her curiosity meant the world to her.

"Perhaps we should put an advertisement in the paper for a new caretaker," Cassandra suggested.

Emily turned to her. "You're terrible."

Cassandra shrugged. "I'm merely looking out for your best interests."

"And who knows," Mary said, "he might just turn out to be a duke in disguise."

Emily met Mary's gaze. "Only one of us could be so lucky." She smiled. "Thank you. Both of you. But I'm actually not sure I'd like my first and possibly only kiss to be with a man whose been procured for that purpose alone."

"Well, if you change your mind," Cassandra said, "you must let us know."

Emily promised to do so even though she knew

that would never happen. If she kissed a man, she wanted it to happen naturally and because he wanted to kiss her as much as she wanted to kiss him.

This certainty grew when she returned to the ballroom and cast her gaze on the dancers. The cotillion reminded her of Lord Langdon, the man she'd once believed she would marry. He'd courted her for nearly a month, had made her feel special and wanted in spite of her less-than-perfect figure. Until he'd called things off by announcing his engagement to Lady Victoria Hewitt.

She'd never figured out exactly what happened, except that her mother, Georgina, was somehow to blame for Langdon's change of mind. There could be no doubt since it had occurred immediately after Georgina had gone to 'discuss a few things' with him. And then, as if that hadn't been bad enough, her mother had made a spectacle of herself later by confronting Langdon openly at the Dawset Ball, immediately after he'd announced his betrothal. This, coupled with the mocking comments other young ladies her age had made at the time about Emily not being good enough for Langdon anyway, had compounded her shame.

Emily had left London the very next day, unable to bear the humiliation or the pain. And as the days had turned into weeks, months, and eventually years, returning to London had become increasingly impossible. More so because of the happiness she'd found at Clearview. There, she could be herself without the fear of censure and without always worrying about the opinion of others. There, she'd found the true friendships she'd always lacked in London.

Now, watching the dancing couples twirling about with smiles on their faces, she supposed Langdon must have realized that she wasn't countess material and that marrying the daughter of a tradesman would not have been wise in the end, even if he did desire the dowry her father had bestowed upon her. Emily's heart still ached, though not because of any lingering affection toward Langdon but because he was proof of how naïve she'd once been. To think that she'd thought he'd actually liked her for herself. It seemed so silly now, in retrospect.

"I wonder if there is still room on your dance card," a low voice spoke at her right shoulder.

Emily glanced up to see one of Camberly's friends, Mr. Bale, regarding her with expectation. "I'm afraid not," she told him since she had no further desire to dance. And then, seeing disappointment in his eyes, she hastened to say, "But some fresh air would be most appreciated."

His face lit up. "Allow me to escort you outside."

She accepted the arm he offered and the welcome distraction from the shattered hopes and dreams of her past. Mr. Bale was a handsome man and quite unattached. If he wanted to keep her company, she would not say no.

Griffin Nathaniel Finnegan Crawford stood in one corner of the crowded ballroom, conversing with his brother, Caleb, and Caleb's friend, Viscount Aldridge.

"I cannot wait for this Season to be over so Mary and I can return to Montvale," Caleb said. The couple had decided to build a cottage for themselves on the Montvale grounds so they could enjoy a simple life while away in the country. The manor itself would be turned into an orphanage so Mary could continue caring for children in need.

"It has only just begun," Griffin remarked. Contrary to his brother, he missed the busy city life whenever he was away from it. He missed Vienna, with its culture and music and picturesque streets. By comparison, London felt like a grimy slum.

"And it will only get busier once parliament is in full swing," Aldridge said.

"Don't remind me." Caleb crossed his arms. He glanced at Griffin. "At least Devlin had the foresight to escape while he could."

Devlin was the third brother, born only five minutes after Griffin. All three were identical in appearance save for a few slight differences between them. But Caleb was the oldest, so he'd been the one burdened with the dukedom when their father and older brother had died. It was a responsibility Griffin didn't envy, though he admired Caleb's effort to find a balance between his duty and a less demanding existence. Mary's love and support had undoubtedly helped.

"I plan to do so as well," Griffin said. "I've already been away from my place of business longer than I ever intended." Years ago, when he'd first left England after arguing with their father about not wanting to join the army, he'd gone to Germany where a chance encounter with a man in a tavern had put him in touch with a clock-maker named Herr Fritz.

Intrigued by Herr Fritz's craftsmanship, Griffin had inquired about a position and had quickly become the man's apprentice. Seven years later, when Herr Fritz had retired, Griffin had travelled to Vienna where he'd opened his own shop, selling not only clocks but mechanical toys to the marvel of all his customers.

"Who's managing it right now while you're here?" Aldridge asked.

"My assistant, Edvard Dreyden." He was a serious and hard-working young man whom Griffin trusted to run things until he returned. But Griffin had to acknowledge that his extended stay in England was pushing the limit of how long he could afford to be absent. In Edvard's most recent letter, he'd informed Griffin that the archduchess Marie Anne wished to place a special order, though only if Griffin himself was available to carry it out.

"If only you could relocate here," Caleb said. "I've enjoyed your company immensely and will be sorry to see you go."

"Yes, but you have a home to build now, a wife to take care of, and a child on the way." Griffin snatched a glass of champagne from a passing tray and took a quick sip. "You'll hardly notice I'm gone."

"And you can come back to visit," Aldridge pointed out.

"Or you could all come to Vienna," Griffin suggested while glancing across the room.

A flash of blue caught his eye, and he followed

the movement until a familiar face appeared from behind a cluster of guests. It was Miss Emily Howard, a close friend of Mary's. Griffin had met her a few times already, most notably at Clearview when he'd gone in search of his brother back in November. She'd stolen his breath once she'd opened the door to admit him, for he had not been expecting to find the most beautiful woman in the world when Aldridge had told him where Caleb had gone.

He narrowed his gaze as she exited onto the terrace, escorted by Mr. Bale, who grinned in response to something she said. An uncomfortable squeezing sensation beneath his ribs had him straightening his posture. He didn't like the way Mr. Bale's eyes gleamed with the prospect of something illicit.

"If you'll excuse me one moment," Griffin told his brother and Aldridge. "There's someone with whom I must speak." Mr. Bale had always struck him as an amicable fellow. Harmless, by all accounts. But appearances could be deceiving. He'd learned that by falling victim himself to the cruelest form of trickery. Setting his glass on a table as he went, Griffin wove his way through the crowd. By the time he reached the door to the terrace and stepped outside, neither Miss Howard nor Mr. Bale was anywhere to be found. Griffin's stomach tightened. Surely she would have more sense than to wander off with a bachelor? He glanced around, uncertain of where to look for her first. Voices emerged from the left, so he followed, heading straight for the corner where a cherry tree offered a canopy to the bench that stood beneath it.

The voices grew louder, though they could only be described as whispers. And although Griffin could not discern what was being said, he knew everything he needed to know the moment he saw Miss Howard in Mr. Bale's arms, his face moving closer to hers until...

"What do you think you're doing?" Griffin asked in his most authoritative voice.

Mr. Bale leapt away from Miss Howard and spun toward Griffin. His eyes were as wide as his mouth. "I, um...I...that is..." he sputtered.

Miss Howard's hands fisted and Griffin saw she was glaring at him with extreme displeasure. "I think it's perfectly obvious," she told him.

Mr. Bale cleared his throat. "Miss Howard and I—"

"Are not affianced, as far as I know," Griffin murmured. He could not explain why the possibility they might be grated as much as it did, but there was something about Miss Howard... something that tempted him beyond reason. He cleared his throat. "If that situation has recently changed, then I sincerely apologize for the intrusion."

Mr. Bale stared at him. He then glanced at Miss Howard, who sighed as if she had no doubt of how he would answer. "It has not." There was a pause, and then, "I was just—"

"Leaving," Griffin bit out.

Mr. Bale stared back at him for a brief moment as if considering whether or not it was wise to argue. *Don't.* As if hearing him, Mr. Bale turned and gave Miss Howard a curt bow. "Forgive me."

He strode off with an apologetic glance at Griffin.

"I've a good mind to hit you right now," Miss Howard announced as soon as they were alone. "You were horribly rude to Mr. Bale, who was merely trying to be helpful'."

"Helpful?" *Ha!* "He was certainly trying to help himself to something, I'll grant you that. And you were not protesting." He considered the sharp look in her eyes and the way her jaw tightened in response to his words. For some inexplicable reason he needed to know what her intention had been, so he took a step closer and gazed down into her upturned face. "Were you?"

"Of course not." She averted her gaze, and he imagined that if it hadn't been dark, he would have seen her blush.

Still, her blasé response shocked him. "Of course not," he repeated in a low murmur.

She sighed. "Mr. Bale and I are friends. Nothing more."

The relief he experienced in response to that statement caught him completely off guard. He had no romantic interest in Miss Howard himself. To suppose such a thing would suggest he was open to marriage. Which he wasn't. Not anymore. Not after Clara had broken his heart.

The keen humiliation he felt whenever he thought back on how she had fooled him still smarted. He fought the urge to tug on his cravat as the air in his lungs grew hot, and forced his attention back to Miss Howard. A dalliance with his sister-in-law's friend could only lead to the altar, and that was a destination he meant to avoid at all cost.

He tried to keep his voice steady so he wouldn't sound too accusatory. "And yet I caught you embracing him as if you meant to—"

"My earring is caught."

Griffin stared back at her, confused. "What?"

She turned the left side of her head toward him and raised her hand to point at the strands of hair tangled in a dangling collection of diamonds. "Mr. Bale noticed and offered to put me to rights."

"But…" Griffin's thought process stumbled as he considered her words. He'd seen her standing inappropriately close to Mr. Bale, so he'd made an assumption. But it was also dark. So dark, in fact, he could not discern her features very clearly. Which meant it was possible he'd imagined something that had not been there.

He inhaled deeply and accepted that he had been wrong. "I'm sorry." His gaze slid to the asymmetrical mess at the side of her head. "If you will permit, I would be happy to offer my assistance. 'Tis the least I can do at this point."

She shook her head. "Thank you, but it would probably be best if I returned inside before someone else mistakes *your* assistance for something it isn't."

She stepped around him, moving so close he managed to catch a hint of the sweetest perfume. Honeysuckle perhaps? Or peonies? He wasn't quite sure, but there was no mistaking the heady effect it had on him or how it beckoned for him to pull her close and press his nose to her skin.

He quashed that foolish idea as immediately as it had formed.

"I shall ask Mama or Laura for help," she said as

she started strolling away.

He followed behind while wondering how he could make her stay. Which was silly since there was no point in furthering their acquaintance when he would depart for Vienna soon. Nothing good could come of it. If anything, the longer they stayed out here together alone, the greater the risk of others imagining they'd had an assignation. But he found he regretted their rendezvous ending so quickly. And with him having ruined what would probably have been an enjoyable walk for her and Mr. Bale.

"Can you forgive me for thinking the worst?" he asked.

She drew to a halt and turned to him, her face more visible now that they were nearer the light from the terrace. A polite smile captured her lips. "Of course. It was an understandable mistake."

"You're not upset?"

"No."

He registered the mistruth because of how bluntly it was delivered. "Are you sure?" She'd always seemed honest and forthright, so it bothered him that he'd somehow caused her to put up a barrier between them now. "I am not so sensitive that I can't handle a set down." Or at the very least an honest response.

Her chin rose and she crossed her arms, affecting the pose of a woman who was rapidly reaching the end of her patience. Griffin braced himself in anticipation of what she would say. Her words, however, where most unexpected. "You ought to know me well enough by now to realize that I am not the sort of woman who would ever invite a man to ravish her at a social event where anyone might happen to see." Her eyes were almost black, shimmering fiercely in the moonlight. "The fact that you did so is a testament to your opinion of me, which is frighteningly low."

"I did not think you'd let Mr. Bale go quite so far as to ravish you, Miss Howard." And now that she'd put that picture in his head, he was having a damned hard time dislodging it again. Which added a terse element to his voice that she did not deserve.

She marched forward, closing the distance between them "Nor would I throw away a kiss so easily, without a thought or a care in the world."

Griffin did his best to come to terms with her statement. There was something in what she had said. Something meaningful just beyond his grasp. "I take it the men you have kissed in the past were important to you, then?"

A sudden dislike for these men swept through him, and his desire to learn their names and discover who he would have to avoid in the future was particularly unsettling.

She stared back at him for a long, hard second and eventually snorted. "No such man exists, Lord Griffin, which is rather the point, don't you think?" Spinning about, she started toward the terrace once more. Griffin blinked, the relief easing the tension within so soothing, it took him a second to respond. He hastened after her without even thinking and grabbed her wrist before she reached the stairs. She turned, eyes wide with surprise and wonder.

"Kisses are overrated," he murmured, his voice almost breathless. What was it about her that made him so desperate to keep her out here with him and away from the ballroom? He did not know and wasn't even sure it mattered. But the fact that she'd never been kissed...*that* was important. And yet, the only thing he could think to say, most likely in an effort to make her feel better, was, "You have not missed much."

A soft little scoff conveyed her derision. "What a comforting sentiment from someone who's likely enjoyed the experience a dozen times by now."

Griffin raised an eyebrow and watched her surprise sink deeper. "Two dozen times?" His lips quirked. "Three dozen?"

"I believe the number's so high it would take you a while to reach it at this rate," he muttered.

She rolled her eyes. "Oh, for heaven's sake." Her gaze found his and he was surprised to find humor there. "I suppose you're just as roguish as all the ladies claim then?"

He knit his brow. "I was not aware such a rumor existed."

"I'm sure it arose because of your scar," she said as if this was so evident that his not knowing it surprised her.

"My scar," Griffin echoed flatly. He'd allowed himself to forget about that while they'd been talking, to forget the way it slashed his left cheek in an ugly red line. It was thick and uneven, puckering his skin in a way that was most unappealing.

"There are those who find such things attractive."

What about you? he wanted to ask.

He dropped his gaze to her lips and wondered if she would retreat if he made an advance. "We should probably go back inside." Anything else would be a mistake. He meant to return to Vienna, to live a peaceful life there without the complications of marriage. The last thing he needed was to kiss Miss Emily Howard out in the open where anyone might see.

And yet, Griffin desperately wanted to chase away all the anger and pain her comment had stirred by distracting himself in the simplest way possible. *She wants her first kiss to matter. You cannot take that from her.* But when she licked her lips and whispered, "Yes," his restraint took off like an army fleeing a battle. Because the truth was he'd wanted to kiss her since the first time he'd seen her at Clearview. So he did the only reasonable thing he could do when she was standing right there, stunning and utterly tempting.

He leaned in closer and pressed his mouth to hers.

Emily couldn't move, most likely because she was in a bizarre state of shock and dismay. Lord Griffin's lips were pressed against hers in a soft and perfect caress. She wasn't sure why he was doing it. After all, they'd been discussing his scar. Finding a logical transition between that and kissing was something of a challenge at the moment.

A distant warning bell echoed in her head, but she was too caught up in this new experience to heed it.

Especially since this was the man she'd dreamed of kissing since he'd walked into Clearview House with a hint of mischief in his eyes and a bit of a crooked smile. She'd liked him right from the start and had never felt that his scar detracted from his handsome features. If anything, she'd always thought it added an appealing element of danger to his overall appearance.

Beware.

Of what, she could not recall. What reason could there possibly be to end this glorious moment?

She inhaled through her nose, acknowledging a spicy scent of sandalwood, bergamot, and a hint of cloves. He smelled incredible. And now his arm was around her, his hand pressing into her back, and Emily could no longer think of anything at all. Except perhaps to consider the problem this business of kissing posed on breathing. That part of the whole experience was rather awkward and prevented her from enjoying the feel of him as much as she would have liked.

Perhaps if—

A squeal pierced the air, and before Emily could fully realize where the sound had come from, she heard a distinct voice say, "Oh, how wonderful! You are finally to be married!"

A breeze swept across Emily's shoulders, and she opened her eyes as if from a dream. She saw Lord Griffin, but he wasn't looking at her with the same kind of pleasure she'd felt in each cell of her body just seconds before. Instead he was staring to the side, his brow furrowed in a deep frown of pure irritation.

Emily turned and it was as if the world started

to fold itself in on her, for there stood her mother, her sister, and her Aunt Julia, the Baroness of Hoff. All stared at her and Lord Griffin in a way that made Emily feel like she'd just walked into a cage and they'd locked the gate behind her. She glanced at Lord Griffin again and saw that he was about to speak, which prompted her to pull away from him quickly and walk toward the three women. Because the last thing she wanted was for him to confirm or deny anything. Doing so would either involve him sacrificing his future for her or breaking her heart.

"Lord Griffin has not proposed," Emily said, "nor should he feel compelled to do so because of a mere kiss." She glanced over her shoulder and saw that he was frowning more than before, if such a thing were possible.

"A mere kiss?" her mother squeaked while Laura and Aunt Julia raised their eyebrows into four pointy arches. "You were embracing and…" She waved her hands as if to form an image of what she had witnessed.

Emily tried to stay calm even though she knew the situation was spiraling out of control. It had in fact been doing so since Lord Griffin's lips had touched hers. "I am not a debutante," she began. "And besides, Lord Griffin was merely doing me the courtesy of sating my curiosity."

The gentleman in question snorted from somewhere behind her right shoulder while Emily's mother gasped as if this were more outrageous than the actual kiss itself. Which it might well have been.

But then her mother stepped forward to hiss in

Emily's ear. "You must accept his offer of marriage if he asks. What happened here could ruin your sister's prospects."

And there it was. The warning she had ignored in pursuit of her own selfishness.

"There is no need for anyone else to discover what transpired here." Emily's voice shook when she spoke to her aunt and her sister next. "Can I count on you to keep this incident to yourselves?"

Laura responded with an immediate nod, but Aunt Julia hesitated. "I am not sure that would be the best course," she eventually said, causing panic to wrap its way firmly around Emily's limbs. It tightened until she could scarcely breathe.

"Please." God help her, she could feel tears starting to prick at her eyes. How could she have been so thoughtless? So foolish?

"Lord Griffin has compromised you, my dear," Aunt Julia said without any hint of sympathy whatsoever. "Marrying him does seem like the best course of action."

"I would be honored to offer for Miss Howard's hand," Lord Griffin said bleakly. Judging from his tone he might as well have been saying he'd fall on his own sword in order to save her.

And just like that, Emily's heart shattered, destroying the illusion the kiss had somehow managed to create, of him wanting her just as much as she wanted him.

"If you do, I shall refuse," she said, forcing the words past the knot in her throat. Somehow, she managed to stand still even though her legs shook beneath her silk gown. Before he could say anything further, Emily told her aunt plainly, "Keep this between us and I shall retreat to Clearview forever."

Aunt Julia raised her chin a notch. She'd always been the one who disapproved most of Emily's broken engagement, convinced that all blame lay on her shoulders. Since Emily's return to London, she'd made it clear that she viewed her as a blemish on the family that would be better off tucked away in obscurity.

"Marrying a duke's brother could perhaps restore your reputation," Aunt Julia answered slowly.

Emily's heart beat fast. "No. I will not wreck Lord Griffin's life over this." A smile tugged at Aunt Julia's lips, and for the first time in her life, Emily imagined there might be a hint of respect in her eyes. It bolstered her courage and made her path clear. She turned to her mother. "I shall leave at once."

Georgina's eyes widened. "Emily, you cannot—"

But Emily no longer wanted to listen. She only wished to escape Society's foolish rules and her own stupidity. Returning to London had been a mistake. She ought to have stayed away.

"Miss Howard. Please wait."

Lord Griffin was on her heels, but Emily wouldn't have it. Quickening her pace, Emily entered the ballroom and hastened through it. On her way, her gaze collided with Mr. Bale's. He moved toward her as if intent on assisting her somehow. She shook her head, signaling for him to refrain as she hurried toward the foyer.

Mary entered the hallway from the music room,

took one look at her, and frowned. "Are you all right?"

"Not exactly," Emily said with a swift glance toward the ballroom. Lord Griffin was there, making his way through the crowd, still determined to catch her. She gave her friend a quick hug. "I am returning to Clearview."

"But—"

"I don't have time to explain." Pulling away from Mary, Emily hurried out into the street. She could not delay any longer. Not if she was to avoid arguing with Lord Griffin over a matter that she refused to concede to. So she ran toward a parked hackney and ordered the driver to take her to the nearest coaching inn. Hopefully the coins in her reticule would be enough to pay for a ticket.

CHAPTER TWO

"**D**ID SHE TELL YOU WHAT happened?" Griffin asked Mary when he finally reached the front door, through which Emily had made her escape moments earlier. If a few startled guests would only have refrained from stepping into his path for a better look at the runaway lady, he would have stopped her by now.

"No."

Griffin stared down at his sister-in-law. His nerves were tightly strung, his muscles tense not only because of the drama that had begun to unfold as soon as he and Miss Howard had been discovered but because of the kiss.

Christ, they'd scarcely gotten started – he'd only just managed to gauge the shape and feel of her lips when they'd been interrupted, but it was enough to compel him to chase her wherever she went. Because damn it all, he wanted more.

"You should not have let her leave." His voice was clipped, hovering somewhere between anger and fear.

Mary met his gaze with defiance, informing him that she would not be put out by his tone. "She's not a child, but a woman accustomed to living her life on her own terms. If you think for one second I might have been able to stop her, you're wrong." She straightened her spine, growing in height by at least half an inch. The edge of her mouth lifted and then she said, "But perhaps *you* should try?"

"I intend to do precisely that," Griffin said, leaving without even bothering to collect his hat. He'd manage without it. Wouldn't be the first time he'd done so. Right now, speed was more important than fashion. He had to find Miss Howard before she left London and...and what? Returned to the quiet life she enjoyed at Clearview?

A moment's hesitation assailed him as doubt crept in. He'd kissed her because he'd needed to push away all the uncertainty, anger, and pain he'd felt when she'd mentioned his scar. He'd needed *her* to make him feel something else. So he'd surrendered to the temptation more easily than he should have only to find himself drugged by her sweet perfume. And then there had been her body, so soft and tempting and...

He shook his head and quickened his pace. If she was going to Clearview then so was he. For her protection, of course. Letting her travel alone would be ungentlemanly. And besides, he had things to say, things that *had* to be said if he was going to avoid Caleb's wrath and their mother's censure. Even if proposing marriage did not fit well with his plans and the lady seemed reluctant to even consider such an outcome, he would do it. Because that was the honorable thing.

So he found a free hackney and asked the driver to take him to the nearest coaching inn. He'd search them all if he had to, but he wasn't about to let Miss Howard spend the night in one alone while dressed in fine silk. She'd be a target for certain – the notion tightened his chest and quickened his pulse. If anything bad were to happen to her, he'd never forgive himself.

This thought increased when he failed to find her at the first inn they stopped at or at the second. It was now an hour since he'd quit the Camberly ball and... what if Emily had changed her mind? Perhaps she'd gone to her parents' instead? Unsettled by his own increasing uncertainty, he decided to check one more inn and then set a course for the Howard residence. It was one o'clock in the morning, which meant there were still a few hours before the first carriage departed along the West Road. And if push came to shove, he'd collect his horse and ride to the first posting inn on the route and pray that he found her before any danger befell her.

But luck was on his side, it would seem, for when he strode into The Swan With Two Necks, he found her in the taproom, sitting at a table with a couple of rough looking fellows whose leering smiles said all Griffin needed to know. He strode forward, grabbed the nearest one by the back of his jacket collar, and hauled him out of his seat. The other man stood, fists clenched and ready to fight.

Griffin turned his scarred cheek toward him and sneered. "I suggest you take yourself and your friend away from this lady before I ruin your evening."

"I don't think so," said the man whom Griffin

had just released with a shove.

"It's two against one," said the second. "I think we can take a toff like you without too much trouble."

"Does that mean you're going to try?" Griffin asked. His body was already honing itself in preparation for the first blow.

"Damn right," the first man snarled.

Griffin caught a flash of movement. He heard Miss Howard gasp. Leaning sideways, he moved swiftly out of the way so the fist that came flying toward him only struck air. Pulling his arm back, he strained every muscle and pushed his fist forward, hitting his opponent squarely in the jaw. Spit flew from the man's mouth as he yelped and fell onto a bench, slumped over and seemingly unable to counterattack.

"Hey," a broad-shouldered man with red hair yelled. "I won't have you fighting in here. You'll have to take that outside."

Griffin answered with a glare, and the man, most likely the innkeeper, took a step back. "If you'd asked these scoundrels to leave when they started harassing the lady, it wouldn't have come to this."

"Watch out!"

Griffin spun back to face the first man as soon as Miss Howard warned him, allowing him to duck just in time. He caught the man's arm and used his momentum to send him stumbling toward the exit. The innkeeper nodded toward the barkeep who came to remove the men from the taproom.

"Are you all right?" Griffin asked Miss Howard as soon as some order had been restored.

She nodded but refused to meet his gaze. "Yes. Thank you. I'm glad you arrived when you did. It was silly of me to come here like this, dressed for a ball, but I...I just wished to escape as fast as possible and..." She swallowed. "You can return to Camberly House now, I should think. The—"

"Absolutely out of the question." Griffin gestured to the innkeeper and the man approached.

"My apologies, sir. It's pretty busy tonight as you can see. I didn't realize the young lady was being disturbed."

"Perhaps you've a quieter room we can use?" Griffin asked. He did not like Miss Howard's presence amidst the riffraff, for although he was now here to protect her against further harassment, it would not stop the men from ogling her.

"There's a vacant supper room in the back. Allow me to lead the way."

Griffin removed his jacket without even thinking, then offered his hand to Miss Howard. She eyed it for a second before accepting it, her fingers carefully curling over his skin in a way that caused heat to flare up inside him. She stood and he draped his jacket over her shoulders.

"Hold it shut with your free hand," he instructed.

She did not argue, for which he was grateful. Apparently she was not completely devoid of common sense, as her hasty departure from Camberly House and her rash decision to come here would have suggested. He kept her close to his side while leading her forward, past some drunken patrons and into the room the innkeeper had to offer. It contained a table and four chairs, nothing more.

Griffin reached inside his trouser pocket and

pulled out a couple of shillings. "For your troubles," he said, handing the coins to the innkeeper. "Do you have minced meat pie?" The man nodded and Griffin affected a pleased smile. "We'll have two plates of that then and a bottle of your best red wine."

The innkeeper pocketed the shillings without comment and left. Griffin closed the door. He turned to face Miss Howard, her hand still clutching the front of his jacket. "The wine will help ease your nerves," he told her.

"Yes. Thank you." She spoke as if in a daze, then blinked and removed the jacket and held it toward him.

Griffin stared. At Camberly House he'd been so distracted by Mr. Bale, and by Miss Howard's possible reason for venturing into the garden with him, he hadn't really considered what she was wearing. The gown was a vibrant shade of blue, far too bold for a debutante to wear but acceptable, he supposed, for a more mature woman considered to be firmly on the shelf.

He flexed his fingers and tried not to let his gaze linger too long on the low dip of her décolletage or on the swell of her perfect bosom. "You should keep that for now. Until you reach your destination."

Her eyes widened. "I couldn't possibly."

"I insist."

"But won't you be cold without it?"

He snorted. "Not in the least." Indeed he was hot as hell at the moment. "Certainly no more than you."

She pressed her lips together, and he could practically hear her mind trying to come up with further arguments against his effort to cover her up, but then she sighed and put the jacket back on, and Griffin breathed a sigh of relief. Her beauty alone would likely drive him mad by morning. The last thing he needed was the additional lure of her body when all he could think of right now was that they were alone, away from Society, and perfectly free to continue where they had left off earlier.

He gestured toward the chair closest to her and waited for her to sit before claiming the one opposite. A waiter arrived with their wine and swiftly departed with the assurance that their meal would be ready soon.

"About the kiss," Griffin said once they'd both had a sip of their wine and he'd spent a good minute or two determining how to best broach the subject. Eventually, he'd decided to be direct, since this would be the most efficient course. "I have no regrets," he assured her.

She met his gaze directly, refusing to shy away even as her cheeks turned a deep shade of pink. He had to admire her for that.

"Thank you."

He hadn't expected her to reciprocate the sentiment, but he realized now that he wished she had. "It would seem that you do, however, for which I am sorry."

She knit her brow as if pondering something important, and then she expelled a long sigh and sagged in her chair. "I could have stopped it from happening, but I did not do so, which means I am just as much to blame."

"And then you ran away." Somehow this was worse than if he'd proposed and she'd turned down his suit. It proved how determined she was to avoid an attachment to him. Which grated, even though it should not do so.

Why did her wanting him matter so damn much?

"If I'd stayed, my mother would have spoken to my father and then he would have had no choice but to make demands which would have led to a duel if you'd refused and—"

"I would not have refused," he told her calmly.

She clenched her jaw, her eyes lit with fierce understanding. And yet, she still mistook his meaning. "I don't want to force any man into marriage. Least of all when it is unnecessary to do so."

"Your mother may disagree with you there."

Miss Howard took another sip of her wine. "She will never accept that I won't be anyone's wife." A hint of pain in her voice caused Griffin's heart to contract. "But I lost my chance at matrimony a long time ago. No," she added when he prepared to point out that the chance she spoke of had just been presented to her, only she'd turned it down. "Being forced into matrimony for the sole purpose of placating others does not count."

"And yet you still chose to give the whole kissing business a go, even though you knew the risk." He spoke with a lighter tone than earlier, deliberately waggling his eyebrows in an effort to lighten the mood.

It worked. More or less.

Miss Howard's lips twitched. "I cannot deny it."

Griffin smiled, content with her answer and happy to see her relax.

"So how was it?" He did not ask because he wanted her to flatter his ego, but because he was genuinely curious to know her thoughts on the matter and, if he were being completely honest, to discover if it had affected her to the same degree it had affected him. With feverish awareness.

She bit her lip. "Honestly?"

He frowned but nodded in spite of his sudden apprehension.

"I don't really see what the fuss is about."

Griffin stared at her, almost missing the fact that the waiter had returned with their food and was placing each plate before them. "Will that be all for now?"

"I believe so," Miss Howard remarked. She stared back at Griffin who suddenly blinked, glanced at his plate, and then waved the waiter away. The door closed behind him.

"In other words, it wasn't as good as you thought it would be?"

Miss Howard was already cutting into her pie. She glanced at him as if considering a puzzle. "Truthfully, I expected more of a sparkle."

"A sparkle?"

"Or a fizz."

"'You're making no sense."

She popped some food in her mouth and proceeded to chew while he started cutting his own pie into tiny little pieces.

"I knew being honest would be a mistake," she murmured. "It wasn't my intention to offend you in any way, merely to inform you that the kiss we shared with each other this evening was…" She drew a sharp breath and returned her attention to her food.

"What?" Griffin asked. He'd completely obliterated his pie by now and was reaching for his wine.

"I dare not say."

"But I am asking you to," he told her in the most patient voice he could manage while this innocent woman destroyed his masculine pride.

"It wasn't unpleasant," she said as if trying to placate a child. "In fact, I do think I'd like to try it again, but considering my…er…your…"

"What?" he asked, no longer able to hide his frustration.

"Well, you're terribly handsome."

Griffin drew a deep breath, the strain on his body relaxing if only a little. She thought him handsome. Now there was a start. "And you're incredibly stunning," he murmured, since it was only fair to let her know she appealed to him as well.

"Right. I mean, thank you." She ate some more pie and drank some more wine while Griffin decided to do the same. But the silence between them was filled with words yet unspoken until she said, "I suppose that is why I expected more. Because of this mutual attraction we've shared since the moment we met."

Griffin almost choked on his food. He'd never heard a woman be so bold as to call direct attention to the obvious, no matter how awkward it threatened to make things. "Ah." Was that really all he could say right now?

Apparently.

She pursed her lips. "Considering everything Cass and Mary have said about kissing over the years, I rather expected to feel like fireworks had been set off inside me."

He gaped at her, unsure which part of that statement he ought to address first. He decided to settle on the part that bothered him most. "There is more to it than I showed you."

Her face lit up. "Well that would explain it then." She drummed her fingers slowly against the top of the table and scrunched her nose as if in thought. "Would you be willing to demonstrate?"

"Er…" Griffin's entire body responded with eager anticipation. His stomach tightened and his heart began to race. He instinctively glanced at the door and forced himself to speak the necessary words. "I don't think that would be wise."

Disappointment filled her eyes even though he could tell she tried to hide it with a smile. "Of course not. One lapse in judgment is more than enough for one evening."

He briefly considered explaining that he disagreed and that his reluctance was solely driven by his desire for more than what she was asking of him. After all, she'd said she and her friends had discussed such matters, and with Lady Cassandra's history taken into account, he was certain Miss Howard must know a thing or two about what could happen between a man and a woman. But that wasn't really the sort of discussion he wanted to have with her right at the moment, so he chose to say nothing and simply enjoy the rest of his meal.

For the first time that evening, Emily was embarrassed. After all, she'd turned him down flat when he'd offered to ask for her hand – had not even given him the chance to do his duty as a gentleman – and had then suggested they kiss some more. As if locking lips with each other was just as normal as taking a stroll through the park. "I think you ought to return to Camberly House and inform everyone that I am all right. Tell Mama and Papa that I shall write to them once I reach Clearview." They'd finished their meal and she'd come to the conclusion that she'd rather be alone than spend more time in Lord Griffin's company.

Wanting him was too painful when he did not want her in return. If he did, he would not have sounded so resigned earlier when he'd spoken of marrying her.

"Absolutely not. I'll send a note to Caleb right now, informing him that I mean to escort you on your journey. Unless I'm able to talk you out of going, which would be the preferable option."

Of course it would be. Anything to put an end to this evening's disaster and quit her company. Emily bristled. "I am not a debutante in need of constant supervision, but a woman accustomed to managing things on her own."

"As you proved most effectively half an hour ago in the taproom."

She glared at him, annoyed by the note of sarcasm in his voice. "I'm sure that was due to the way I am dressed."

He let his gaze roam over her shoulders and down across her breasts until she was tempted to block his view by pulling his jacket closed. But she didn't, because that would show weakness — a sign of defeat — and she meant to win this argument if at all possible.

"Are you planning to change into something less…alluring before you depart?" He asked the question softly, his words sliding across her skin in the most provocative way imaginable.

Emily made a stoic attempt to ignore the hot little shivers his voice evoked. She would not let him turn her into a breathless ninny when he was so calm and collected. "I've nothing else with me and before you suggest it, I will not go back to my parents' house in order to fetch my belongings before I leave."

He frowned. "Because you fear you might find them at home by now?"

She gave a quick nod and averted her gaze. "Mama can be horribly pushy, and with my sister still unwed, she will plot a way to ensure we marry after what happened earlier. Especially if I give her the chance to do so." Forcing herself to look at him, to show her strength and her resolve, she stared straight into his dark brown eyes. "And neither of us wants that. Do we?"

"No." The word was gently spoken, but that did not make it less exact. Like an arrow shot with precision, it confirmed everything she already knew. And then to underline it, he added, "Marriage is the very last thing I want, and I believe it is for you as well."

"Yes." She would not give anything away at this

point. She would not tell him that she might consider marriage if he was willing to do so, that she wouldn't mind getting to know him better during the course of a courtship, that she would welcome the excuse to kiss him some more. Instead, she told him, "I am very content with my life and the freedom I've managed to acquire by living apart from Society. The last thing I want is to lose all of that by subjecting myself to a man's will."

"I don't believe Mary considers herself a victim of Caleb's high-handedness."

"Of course not. Those two are madly in love with each other, which I do believe makes every difference."

"And you don't think such a match is possible for you?" He sounded curious, as if he was genuinely interested in figuring her out.

"No. At least not with the gentleman in question, who happens to be you, in case you'd forgotten."

He looked momentarily uncomfortable. "Right." He stood and glanced at the door. "I'm going to see about sending Caleb a note. Stay here. I won't be long."

And then he was gone, leaving Emily with the uncanny feeling that he'd been more bothered than he had let on by her last comment. Drat it all. She'd been horribly unkind, which wasn't in her nature. But her nerves had been frayed by the kiss, by her mother, aunt, and sister witnessing it, and by Lord Griffin's gentlemanly manners in the wake of it all.

The kiss had been a mistake. But it was too late for regrets now. It had happened and it had not been the marvelous experience she had hoped for. Instead, it had confirmed a huge lapse in judgment on her part, and as much as she wished to forget it, doing so would be impossible when Lord Griffin refused to leave her side.

CHAPTER THREE

THERE WAS NO LOGICAL REASON for Griffin to be put out by Miss Howard's insistence that he and she could not fall in love with each other – that *she*, more specifically, could not love *him*. But her words had speared their way through him nevertheless and caused a deep ache to form in the middle of his chest. Coupled with her low rating of their kiss, he rather felt as if he'd been kicked in the ballocks.

When he'd tried to explain that their kiss had been chaste, that he could most certainly make her feel as if fireworks were exploding all around her, she'd asked him to demonstrate, and he'd been tempted. Incredibly so. But he'd also had the clarity to acknowledge that doing so would be tremendously reckless. For while she presented herself as an unmarriageable spinster whose time for romance had passed, the fact remained that she was still young, only six and twenty years old, with the sort of beauty most men would have trouble resisting.

Marriage was possible for her, no matter how much she wished to deny it. And if the right man came along and proposed, she'd regret squandering her firsts on Griffin. Which meant he would have to keep his distance, escort her to Clearview, and leave for Vienna immediately after. This business tonight had made him realize that he'd overstayed his visit in England. It was time to leave, to put Miss Howard out of his mind and return to the life which had, until now, been both comfortable and rewarding.

So he penned a quick note to Caleb, bought a ticket for the same coach she would be taking, and returned to the room where Miss Howard waited. "There's still five hours until the carriage departs, so I've taken the liberty of acquiring a bedchamber for you upstairs. It will give you a chance to sleep for a while."

"That is…" She pressed her lips together and to his surprise her eyes conveyed a mixture of guilt and gratitude. "Thank you. After what I said to you earlier, I hardly deserve your kindness."

He stared at her, both impressed and unsettled by her ability to set pride aside and address her mistake, for it suggested he'd not quite managed to hide the effect of her insult and that she believed he needed an apology. "You've had a tumultuous evening, Miss Howard."

"That's not an excuse."

He sighed. "You spoke the truth and I respect that."

"Even so, I would like to apologize." She bit her lip and furrowed her brow. "You're perfectly nice and—"

"Apology accepted," he said, preventing her from making matters worse by pointing out all his wonderful qualities – none of which would cause her to fall in love with him. Not that he wanted her to, because he most certainly didn't. "Now about the bedchamber. Shall I show you up?"

She stood and gave him a nod. "Yes. Thank you."

He went to help her rise and saw that his jacket collar was flipped up at the back. Instinctively, he began to adjust it, his knuckles grazing the back of her neck. She shuddered slightly and moved away from his touch. "Sorry," he murmured, completely overwrought by her sudden disinterest in him when his own awareness of her only seemed to be growing.

Hell.

He was in absolute hell.

Because he'd kissed her and liked it in spite of its chasteness, and now, damn it all, he wanted more. Except she clearly didn't, even though she'd invited him to kiss her again. But that had obviously been to appease her own curiosity and not because she actually wanted him. Indeed, she hadn't seemed to care one way or the other that *he* had kissed her. For all he knew, Mr. Bale's lips would have served just as well from an educational standpoint. Which made him want to hit something. Like, Mr. Bale. Even though he knew damn well that the man did not deserve it.

Frustrated, Griffin opened the dining room door and escorted Miss Howard toward the stairs. They climbed them together until they reached the bedchamber she'd been allotted.

"Where will you be sleeping?" she asked as they paused outside her door.

"Right there." He jutted his chin toward the

room next to hers. "Lock your door, Miss Howard, and shout if you need me."

She licked her lips then, which gave an entirely different meaning to what he'd just said. Although only in his own depraved mind, he wagered. "Good night," he told her swiftly, before he did something stupid, like give her a more thorough lesson in kissing.

"Good night." She slipped inside her room before additional words could pass between them and closed the door behind her with a click.

Griffin blew out a breath. He could finally escape the charged sensations assailing his body while he was near her. His muscles, which had been strained since he'd seen her with Mr. Bale in the Camberly garden, could relax at last. But as Griffin climbed into bed and laid his head on the pillow, closed his eyes and prepared for sleep, he could not rid his mind of Miss Howard. She was like a lighthouse blazing brightly in the night, impossible for him to ignore.

When Emily woke a few hours later, it took her a second to figure out where she was. But then she spotted her discarded ball gown, hung across the back of a chair, and it all came tumbling back with the force of an oncoming carriage. Oh God. Lord Griffin had kissed her and now he meant to escort her to Clearview.

Taking a long, deep breath, she tossed the counterpane aside, flung her legs over the edge of the bed, and stood. His jacket was visible beneath her gown, the dark wool a stark contrast to the smooth silk. Masculine versus feminine.

She shook her head, reminding herself there was no time for fanciful notions. Only practicality would serve her well in this instance. So she dressed with crisp movements and put on his jacket to cover herself, even though it was much too wide across the shoulders and the sleeves so long they hid her fingers.

A knock sounded at her door, followed by a low, "Miss Howard?"

Emily's pulse quickened in response to Lord Griffin's voice. She took a deep breath and swung the door open. And froze. Because there he was, exactly as she'd expected, except he was somehow more masculine, more roguish, more tempting than ever before.

Emily swallowed. It had to do with the fact that he hadn't shaved, which lent a surprisingly attractive ruggedness to him. She couldn't help but stare.

He did not seem to notice. "Forgive the intrusion but I feared you might still be sleeping, and our coach departs in less than one hour."

"Do we have time for a quick breakfast?"

"I expect so." He gave her a once over and nodded as if she'd just passed inspection. "Ready?"

"Yes." She grabbed her reticule and followed him into the hallway. "Do you know if anyone came looking for us?"

He shook his head as they started down the stairs. "No. They did not." He glanced at her briefly. "I'm sorry."

"You need not be." They reached the foyer and she stopped there to add, "It does not surprise me is what I mean to say. And since I am not surprised, I am not disappointed either. Truth is, I'm rather glad to avoid an argument with my parents and to just be on my way. It simplifies matters."

"It also suggests that they're not especially worried about you, which ought to be of some concern, don't you think?"

She scoffed and crossed her arms. "I'm the disappointing daughter – the one who cannot be saved." Lord Griffin raised an eyebrow at this and opened his mouth as if to comment, but Emily cut him off by adding, "My mother may have glimpsed a brief chance at doing so last night, but she will have realized that attempting to make us marry because of a mere kiss would have been a futile endeavor. After discussing matters with my father, I'm sure she will have acknowledged that the best way forward is to let me go. As far away from them as possible so my indiscretion in the Camberly garden can quickly be forgotten."

"For the sake of your sister," he murmured.

"Precisely." Emily's stomach grumbled, reminding her that she was really quite hungry. "Perhaps we should eat something now?"

He nodded and led the way to the same supper room they'd used the evening before. Their breakfast was simple, consisting of toast, ham, and cheese, which they washed down with tea.

"No milk or sugar?" Emily asked when Griffin refrained from adding either.

"I'm not particularly fond of sweet drinks and milk just dilutes the flavor."

She couldn't help but smile. "I quite agree."

He glanced at her cup and the edge of his mouth

lifted. "I didn't expect to have that in common." His expression turned pensive. "You might actually be the first woman I've met who takes her tea plainly."

Emily gave him a rueful look. "My mother used to feed me cakes because she believed I'd do better on the marriage mart if I had some meat on my bones."

"Which is probably true to some extent. I don't care for scrawniness myself."

Emily snorted. "Oh, there was never any danger of me ending up at that end of the spectrum." She sobered as she thought back on the years when her mother had fretted over her future. "As the eldest daughter, I was something of an experiment."

"I'm sorry. That must have been very trying for you."

She nodded. By the time her second season had begun, she'd doubled in size. "Clearview was the best thing that ever happened to me."

A horn sounded, causing Lord Griffin to glance at the door. "Time to go." He stood and offered Emily his hand.

Heat darted up her arm as soon as she made contact with him, and for a second she was tempted to pull away as if scorched. But her refusal to let him see how easily he affected her compelled her to close her fingers around his instead.

There.

Not an impossible feat.

She raised her gaze to his and sucked in a breath. The way he looked at her caused her legs to grow weak and her belly to flutter.

A knowing smile tugged at his lips, and a gleam

appeared in his eyes. Emily realized in that instant that he was aware of her visceral response to his touch, but before she could think of something to say, some means by which to distract from the truth, he was leading her out to the courtyard and to their awaiting coach.

As the last passengers to board, Griffin and Miss Howard were forced to take the remaining seats, which were on the same bench, closest to the door. "I'll sit in the middle," he told her when he handed her up.

Standing with one foot on the step and the other in the doorway of the coach, she leaned forward to peer inside and then glanced back at him over her shoulder. "I think you will have more space if I take the middle."

"That is irrelevant."

"But—"

"I will sit in the middle." Because the alternative would be to let her sit pressed up against a scruffy looking fellow whom Griffin didn't trust to sit shoulder to shoulder with a beautiful woman.

"Very well," Miss Howard agreed. "But only because I do not wish to trample on your good intentions."

She disappeared into the coach and Griffin followed her inside. He greeted the other passengers, a portly man in a brown suit, an old woman who stared at him through her spectacles, and a young, eager-looking lad. "Good morning," he said and lowered himself to his designated spot. The scruffy fellow next to him shifted, politely adding more space.

Griffin thanked him as the door slammed shut. Perhaps he'd misjudged him, but even so, he knew he'd made the right decision by preventing Miss Howard from sitting beside him, for although his manners were good, his odor was not.

The coach rolled forward with a jolt, and Griffin averted his face from the man beside him in a pointless attempt to ignore the smell of sweat wafting off his person. He smothered a cough and gave his attention to Miss Howard. Perhaps a bit of conversation would distract him.

"Do you think you would have married if your mother had not been so..." He searched his brain for an appropriate word to describe the woman without causing insult.

"Domineering?" Miss Howard asked before he could think of one.

Griffin shrugged, which caused his arm to move against the entire length of her side. She shifted against him, undoubtedly trying to give him more room, but the tight space would not allow it. Instead, her thigh rubbed against his in the most seductive way.

Christ.

This was not the time or place for arousal. He tried to focus on what they'd been talking about before she'd drawn his attention to their close proximity with each other. Ah yes. Her mother.

His ardor cooled with unsurprising swiftness.

"Yes," he said, not bothering to contradict her description.

"Possibly. That is to say, I did have a suitor during my second season, but he lost interest and eventually married someone else."

"Then he's a fool." Her wistfulness settled heavily across his shoulders. He did not like knowing that she'd been rejected, perhaps even hurt by some unappreciative man. "Did you care for him?"

It took a while for her to answer, and for some absurd reason this made him edgy. The carriage rattled in response to an uneven spot in the road. Griffin clenched his fists and braced for her response.

"I believed we would get on well with each other." She sighed with a hint of sadness that tore at his heart. "It would not have been a love match, but it was a chance for me to have a family of my own."

"Did you ever discover what happened? Why the gentleman in question changed his mind?"

"Not exactly, though I do think my mother managed to frighten him away." She took a deep breath and attempted to meet his gaze, which pushed her knee more firmly against his own. The contact was brief since she quickly changed her position, but the effect lingered like hot little embers scattered across his skin. "But I'm no longer sorry the attachment ended, for it allowed me to choose a different path, one which includes Cassandra and Mary and the children we've taken into our care."

Griffin expelled a deep breath. For a second, he considered asking who her suitor had been, but then she began regaling him with stories about the orphans and it no longer seemed appropriate. Nor did it really matter. She'd clearly moved on and was happy with the life she'd built for herself together with her friends.

He ought to be pleased for her. After all, he had his own life to return to.

So then why did he wish that she'd want something more? Something that might include him in the picture? It made no sense. Especially since this wasn't something that he was prepared to offer.

"What about you?" Emily asked Lord Griffin a couple of hours later. They'd just left another coaching inn where they'd stopped for a change of horses.

"How do you mean?" he inquired.

His question made sense considering she'd just finished telling him about the time when the oldest boy in her care, Peter, had gone missing, and Caleb had found him and brought him back to Clearview.

"Have you never considered marrying?"

Lord Griffin grunted. "Marriage demands a certain degree of trust in the other person. I've not yet found such a person."

Emily took a moment to let that cynical impression of marriage sink in before saying, "I take it you've never been in love?"

There was a pause. And then, "Your assumption is quite correct, Miss Howard. I also don't expect to be, which is why I'm not eagerly looking to settle down. Even though my mother would be thrilled to have me do so." He gave a humorless chuckle. "She even has a list."

Emily couldn't help but smile. "Of suitable

brides?"

"It was meant for my brother, but now that he's safely married, it's been passed on to me."

Emily laughed outright. "Judging from the lack of enthusiasm in your voice, I take it you're not enjoying her matchmaking efforts."

"To put it plainly, I cannot wait to escape them."

His comment compounded the inconvenience she'd caused him. Guilt threaded its way through her heart. "I'm sorry if I've delayed you. Caleb did say you were planning to return to Vienna soon."

"I've no fixed schedule for my departure. A quick trip to Clearview won't make much of a difference."

She was pleased to hear it and yet she wasn't, because his assurance, as comforting as it was, confirmed he would leave for Austria once he'd completed his gentlemanly duty toward her. Which was something she found to be rather depressing.

She'd grown accustomed to his presence, even though they'd only interacted occasionally. But it had been enough for him to become the man she looked forward to seeing. Not because she imagined he'd ever feel for her what she felt for him, but because she enjoyed the spark he instilled in her. It made her feel alive and because of this, she could not quite imagine England without him.

"I'm glad to hear it," she said, pleased with the level sound of her voice. The carriage bounced as it followed a bend in the road. Emily leaned her head back and closed her eyes. "I think I'll try to sleep for a while now if you don't mind."

"By all means," he murmured.

Emily said nothing further. She was actually quite exhausted, both physically and emotionally. Because she could no longer claim an innocent appreciation for Lord Griffin's company or even a slight attraction. What she felt for him now that she'd kissed him was far more complicated and not at all easy to unravel.

CHAPTER FOUR

GREY CLOUDS WERE DRAWING TOGETHER when the carriage reached their destination three days later. "It looks like it's going to rain," Griffin said as they started their one mile walk to Clearview. In spite of the foreboding weather, he was glad to exchange the pungent smell of the carriage with clean country air.

"We'd best hurry then," Miss Howard said. She strode forward with long strides, a caricature of elegance in her billowing evening gown and his much-too-large jacket.

Griffin forced back a grin and hurried after her. She was an interesting person: beautiful, independent, and very determined in her pursuits. Which of course made him wonder if she would approach all things in life with the focus she'd given to convincing her mother she needn't marry on account of a kiss before heading off on a cross-country journey with the very same man who'd just compromised her. Would she dedicate herself to making love with equal zeal?

Not the right question for him to be asking while trying to give her protection.

He set his jaw and glanced across at her profile.

Her gaze was fixed upon the horizon with fierce determination, her chin jutting slightly forward beneath a full pair of rosy lips, and her cheeks flushed by vigor. Strands of loosened hair tangled in the wind, flung out behind her in a haphazard display of careless abandon.

Most people who saw her like this would likely say she looked a mess, but Griffin disagreed. In his opinion he'd never encountered a lovelier woman, nor one he'd rather take a walk in the rain with.

And it was raining now. Only a little, but enough to warn him that more was to come. "We'll be soaked before we get there," he said, stating the obvious.

"Do you not like the rain?"

A flash of light lit up the sky, followed shortly after by a boom in the distance. The drizzle came faster and heavier until it became a rapid downpour.

Griffin was drenched before he'd taken another five steps.

"I like it well enough as long as I'm sitting inside by a blazing fire."

She laughed in spite of the wind and the rain streaking over her face, which made Griffin laugh as well. Miss Howard was good company. There was a carefree honesty about her that most people lacked.

"That does sound lovely, but since we've still got some way to go, I would suggest finding pleasure in our current circumstances."

"My clothes are clinging to my skin, Miss Howard."

"So are mine. But if you try to ignore that for

a moment and direct your attention toward the drops of water spilling onto your face and the wind blowing over your cheeks, you should start feeling revived. The energy found in nature should lift your spirit, not repress it. It should wash away all restrictions and make you feel free."

God, he wanted to kiss her right now. He wanted to taste the raindrops on her face and feel the drenched fabric of her gown bunched in his hands as he pulled her against him.

He took a deep breath, conscious of the water trickling over his own lips. It cooled there in response to a harsh gust of wind blowing in from his left. Griffin's senses sharpened, bringing about a new awareness and appreciation for how the cool air mixed with the rain invigorated every cell in his body.

"I never considered that before."

"When we allow ourselves to abandon the rules we've been taught to adhere to, like taking shelter at the first sign of rain, we open ourselves to new experiences and a freedom that cannot exist as long as we let ourselves be restricted."

"Do you know how revolutionary that sounds?"

She swiped some water from her eyes with her hand and said, "It is the most compelling argument for my present situation." A grin tugged at her lips. "We would not be here together like this, you and I, if we'd chosen to follow the rules."

"We'd likely be arguing with friends and family about the repercussions of our kiss."

"Which would have been a dull way to spend a Monday, would you not agree?"

He laughed. How could he not when she was so

marvelously refreshing? "You make an excellent point, Miss Howard." Spending a brief reprieve with her at Clearview would not be so bad. In fact, he was rather glad things had turned out the way they had, for it meant he would now have a chance to get to know her better.

But to what end?

You don't wish to marry and you plan to leave England.

He chose to ignore that nagging thought for the moment and simply enjoy the company of a woman who was proving to be far more entertaining than he'd ever anticipated.

In spite of what she'd said to Lord Griffin, Emily was actually quite glad to arrive at Clearview when they did because she'd still been wearing her silk slippers from the night of the ball, and they weren't meant for walking through mud and puddles.

"I wish you could see this place in a few weeks when daffodils bloom," she said as she entered through the garden gate.

"I imagine it must be very picturesque." The gate squeaked on its hinges as he closed it. "I've always been fond of daffodils myself."

"They're my favorite flowers. Along with peonies." Turning right, she made her way toward the cottage where Caleb had stayed during his time there.

"Where are you going?" Lord Griffin asked as she sloshed her way forward.

"To fetch the spare key." Reaching the overhang next to the cottage, she reached up under a wooden beam and unhooked a key from a nail there. She held it up for Lord Griffin to see. "Victory. Come on."

"You came all this way without being sure you'd be able to get inside the house?" He sounded incredulous.

"Of course not. I knew the key would be here." She made her way back toward the front door of the main house. "Or at least I was very certain it would be." He muttered something inaudible behind her, and she grinned in response. "Cassandra has the other copy, and I did not stop to think about asking her for it during my escape from Camberly House."

"Are you always this spontaneous?"

She placed the key in the lock and turned it, then pushed the door open and entered the foyer. It wasn't warm, but at least it was dry. "I don't think so," she said, answering him after a moment's consideration.

He closed the door, shutting out the rain and the wind. Puddles started forming at both their feet, and Emily suddenly felt the chill more severely than when she'd been outside walking. "We should light some oil lamps and start a fire."

"I'd recommend doing so in the kitchen so we can prepare some hot tea as well."

"Agreed." She led the way and then pointed out where the wood was kept so he could start making the fire while she lit a couple of oil lamps. Their glow illuminated the interior and brought Lord Griffin's lack of a jacket into sharp focus. His shirt and waistcoat clung to his back as he bent before the fireplace, the shirtsleeves gripping his arms to accentuate his toned muscles.

Emily swallowed and realized her throat had gone dry. She took a step back, almost stumbling over a chair. "I'll fetch some water," she muttered. "For the tea." As if that needed explaining.

She spun away and went to collect a couple of bottles that were kept in the pantry. The water inside them wouldn't be fresh, but that didn't matter since she would be boiling it anyway. And it was better than having to go back out into the storm in order to pump water from the well.

Collecting a kettle, Emily filled it and set it on the kitchen table. "This is ready to be hung above the fire," she said while trying not to stare at Lord Griffin. He'd risen from his crouched position and was standing by the fireplace, prodding the wood there with a poker, and dear God, she could not think straight. Not with his wet trousers hugging his thighs in the most incredible way and...

She cleared her throat. "I'm off to get changed. Make yourself comfortable. I shall see you in a bit." Grabbing one of the oil lamps, Emily fled upstairs to her bedchamber and shut the door firmly behind her.

Inhaling deeply, she took several breaths in an effort to slow her rapid heart rate. The most gorgeous man in the world was presently in her kitchen, and she was in serious danger of making a fool of herself. Sighing, she pushed his jacket off her shoulders and hung it across the back of a chair. If they were going to make this bizarre partnership of theirs work, she would have to be able to look at him without losing her wits. Which would likely become a lot easier once his clothes dried and he could be properly attired again.

With this in mind, Emily went to work on the buttons of her gown, which involved a bit of contorting. Eventually, she ended up tearing some of them off, but since the alternative was to ask Lord Griffin for help, she decided the extra work spent with her sewing kit later would be the better option.

Crossing to her chest of drawers, she found a clean chemise, stays, and stockings, which she put on before selecting a plain indigo dress with long sleeves from her wardrobe.

Reminded of the fact that Lord Griffin would not have any dry clothes to change into, she found a large blanket in the chest at the foot of her bed and hurried back downstairs. What she was not prepared for when she returned to the kitchen was to find him sitting before the fire without his shirt or waistcoat on. Indeed, he was totally naked from the waist up, which was something of a shock since she'd never seen any man so scantily clad before.

Being the practical sort, Emily knew that accepting the situation for what it was would be the only way for her to have some tea, so she took a step forward and ignored the riotous nerves in her belly. They would not help her any more than the soft little shiver that tickled her spine when Lord Griffin heard her and glanced her way. Her determination to remain unaffected by him was rapidly proving as useless as her soggy slippers upstairs.

And then he stood, as gentlemen were trained to

do when a woman entered a room. Except most gentlemen did not put their nipples and chest hair on bold display. Even as she feared her heart might seize, Emily's fingers tingled with the most absurd desire to reach out and touch him. Without even thinking, she lowered her gaze and was briefly distracted by a fainter dusting of hair leading from his naval toward his waistline.

She snapped her gaze back to his and held the blanket toward him as rigidly as if she were holding a rotting cabbage at arms length. "This should help keep you warm," she muttered while brazenly staring straight into his dark brown eyes. Looking away would show embarrassment and weakness, and she refused to let him think she might be suffering from either. Even though she was well aware of the heat rushing into her cheeks and the wobbly uncertainty of her knees.

"Thank you." He accepted the offering with a smile, his fingers grazing hers as he took it.

Emily counted to five in her head and then finally did turn away, more eager than ever for a cup of hot tea. She searched the table for the kettle, but it wasn't there.

"It's already hanging over the fire," Lord Griffin told her, apparently well aware of what she sought. "The water should be boiling soon, so all we need is a pot and some tea."

"I'll see to it." Emily rummaged around until she found the items. She looked at Lord Griffin from the corner of her eye and saw he was wrapped up quite nicely now in the blanket. A smile tugged at her lips. This was by far the most unexpected situation she'd ever thought to find herself in.

A thought struck her. "Are you hungry? There should be some cured meat, some preserves, and a bit of cheese in the larder."

"That would be welcome until we're able to buy fresh supplies tomorrow."

"All right then. If you can add the boiling water to the pot here, I'll prepare a couple of plates for us to enjoy."

Intent on focusing on the task she'd set herself instead of on Lord Griffin's unavoidable presence, Emily went to find as much variety as she could among the supplies. Everything she'd mentioned to him could be found, including a tin containing a few remaining biscuits she'd baked last month.

Piling everything into her arms, she returned to the kitchen and almost dropped it all on the floor when she spotted Lord Griffin's trousers hanging across the back of a spare kitchen chair. Were those his smalls, right beside them? She gulped, which was something she never did. But really, how could she not when the only thought spinning inside her head was that he was now completely nude beneath that blanket.

Dear God in heaven, she could even see his shins and his feet, just as bare as the rest of him. Closing her eyes for a second, Emily inhaled deeply through her nose.

What was it with the Crawford men, wet clothes, and blankets? Mary had experienced a similar incident with Caleb while he'd been staying here, and since Emily and Cassandra had been aware of an attraction brewing between them, they'd made her handle the situation on her own.

The reminder gave Emily a newfound respect for Mary's fortitude since she herself was starting to fear that the only way for her to cool down was to step right into the fire.

"Miss Howard?"

Emily blinked. "Huh?"

"Are you all right?"

She blinked again. Apparently that was what one did when one was thrust into the complete unknown and began suffering from shock.

"Ye-yes," she stammered like the foolish ninny he'd turned her into. Her brow furrowed and she clenched her jaw. No. He would not divest her of all reason. She would not allow it. So she tightened her hold on the supplies, just to be safe, and crossed to the kitchen table.

"Would you like some help with that?"

"No thank you." He raised an eyebrow and she realized she sounded terser than she'd intended. Great! The balance between portraying a light-headed dunderhead and a difficult harridan was proving a chore to master. She exhaled slowly, intent on regaining some semblance of control over all the emotions he'd stirred in her since their kiss.

Finally, she said, "I believe I can manage if you'd be kind enough to pour me a cup of tea once it's done steeping."

"Certainly." He went in search of cups, allowing Emily to relax even further. Yes, she found him impossibly attractive, but in all fairness she did not wish for him to catch cold which was what he risked doing unless he got dry. She could not fault him for removing his clothes. Least of all when he'd done a good job concealing as much of himself as possible. Which now made her miss the sight of his torso, so beautifully sculpted by smooth skin and muscle.

Stop it.

There's food to prepare.

She grabbed a knife and proceeded to slice thin pieces of ham, arranging them neatly on two plates. Next, she cut some chunks of cheese, divided the biscuits equally between them, and finished off with a dollop of cherry preserves.

"The food is ready," she told Lord Griffin.

"So is the tea. Shall we sit at the table or in front of the fire?"

Emily's heart skipped a little with appreciation. There was no denying the hopeful look in his eyes when he mentioned the fire, but he was prepared to forego comfort in favor of protocol if she desired.

"As long as you're able to balance a plate in your lap, then I am too," she told him sincerely.

His smile was immediate and so warm that she could practically feel the heat of it all the way down to her toes. "I'm glad to hear it." He turned the edge of the blanket over and tucked it firmly into place, then arranged their respective chairs and set each of their mugs on the low stone ledge in front of the fireplace.

"You should sit down first so I can hand you your plate," Emily said.

"Or you could give me the plates so you can sit first."

She thought of arguing and then decided against it. He was after all just trying to adhere to some semblance of normalcy even though there was nothing normal about their current situation.

"Very well." She did as he suggested and was quickly seated in front of the welcoming heat from the flames and ready to enjoy her meal.

"This is not where I imagined I'd be today when I readied myself for the Camberly ball on Friday," he said when they'd both had a chance to eat some of their food.

Emily glanced across at his profile. Each line of his face was highlighted either by light or shadow. As if sensing her perusal, he tilted his head, angling it toward her. "Nor I," she confessed.

"Oh?"

She laughed in response to his obvious attempt at feigning incredulity. "It was not my intention to kiss anyone…" She averted her gaze, dipped a biscuit into the cherry preserves and took a large bite. The lie made her insides squirm with discomfort. So she swallowed her food and sighed. "That's not entirely true."

"How do you mean?"

He sounded both curious and hesitant, as though he wasn't quite sure that he wished to hear her answer.

And yet she was somehow compelled to confide in him. Perhaps because this was home. If Cassandra had been here, she would have told her everything. But both she and Mary were back in London and that left Emily with Lord Griffin.

"I did mean to encourage Mr. Bale to kiss me after he'd helped me untangle my earring."

A rough sound rose from Lord Griffin's throat. He was staring at his plate. "Why?"

Emily shrugged. "He's very agreeable and discreet. Of all the gentlemen I'm acquainted with, I believed him the most likely one to show me what kissing is like without making demands after."

"I see."

"Do you really?" She set her plate aside and picked up her cup. "Are you really able to imagine what it is like to be six and twenty years old and not have experienced kissing? To fear you might never do so or that if you do you'll end up trapped in an unhappy marriage? That the action, no matter how simple, could have dire repercussions for your sister?" She shook her head. "Men are able to learn about these aspects of life without anyone caring one way or the other. Indeed, they are expected to do so and more."

"More?"

"Well, yes. All young gentlemen have mistresses, and if they do not then they visit the brothels. By the time they marry, they have acquired a wealth of knowledge that young women completely lack."

If there was one thing Griffin could say with confidence, it was that Miss Howard did and said the most unexpected things. It had taken considerable restraint on his part to stop his mouth from falling open in response to her rather outrageous remark.

"Do you deliberately aim to shock people?" He honestly wasn't sure since he did not know her well enough yet to have discovered if this was a permanent characteristic of hers or merely the result of being too put out by circumstance to care.

Her eyes widened. "Oh, I do beg your pardon. I'm not usually so blunt." She smiled then, with a wryness he found incredibly charming. "Except when I'm with Cass and Mary. We've grown so close over the years, I feel I can say whatever I like to them without reproach."

Griffin felt a sharp pang in the middle of his chest. He envied that sort of honesty and the bond it forged. The years he'd spent apart from his brothers made him feel foreign to them, in a way. Which was yet another reason why he wanted to leave; so he could escape the lack of closeness he experienced with his family.

When he'd returned, he'd foolishly imagined they'd all pick up where they'd left off. But of course that wasn't possible. Too much had happened in the years since. They'd lived different lives from the one they'd once shared. Their father and older brother were dead, and Caleb was now the duke.

Nothing would ever be as it once had been.

Which was probably why Devlin had already gone away.

Smart man.

"Lord Griffin?"

Griffin shook his head at the sound of Miss Howard's voice. He looked at her and saw that she stared back at him with a question in her green-gold eyes.

What was it she'd been saying?

Ah, yes. She could be open with Cassandra and Mary.

"I'm not judging you," he said, even though he clearly had. Her deepening frown confirmed that she shared this opinion. Griffin sighed. "I was caught by surprise, but I actually..."

He considered how much to reveal. Was it wise to encourage additional closeness with her? Probably not, but he also didn't want to stifle her true nature. That would be wrong.

Or so he told himself.

"Yes?"

Griffin cleared his throat. "In spite of my initial reaction, I actually like how straightforward you were before with your comment. If you will permit, I would welcome the opportunity for us to be completely candid with each other for as long as I'm here. It would make a refreshing change, I should think."

"From putting on airs?"

He nodded slowly. "From feeling as though I'm walking around in someone else's skin."

The snort with which she responded became a laugh. "That's rather morbid." Her amusement was brief, however, and quickly transformed into a more serious expression denoting respect and thoughtfulness. "I actually like the idea. And I agree with your suggestion since I would rather be myself than the carefully polite miss Society insists I must be."

"In other words, we shall be respectful but brutally forthright with each other."

"As long as you promise not to judge me."

"If I do," he told her sincerely, "it will be in the best way possible."

She seemed to like that response, for she smiled

as if he'd just set a plate of treats before her.

"Now then," he continued. "Which topic shall we address first? The injustice of young men knowing what to expect when they enter the marriage bed or the anatomical differences between the sexes?"

Emily's face grew instantly hot. Oh, she was in trouble now and with no one else to blame for it but herself. She eyed Lord Griffin, whose cheeky grin and gleaming eyes bore evidence of a deliberate attempt to tease her. Clearly, she had overestimated her ability to face his straightforwardness because she could not even think of how to respond. Except perhaps with a squeak of dismay, which would not do at all since she was the one who'd initiated this peculiar dialogue.

And now the annoying man was openly laughing.

Emily glared.

"Oh, you must forgive me, Miss Howard, but your face..." Warmth flickered in his eyes along with a hint of regret that made guilt spark in Emily's heart. "Forgive me, but I could not resist."

"You did what we agreed to. If anything, it is I who should ask forgiveness for not being able to meet the challenge."

"I went too far," he argued. He blew out a breath and knit his brow in a way that made him look slightly lost. "I spoke to you as I once would have done to my brothers. It was a mistake."

"I gather you're not as close as you were before you went your separate ways?"

"We've lived different lives for the past ten years. Our experiences have been dissimilar and..." He stared into the flames. "It is as if we share a common point in the past from which we've all diverged."

"Do you regret leaving?" she quietly asked.

"No. Staying would have meant following the path my father intended for me." He met her gaze directly. "He wanted me to be a soldier."

"And you wished to build mechanical things."

A grin curved his lips. "I suppose so, even though it took me a while to realize it."

"So you just went out into the world, unsure of what would become of your life." She marveled at his courage and his ability to stay away. And then she marveled at her own.

As if reading her mind, he raised his chin a notch. "We're not so dissimilar, are we? Both running from the mold our parents meant for us to fit into."

His comment hung in the air for a moment. Accompanied by the dim lighting and the warmth emanating from the fireplace, it added an intimacy between them that made Emily feel uncomfortably vulnerable.

She nodded. "I suppose." She glanced at their empty plates and mugs. "It's been a long day and it's getting late. I think I'll start cleaning up."

"I'll help," he offered.

Even though they washed and dried the dishes in silence, Emily's mind whirled with the keen awareness of how undressed he was, his close proximity as he dried the items she handed to him, the intoxicating scent of sandalwood wafting off his person, and the very critical question of where he would sleep.

"If you agree," he said after putting the flames out in the fireplace so only a few hot embers remained, "I'll stay in the parlor tonight. On the sofa."

"I think that would be acceptable," she said and then winced at how prim she sounded. But relaxing was no easy feat when she and the most gorgeous man in the world would be spending the night together. Beneath the same roof, at least. "I will go find a pillow for you. And an extra blanket."

The edge of his mouth curved, producing the smile that invariably caused her stomach to flutter. "I would appreciate that, Miss Howard."

His eyes held hers for a moment, the intensity of his gaze so acute she found herself scorched to the depth of her soul. Unnerved, she turned away and went to locate the items he needed for a good night's rest, all the while wondering if coming here with him alone would lead to her biggest regret.

CHAPTER FIVE

"WE NEED TO MAKE A plan," Griffin told Emily the following morning when she came to join him in the kitchen. He'd slept abominably on the sofa since it had been at least a foot too short to accommodate him comfortably. So he'd risen early, put on his clothes which were now blessedly dry, and set about preparing some breakfast while pondering his circumstances.

The attraction he felt toward Emily couldn't be denied, which meant staying here with her like this posed a serious threat, not only to her reputation but to her virtue and his peace of mind. Since he only meant to secure her safety and had no desire to find himself tied down in England through marriage, they would have to act quickly.

"How so?" she asked, stepping further into the room.

Directing his attention away from the eggs he was frying, he looked at her more fully. She was dressed in the same slate blue dress she'd changed into the previous evening, so he ought not have marveled over her appearance. But now, illuminated by the fresh beams of sunlight falling through the beveled glass windows, she made him forget himself for a moment. Instead he considered the way her skin glowed, the fact that her hair, which he'd always considered a plain shade of brown, was more reddish in tone, and how he longed to feel her plush, velvet lips pressed against his once more.

The smell of something burning snapped him out of his reverie, and he hastily removed the pan from the stove. Clearing his throat, he deliberately tamped down the surge of desire rising inside him. Whatever he felt for her was temporary, he told himself. The result of their being alone together without a chaperone. It had nothing to do with the fact that he'd kissed her, that she'd been disappointed by his effort, or that he wanted to prove himself capable of giving her an unforgettable experience. Only danger lay in that direction. Which reminded him of what he'd concluded this morning before she'd risen.

"We cannot remain here together," he said as he slid the eggs onto a couple of plates. The eggs were slightly blackened around the edges – a testament to the distraction Emily posed.

"I agree." Her response was swift, as if she had arrived at the same conclusion. Before he could come to terms with the disagreeable effect that had on him, however, she moved in closer to where he stood and said, "I've never seen a man cook before."

His chest expanded. "Necessity can be quite motivational." He placed two slices of bread on the pan and let them toast in the leftover grease while he poured the tea he'd prepared into cups. "I had no one to rely on for food but myself when

I left home." He shrugged at the memory. "It was actually nice not having servants around all the time, ready to tend to my every need. So I chose not to hire any even after I got myself settled in Vienna."

"Then you also clean?"

"And launder my clothes." When he caught her staring at him in dismay, he couldn't help but chuckle.

"You don't send them out to a laundress?"

"I'm just one person, Miss Howard. I find it's not really worth it, though I did try doing so once in the beginning. When my shirts came back two sizes smaller, I decided never to do it again."

She blinked. "But you're a duke's son."

"And you are an affluent businessman's daughter." He set their teacups on the table, retrieved the toast from the pan, and placed each slice on a plate beside the accompanying egg. "I doubt you were raised to cook and clean and tutor orphans."

"I suppose you have a point." Her brow puckered as if in thought. She went to the table and took her seat. "Moving here was the best decision I ever made for myself. I've never felt freeer."

"It cannot have been easy, though." He sat opposite her and took a sip of his tea.

She did the same, directing his gaze once again to her lips, now carefully poised against the rim of her cup while she drank.

A rush of desire swept through him again, this time tempting him with erotic visualizations of how those lips might give him the most divine pleasure.

"On the contrary, it was extraordinarily challenging," she said, her precise tone suggesting that she was completely oblivious to the forceful effect she was having on him. "Not just for me, of course, but for all of us." She set her cup aside, picked up her knife and fork, and proceeded to cut her toast into narrow strips. "We had to learn new skills." A smile tugged at her lips. "The first meal I made was an utter disaster. The meat caught fire and blackened while the water I was boiling vegetables in overflowed." A sigh accompanied by a small shake of her head conveyed her self-deprecation. "I burnt my hands badly in the process."

"Dear God." The arousal that had been building inside him was swiftly banked by concern. He instinctively looked at her hands, and she turned them palm up to reveal three dark lines of discoloration.

An ache took hold of his heart. "How?" It was all he could manage to get past the sudden knot in his throat.

"In my haste to remove the burnt roast from the spit, I did not think to use a dishtowel or anything else to protect my hands." She laughed lightly, forcing his gaze back to hers. "You need not look so serious. I'm quite all right and have learned from my silly mistake. Haven't burnt a roast or myself since."

"I'm relieved to hear it." He studied her for a second then asked, "Do you like doing it? Cooking, that is."

"Yes." There was no hesitation in her answer. "I've improved a great deal over the years. Acquiring a couple of recipe books helped. And some of the women I've met in these parts, especially the vicar's wife, have provided me with some wonderful advice." An almost shy smile tugged at her lips as she shrugged one shoulder. "I'm especially fond of cooking new dishes and have started compiling a book of my own recipes."

She dipped a strip of toast into her egg yolk and took a bite while he stared at her in wonder. "Thank you for making breakfast."

"You're welcome," he said before popping a piece of egg on toast into his mouth.

They ate for a moment in silence before she eventually asked, "What about *your* scar? It doesn't look like the sort of thing you acquired by accident."

Griffin winced. He didn't like being reminded of the poorest lack in judgment he'd ever had. "I came too close to another man's blade once," he grumbled.

"I thought as much." Miss Howard hesitated briefly and then posed her next question. "Why were you fighting?"

"I prefer not to discuss it." He met her gaze boldly. "It isn't a suitable subject of conversation for a lady."

"If you recall, we promised each other honesty."

A sigh forced its way up his throat. Devil take it if she wasn't correct.

Right.

If honesty was what she wanted, then that was what she would get. "Years ago, a woman came into my shop." He sighed at the memory of golden curls framing a heart-shaped face and eyes as blue as the summer sky. "She was the loveliest creature I'd ever seen."

"What happened to her?" The words were gently spoken. Almost a whisper.

"She..." He swallowed. Already his heart was pounding while tremors raked his skin. Gripping the edge of the table, Griffin struggled to calm the riotous flare of emotion this conversation had caused. "As a widow, she was free to enjoy certain liberties." He gave Miss Howard a pointed look.

"So you became lovers."

Surprised by her matter of fact manner and the lack of surprise on her face, he could only nod in response. "Yes."

"I see nothing wrong with that."

No. Of course she wouldn't. Except... "I made the mistake of falling in love with her though."

"You told me in the carriage that you have never been in love."

"I lied."

Her jaw tightened ever so slightly, with what appeared to be disapproval. But then she asked, "And why would loving this woman be so bad?"

For some absurd reason he chuckled, only the sound was not at all humorous. "Because it turned out that she wasn't a widow at all. Just a married woman seeking a bit of adventure."

Miss Howard inhaled sharply. "She tricked you!"

"Indeed she did," he said softly. "And when her husband found out about it, she accused me of seducing her and even demanded that her husband challenge me to a duel."

"That scheming little harlot." The words dripped from Miss Howard's tongue like venom. Her eyes, he saw now, were dark with anger.

Anger directed at Clara. Anger for what she had done. Anger on his behalf.

He almost laughed in response to her outrage. Until she added, "That woman never deserved you. So I'm glad you're rid of her. Even if she hurt you."

Ignoring the warmth her words stirred in his heart, he told her gruffly, "I was stupid. In retrospect there were signs, indications of her duplicitous nature that I chose to ignore. And as a result, I ended up deformed." He touched one finger to his cheek, allowing it to slide against the raised line of flesh.

A snort was her first response. And then she said, "There is nothing deformed about you. And besides, it is my understanding that many young ladies find scars incredibly dashing."

"Really?" For some peculiar reason, his voice was lower now, with an unintentional seductiveness to it. And yet, he could not help but ask, "And what is your opinion?"

She started a little as if unprepared for such a forward question. And then her cheeks turned a lovely shade of pink. Swallowing, she averted her gaze from his. "I'm not entirely sure."

Intrigued by her response, he leaned forward in his seat. "Come now, Miss Howard. You can do better than that." He allowed an encouraging smile when she glanced his way once more. "After all, we did say we would be both direct and honest with each other."

Her blush deepened and Griffin's whole body tightened in response. He held his breath, both dreading her answer and longing to hear it.

"Very well," she acquiesced. Her eyes sharpened, focusing more intensely on his face. Her scrutiny caused his skin to prick with awareness. "The scar does not detract from your handsomeness. If anything, it adds character and perhaps an element of ruggedness that suits you rather well." She tilted her head. "I also think you would be less intriguing without it."

"Are you saying that you like it?" Surely not. He'd spent the last six years regretting the wound he'd sustained at the hands of a man who'd had every right to kill him. The awareness that it was the first thing people noticed about him had been at the front of his mind ever since.

Miss Howard grinned as if by surprise. "Well yes. I suppose I am."

Griffin expelled a breath. His muscles relaxed. Her open acceptance of him was a balm to his soul. It made him feel light and unburdened. Furthermore, it made him feel very comfortable in her presence, which reminded him of what he'd wished to discuss with her earlier. She'd managed to distract him by redirecting his attention elsewhere, but it was time for him to focus now. For both their sakes.

"About our circumstances…" He waited for her to adjust to the seriousness of his tone before continuing. "As I mentioned earlier, we cannot remain here together."

"And if you'll recall, I agreed."

"Quite." For some absurd reason, her chirpy response made him irritable. He grabbed his cup a little too roughly, causing tea to spill onto the table. Whatever relaxed state he'd been in a second earlier was gone now. He knit his brow. "I will return you to your parents' home immediately. With any luck, no one besides your own family will have noticed that you have been travelling unchaperoned and spending the night with a man to whom you are not related."

Her lips twitched and he saw that her eyes sparkled with amusement. Glowering, he took a sip of his tea which was now completely cold. His irritation grew until he was sure he would shout at her, reach across the table and shake her, or worse, kiss her.

"What?" he growled, like the frustrated beast she was turning him into.

"Oh, I just love how you refer to yourself in the third person, not to mention your boorish assumption that I will have any compulsion whatsoever to do as you demand."

"I did not demand anything. I merely made a suggestion."

"No, you did not. You told me what you would do, which is to return me to London. You did not ask me if I would agree to come with you. And just to be clear, I will not."

Griffin stared at her. "But you must!"

"Why?"

He blinked. "To save your reputation. To—"

"My reputation is of little consequence to me because of the life I have chosen. I live remotely, away from London society. Considering my age, I am also firmly on the shelf and very unlikely to become the focus of any gossip monger's attention. No one besides my mother, sister, and aunt witnessed our kiss, and they will not breathe a word about it since that would ruin Laura's prospects. Furthermore, only my friends and your brother are aware of the fact that you accompanied me here, and I don't believe any of them will say a word about it to anyone."

"But…" Griffin searched his brain for a logical argument that might rival hers. "I cannot leave you here on your own. It would not be safe." There. Perfectly valid.

"On the contrary, I cannot think of a safer place considering the last crime committed in these parts involved the theft of a chicken, took place long before I ever moved here, and was discovered to be nothing more than a misunderstanding."

"Very well, I will concede that you have a point, but I'm still not letting you stay here alone."

Her pleasant smile dropped from her face, and she leaned toward him so she could glare at him properly. "You are not *letting* me stay here alone?"

"Any number of things might happen," he explained while doing his damndest to ignore the quickening of his pulse and the tension now simmering between them. "What if you fall and hurt yourself?"

"I have never done so in the past."

"Accidents happen."

"And I am starting to pray that one might befall you," she grumbled beneath her breath, though not quite low enough for him to miss it. He pressed his lips together to hide the surge of laughter bubbling up inside him. Her eyes sharpened. "I know you have plans to return to Vienna and I would hate to be the cause of any delay. Cassandra will join me here soon enough, so you need not worry on my behalf."

He frowned. "When, if I may ask, do you expect her to arrive?"

She clenched her jaw as if trying to trap the answer in her mouth. "On the twentieth."

"But that's at least two weeks from now."

"And I shall be fine until then."

There was no denying the fact that she was now trying to rid herself of his company completely, and *that* realization instilled in him an inexplicable stubbornness. It was as if she'd thrown down a gauntlet and challenged him to a contest of wills.

"That is not a chance I'm prepared to take. If I were to leave and something happened to you, I would never forgive myself. Nor would I be able to face your friends or Caleb again after promising them that I'd see to your safety." He paused for a second to consider the choice he had already made. Somehow returning to Vienna held less appeal than it had three days earlier, though he refused to consider the reason for that too closely at present. Instead, he forged ahead with his decision. "If you insist on staying, then I shall remain here with you until Cassandra arrives."

Miss Howard's mouth dropped open. Her eyes widened with dismay. "But...You cannot. I mean... It would not be proper."

"By your own account a few short minutes ago, propriety is not much of a concern to you."

"If you leave!" The glare was back in her eyes, even fiercer than before.

He understood her completely. "You worry what the locals will think if they discover that you and I are living together." It was a fair point, he had to admit. And since ignoring it would defeat his reason for staying, it was also one he could not deny. Least of all if he was to call himself a gentleman.

Seeing the look of despair in her eyes, the compulsion to keep her safe grew alongside his longing to stay, so he grasped at the only plausible option that came to mind. "None of the locals met me when I was last here, so I would suggest we allow them to think that I'm Caleb."

She shook her head as if trying to rid herself of an itch attacking her brain. "What?"

"We look identical to each other, save for the scar, which Caleb could have sustained a couple of months ago while fixing something or other on his London home."

"But why on earth would you...Caleb...be here instead of there with his wife?"

"Because some of the rooms here need a fresh coat of paint," he explained, warming to the idea. "Getting the work done while the children are away would be safest as it prevents them from being exposed to the fumes. And you have kindly agreed to oversee the project."

"But wouldn't Mary have come with you?"

"Not when she is expecting. It wouldn't be safe for her or the child."

Miss Howard did not look the least bit convinced. "Even if we managed to sell such a fib, there is still the matter of you and me living together."

"Except it would not be you and me. It would be you and Caleb, a married man who's practically your brother-in-law for all intents and purposes.

Certainly, there are those who will find it odd, but bearing in mind your status as a spinster, I don't think it will lead to scandal."

"I don't know…"

"The most important thing will be to prove our story, which means that I will actually have to do some painting while I am here." He smiled at that thought. "Surely that's too good an offer for you to pass up."

She drummed her fingertips lightly against the tabletop while considering. Griffin's heart thrummed with the sort of excitement he hadn't felt in years. Not since opening his shop and selling his first mechanical bird. But it was back now, and he could only hope that the woman who had the power to grant him a bit of adventure, no matter how brief, would not deny him the chance.

Her eyes met his and he saw in them a resolve that caused him to hold his breath. "You will have to stay in the cottage, just as your brother once did." Griffin expelled his breath and gave a quick nod. "Considering your rank, you should know that I am not comfortable with that demand, but it is a necessary precaution. I hope you understand."

"Of course. And you must not worry. I'm accustomed to living modestly."

She did not smile. Indeed, her entire demeanor had turned inscrutable. "You should also consider trimming your hair." Reflexively, Griffin ran his fingers through his dark locks. "Caleb's was shorter when he was here. Trimming it will make you more closely resemble the man the people here remember."

"An excellent point. Anything else?'

Hesitating briefly, she then slowly nodded. "If we are to do this successfully, we must start right away. We'll go into town so I can shop for some food while you purchase your supplies. This will give us a chance to establish the façade we wish to present."

"And prevent suppositions from being formed."

"Precisely."

He liked her logical reasoning. "Then we are in agreement?"

She inhaled deeply, as if preparing to dive to the bottom of the ocean. A swift nod followed, and then, "Yes. I believe we are."

Griffin almost whooped with the thrill that raced through him the moment she gave her consent. Vienna could wait. Staying here with Miss Howard, however, was the sort of opportunity he instinctively knew he ought not pass up. Because of duty and honor and the promise he'd made to protect her. To suppose there was any other incentive wasn't something that he was prepared to admit.

CHAPTER SIX

THERE WAS ONLY ONE REASONABLE explanation for why she'd agreed to Lord Griffin's mad scheme, Emily decided as they walked to the village together after breakfast. She was obviously cracked in the head. If randomly kissing him at a ball did not confirm this, then letting him stay with her at Clearview for two weeks most certainly did.

But the truth of the matter was that as adamant as she had been about trying to send him away, part of her had hoped he'd stay. It was selfish, she knew, for her reasoning had everything to do with the way he made her feel. For the past six years she'd come to the gradual realization that she would probably never marry and that she was destined to dedicate herself to the children she and her friends had taken into their care

It was a purpose that filled her life with meaning, and she knew it ought to be enough. But as much as she loved the boys and girls who depended on her, she longed to experience the sort of passion that Mary had found with Caleb. And Lord Griffin offered that chance. Being the subject of his attention made her feel beautiful and wanted.

She glanced at him briefly, at the firm outline of his jaw set in profile. The attraction between them had to be mutual. She was certain of it. And as much as it unnerved her because of her limited experience with men and flirtation, it also instilled in her the desire to explore, study, and learn.

Two weeks.

That was the time they would have together.

Alone.

At Clearview.

Her heart fluttered rapidly against her breast. Any number of things could occur between now and Cassandra's arrival. Presently, her most fervent wish was for him to give her a proper lesson in kissing. Because she already knew that there had to be more to it than what he had shown her in London. And since it was highly unlikely that she'd ever have a better opportunity to learn what all the fuss was about, she could not afford to pass up this chance. Even if it did mean risking her heart. Which was something of a problem since he did not seem the least bit inclined to repeat the effort.

"Penny for your thoughts?"

The sudden sound of his voice almost caused her to trip. "What?" She glanced at him and nearly lost her footing again on account of the warm, coffee-colored eyes gazing back at her from beneath a fringe of black lashes. His lips curved with a hint of amusement, and Emily's stomach dipped in response.

"You've been very quiet since we left the house, except for the occasional sigh which suggests something's troubling your mind."

"It is nothing." She deliberately coughed to conceal the bluntness of her words. And then, to ensure he would not press her further, she infused her voice with brightness as she added, "I was merely trying to decide what to make for dinner in the coming days. Is there anything you would rather not eat?"

He narrowed his gaze as if seeing straight through her attempt at directing the conversation toward him instead. A pause followed and for a second Emily feared he would once again insist on honesty from her.

To her relief, he shrugged and turned his attention toward the road ahead. "I am not partial to animal organs. And I cannot stand cabbage, cooked carrots, or brussels sprouts."

Emily smiled at the way he shuddered as he mentioned those items. "In that case I shall pretend I am cooking for one of the children, for I do believe your tastes are quite similar."

That comment earned her a scowl. "If I didn't know any better I'd think you were having a laugh at my expense."

"I would never," she said without any attempt at hiding her effort to tease him.

He shook his head, though not without adding a smile. "You're unrepentant."

She chuckled. "I'll take that as a compliment."

"Good. For it was intended as such." His voice was a low sensual murmur, causing sparks to fly over Emily's skin as it teased it into awareness.

She glanced away, unsettled by the powerful effect he had on her, for although she would readily accept his advances for educational purposes, she had no desire to be seduced. Which meant that if they did kiss again, it would have to be with pre-determined parameters. It would be the only way for her to remain detached and not lose her heart to a man whose life would never include her.

This thought lingered as they entered the town a few minutes later, but was quickly dislodged when Lord Griffin asked her to direct him to the paint and hardware shop. She did so and they parted ways with the agreement to meet one hour later at the inn across from the church.

Basket in hand, Emily made her way to the butcher where she purchased a pork loin roast and a chicken before continuing to the green grocers and cheese shop. She was just exiting Wilson's Bakery when she spotted two familiar faces.

Panic bubbled up inside her and she instinctively glanced around, searching for Lord Griffin.

When she saw that he was nowhere in sight, she allowed herself to relax. There was nothing to worry about. She would simply greet Mr. David Partridge and his sister, Miss Amanda Partridge, exchange a few pleasantries with them and be on her way.

Forcing a smile, she walked toward them.

"Miss Howard," Mr. Partridge said, tipping his hat politely in greeting. "What a pleasure it is to see you again."

"You too," Emily said, with a nod directed at the siblings. "I trust you are both doing well?"

"In a manner of speaking," Miss Partridge said. "Unfortunately we lost our beloved grandfather last month."

"Oh. I am so very sorry to hear that," Emily said, replacing her smile with a somber expression. "Please accept my condolences."

"Thank you," Mr. Partridge murmured. "It has been a trying time. If you recall, I have been managing his estate in Dorset since he went blind a few years ago. The place has felt a bit too somber lately, which is why I decided to come here and visit with the rest of my family for a while."

"I've been entertaining him with card games and charades," Miss Partridge added with a smile, "but after the rain we suffered yesterday, we decided to take advantage of the improved weather and go for a walk instead."

"And what a good choice that was," Mr. Patridge said, his gaze settling more firmly on Emily, "or we would not have happened upon you, Miss Howard."

Alerted by an increased degree of interest in her since their previous encounter with each other, Emily felt her cheeks heat in response. She was still determining how to respond when Miss Partridge's face lit up with pleasure. "Why, Mr. Crawford! How delightful to find you here as well."

Emily stiffened and then she turned until Lord Griffin came into view, his tall, broad-shouldered form a testament to his strength and solidity. The heat in her cheeks fanned out across the rest of her body, and her heart began to race with anxious awareness. She held her breath, uncomfortably alerted to the fact that this was the first test of their ruse.

Griffin tightened his hold on the parcels of ready-made clothing he'd purchased. "I should say the same to you," he said, responding to the blonde-haired lady with what he hoped was flawless credibility. "May I add that you look even lovelier than when I last saw you?"

The lady's lips curved with pleasure. "If you weren't already married, I daresay I'd set my cap for you myself."

Griffin smiled, not because of the flattery, but because he was glad to know that whoever these people were, they seemed to believe that he was Caleb. Both were dressed in a manner suggestive of wealth and good taste. He glanced at the man who could not be described as anything other than very attractive. When Griffin had rounded the corner and seen him addressing Miss Howard with a sparkle in his eyes, Griffin's insides had twisted beneath the tightening of his chest.

An immediate dislike of the man had erupted inside him – a dislike so intense there could be no logical explanation for it, except to suppose that it came from his duty to protect Miss Howard. And since he did not know who the man was or what his intentions might be, Griffin must have subconsciously chosen to err on the side of caution by considering the man a threat until proven otherwise.

Having made sense of this initial reaction, Griffin allowed himself to relax. He also did his best to behave as cordially as possible since the manner in which both the man and the lady had greeted him suggested they'd both been on good terms with Caleb. So he smiled while the young lady spoke of the weather and how she and her brother were very relieved to get out of doors after the previous day's rain. Every now and again she would give his cheek a curious look, but she was apparently too polite to inquire about his scar, denying Griffin the need to address it.

"What brings you back to Clearview, Mr. Crawford?" The gentleman inquired with interest.

The pair clearly stayed away from London society, or they'd have known that Caleb was in fact the Duke of Camberly and not the mere Mr. Crawford they'd known. Sticking to the role he himself was meant to play now, Griffin said, "Clearview still needs a few extra touches. When I left and married Mary, I promised Miss Howard and Lady Cassandra that I would return at the first available opportunity in order to see to it."

"You must join us for dinner one evening," the young lady said when Griffin had finished explaining his reason for coming to Clearview and why his 'wife' had not joined him. "It would allow us the opportunity to become better acquainted."

"Indeed," her brother murmured, his warm gaze fixed on Miss Howard in a way that caused Griffin to ball his hands into tight fists.

He deliberately flexed his fingers, tamping down the rising tension inside him, and turned to Miss Howard. Her lips were set in a firm line and although the edges were drawn up as if in a smile, he wasn't fooled. Something was bothering her, though he wasn't sure what.

Perhaps the invitation?

He prepared to offer their regrets when she accepted with a nod and a hastily spoken, "Thank you. That sounds lovely."

"Would Friday evening at six suit you?" the young lady asked, her eagerness to entertain them bubbling around her words.

Miss Howard's smile stretched in a way that caused Griffin to wince with discomfort. "Yes," she said. "We look forward to it already." They parted ways, with Miss Howard and Griffin continuing toward the inn where they had initially agreed to meet.

After going a few paces, Miss Howard glanced over her shoulder before quietly saying, "I'm sorry, but I could think of no reasonable way in which to tell you that the lady and gentleman with whom we were speaking just now were Mr. David Partridge and his sister, Miss Amanda Partridge."

"His interest in you was very apparent," Griffin said, not liking the clipped undertone sharpening his words.

"I could say the same of the attention Miss Partridge paid you. It was highly inappropriate, considering she believes you to be a married man."

The tightness in Miss Howard's voice gave Griffin pause. It struck a chord with which he could all too easily relate, and while he liked the idea of her getting slightly jealous, he did not want to believe that he might be susceptible to such an emotion himself.

Discomforted by this line of thinking, Griffin chose to circle back to the subject of Miss Howard and Mr. Partridge. "Perhaps you ought to flirt with him a little."

Where the hell did that suggestion come from?

Even as he said it, he felt his nerves pinch together tightly with displeasure.

"I beg your pardon?"

Begging his pardon was right, but for some unfathomable reason, Griffin's mouth had detached itself from his brain. "If you wish to marry..." *shut up, you fool* "...I daresay you could do worse." Oh hell. He knew he'd jammed his entire boot down his throat when he heard her sharp inhalation. When he realized she'd ceased walking, he stopped and turned hesitantly toward her, only to curse himself for the cad that he was.

Indignation burned in her eyes, brighter than the pain which she failed to hide from him completely. But she did tilt her chin and she did square her shoulders, for which he could only applaud her. And then she stepped toward him and for some peculiar reason, he felt like a small boy about to be soundly told off. He wasn't completely wrong to feel that way, he realized, for the words she spoke next made him feel half as tall as he actually was and less of the man he wanted to be.

"The fact that I might want to experience kissing does not mean I long to get married. I do not sit about pining for a husband, nor do I think of each man that I meet as a potential match." She inhaled deeply. "I certainly never considered you in that way, and we have done more than exchange a few words with each other."

Griffin blinked. "But you kissed me."

She glanced up at the sky, and he realized in that

instant that he was about to feel even smaller than he already did. "Actually, if you will recall, you kissed me. My intention was to share my first kiss with Mr. Bale. And so I probably would have if you hadn't chosen to interfere."

"I only did what I thought was right," Griffin said. The memory of how she'd looked together with Mr. Bale made his teeth gnash in annoyance. "And when I realized what I'd done, I did what I could in order to fix it."

"By providing me with the sort of demonstration that even a nun would find boring."

Christ!

Griffin straightened his spine. His pride was taking a beating, and it was high time for it to stop. "Anything else would have been both ungentlemanly and unforgiveable." What he would not tell her was that he'd been sorely tempted to give her precisely the sort of kiss she craved.

She closed her eyes briefly and pushed out a breath. "Quite so." A nod followed as if to underscore her approval of her own statement, and then she continued walking.

Griffin stared after her for a second before hurrying to catch up. "What do you mean by that?"

They passed the inn and continued toward the road leading back to Clearview. She shrugged. "It no longer matters."

"Are you sure about that?"

"Absolutely."

Griffin didn't believe her, but since he did not feel like arguing any more, he let the matter rest. Instead, he told her of the paint and the brushes he'd bought. Everything would be delivered the next morning, and as they walked home, he decided that painting the rooms at Clearview would not only help explain his presence, but would also offer the perfect distraction from Miss Howard and all the tumultuous feelings she stirred in him.

Flirt with Mr. Partridge.

That was Lord Griffin's suggestion?

Emily moved about the kitchen, putting away her shopping with jerky movements while cursing the stupid man who'd somehow managed to make himself her houseguest for the foreseeable future.

His comment had bothered her to no end, partly because it had not been as misplaced as she'd insisted, but mostly because she didn't want him to think of her as some desperate woman ready to leap at even the slimmest chance of forming an attachment. And to be fair, Mr. Partridge, however kind he might be, would hardly set his sights on a spinster without a dowry or any other advantageous incentive to warrant a proposal of marriage.

Not that she wanted him to.

In truth, if she were being brutally honest with herself, she would rather have Lord Griffin's attention. Which was yet another reason for her increased irritability—namely his effort to push her toward another man.

Even though her chance of ever becoming more to him than the forward woman who inappropriately tried to secure a kiss from a man she had no intention of entering into a courtship with was possibly slimmer than it was with Mr. Partridge. As evidenced by the fact that Lord Griffin had made it abundantly clear that he and she would not be engaging in any more kissing. At least not with each other.

She blew out a frustrated breath and leaned against the pantry door. The opportunity to experience a bit of passion had never been more available to her than now. A pity then that the man with whom she was able to experience it had seemingly little interest in her. But to let herself fixate on the issue would lead her nowhere, so she pushed away from the door and went to select a few herbs for the roast she planned on preparing for dinner.

When she returned to the kitchen, Lord Griffin was there, lounging in one of the chairs with casual abandon and looking as handsome as ever. Emily set her jaw. She could not afford to want him. Not when the last thing she wished to experience was disappointment and regret over his eventual departure. So she squared her shoulders and went to collect a bowl in which to rinse the herbs.

"You're still upset with me," he said after a moment of silence.

Emily dried off the herbs and placed them on a cutting board. She absolutely refused to look at him directly, for she knew that if she did, her knees would grow weak and her stomach flip over. "No. I'm not."

"Are you sure about that?"

"Of course." She grabbed a knife and proceeded

to chop the herbs into miniscule pieces. "And I apologize. For overreacting earlier when you were simply trying to be helpful."

He said nothing to this, and the sudden temptation to glance at him and read his expression was overwhelming. She marveled over her ability to resist it as she set about starting a fire in the hearth. When he offered to help, she allowed it and quickly gave her attention to rubbing the chopped herbs, salt and pepper into the roast.

"I realized when I was preparing the parlor for painting tomorrow that this clock is no longer working," he said a while later, breaking the silence.

Reflexively, Emily looked at Lord Griffin properly for the first time since entering the kitchen. The effect he had on her was just as visceral as she'd predicted it would be, and as a result, she found herself gripping the roast more firmly in a futile effort to steady herself. Whatever preparing the parlor for painting had entailed, it had caused his hair to get mussed. Haphazard locks shot upward in opposite directions while one fell randomly over his brow. It ought to have made him look ridiculous. Instead, it made him more attractive than ever.

And that was without considering the scruffy twist of his loosened cravat, the fact that his jacket was missing and his shirt sleeves rolled up past his elbows. Emily swallowed as her gaze swept over the dark dusting of hair on his forearms. Of course, she'd seen a lot more of him last night after they'd arrived and he'd been wearing nothing but a blanket, but the state of abandon with which he presented himself right now – the awareness that his appearance resulted from physical work – held greater appeal.

A movement drew her attention to his hands and the clock he was holding. "Oh. Right." She dropped her gaze to the roast and chastised herself for fawning over him like a nitwit. "My grandmother gave that to me for my tenth birthday. It was one of the few things I chose to bring with me when I came to live here. Even though it no longer responds to getting wound up, I keep it on display for sentimental reasons."

"If you like, I believe I am able to fix it for you."

In spite of her effort to maintain composure, Emily's eyes began to sting. Determined to hide it, she set about fetching a metal rod and spearing it through the roast. "Thank you," she said when she felt herself able to speak without her voice cracking. "I would be grateful for that."

He said nothing more for a while. And then she heard his chair scrape across the floor as if he were getting up. "I'll get started on it right away then. Please let me know when dinner is ready and... if there's anything else you would like me to help you with while I am here."

Emily could only nod in response. She was far too overcome for anything else.

CHAPTER SEVEN

DUSK FORCED GRIFFIN TO LIGHT a candle in order to better see the tiny pins, wheels, and other mechanical parts of the clock. From what he'd discovered after removing the movement from the housing, the power from the mainspring was unable to flow through the gears on account of the teeth being jammed too tightly together.

This would be a relatively simple fix. A trickier task would be to pre-load the tiny balance wheel spring which had come loose and add the right amount of tension to it. He would have to remove the regulator and balance cock in order to gain access, and this would most likely require an additional trip into town since he'd need some specific tools.

For the moment, Griffin added some gentle pressure to one of the stuck cogs. When it popped free with a click, he rotated it slowly to make sure the teeth were moving easily between each other once more. Oiling them would probably be a good idea, as would a proper cleaning.

He set the movement down and prepared to go and ask Miss Howard if she had any oil available, when a knock at the front door made him pause.

He stepped out into the hallway just as Miss Howard arrived from the kitchen. She gestured for him to return to the dining room where he'd been working, and he did so, easing the door shut behind him until a thin gap remained between it and the frame, allowing him to see who had come to call.

With a swift glance over her shoulder, Miss Howard went to open the front door just as another knock fell against it. She eased it open to reveal a young man with flushed cheeks and a cap pressed down over his forehead. "Letters from the Duke of Camberly and Mrs. Howard," he said.

Miss Howard took the letters, appeared to study them for a moment, then asked the man to wait. She went to collect a coin which she then handed to the messenger with her thanks.

He wished her a pleasant evening and departed, leaving Miss Howard alone in the hallway. Slowly, as if her mind was too busy for hasty movement, she closed the door and turned to face Griffin, who'd stepped back into the hallway.

"I think this must be for you," she said, handing him one of the letters. No recipient was specified, only the address, and since it was from his brother, Griffin believed she was probably right in her assumption.

"Thank you." Letter in hand, Griffin followed Miss Howard into the kitchen where the most delicious aroma now filled the air. His stomach grumbled in response, and he realized that he was quite ravenous. "Whatever it is you're cooking, it smells incredible."

She answered his compliment with a grin. "I

added some cinnamon to the root vegetables in the oven. Together with the roast meat and other spices and herbs, it creates both an aromatic scent and flavor."

"I can't wait to taste it," Griffin told her honestly as he dropped into one of the chairs, stretched out his legs and tore the seal of his letter.

"And so you shall very soon. Dinner ought to be ready within ten minutes." She turned away from him slightly and gave her attention to the letter she'd just received. Griffin could tell by Miss Howard's stance and by her hesitation to tear it open that she was reluctant to learn of its contents.

So he decided to offer her privacy and returned his attention to his own correspondence. Unfolding the piece of paper, Griffin stared down at Caleb's bold script as it came into view. There were only a few brief lines, but they were enough to make Caleb's muscles draw tight with agitated concern.

Griffin,

I trust that you and Miss Howard have arrived safely at Clearview. As commendable as your escort of her may be, however, I must point out that it is not without consequence. Having discussed the matter with her parents, we have concluded that the only way forward is for the two of you to marry. Any other solution would risk a permanent blemish on not only her reputation, but that of her unmarried sister as well. With this in mind, I have proposed a house party at Montvale, commencing on the seventeenth. Marrying there will ensure the privacy I'm sure you prefer.

I offer my sincerest apologies if this news is not to your

liking and look forward to seeing you soon.
Caleb.

Griffin re-read the letter twice before letting it fall to the table. He glanced across at Miss Howard whose shoulders now held a stiffness to them that suggested her letter was equally unpleasant.

Seeing no point in hiding the contents of his own letter, he told her plainly, "My brother says we must marry."

Startled, she let out a gasp and spun toward him. Her eyes were wide, her lips slightly parted as if it surprised her to find him there. She blinked and considered the piece of paper still clutched in her hand before setting it aside on the counter. Inhaling deeply, she then began taking the roast off the spit and removing the vegetables from the oven.

Griffin watched her stiff movements and considered the sharpness with which she sliced the meat a few minutes later. Her lips were now pressed firmly together, her chest rising and falling as if it took immense effort for her to contain her emotions. Eyes flashing, she scooped the vegetables into a bowl and set it down hard on the table. Her hands went to her hips as she glared at him with undeniable anger.

"My parents insist on the same." She spun away, collected the serving dish holding the meat and placed it in front of Griffin before sitting down with a jolt. "We must explain to them how unnecessary it would be. You…" She pointed her finger at him as if he were to blame for the current mess they were in. "You must return to London and talk some sense into your brother. Explain to him that I haven't been compromised, that we have taken precautions, and that there's no reason for anyone to find fault with your staying here with me. For God's sake, I have been living separate from my parents for several years. To think that my reputation could possibly be so easily endangered at this point is nothing short of silly."

"I believe my brother and your parents disagree," Griffin muttered. He stared back at her, at her horrified expression and the stubborn set of her jaw. She would fight this. Of that he had no doubt. And for some peculiar reason, this bothered him more than he cared to consider. "If you recall, I also warned you it would come to this."

Her mouth dropped open. "But it is preposterous!" She shook her head and proceeded to serve him, the rising mountain of food on his plate a testament to her scattered thoughts. When no additional vegetables would fit, she sat back and blew out a breath. "I would understand it if I were a debutante or if all of London had witnessed our kiss, but since neither is the case, I simply refuse to accept a solution as drastic as marriage."

Griffin nodded. "I must confess I agree." Slowly, he returned some of the vegetables to the bowl and two slices of meat to the serving dish.

"Of course you do," Miss Howard said with a burst of emotion. "You must return to Vienna. Getting married and staying in England would hardly work in your favor." Her brow puckered as she started serving herself. "Perhaps you ought to leave directly from here."

Her comment caused Griffin to sit up straighter, his fork halting en route to his mouth. He set it back down while battling the sharp stab of protest attacking his chest. "As we previously discussed, leaving you alone without any protection is not an option."

"But—"

"I am staying," he clipped, not caring that his comment made her glare at him like a petulant child reprimanded by a parent. Softening his tone slightly, he added, "Caleb will host a house party at his estate in Dorset on the seventeenth."

"Yes, I know. My mother mentioned it in her letter."

"Right." He gave her a firm look. "When it is time to depart for Montvale Manor, I shall escort you."

"You cannot be serious."

"Trust me when I tell you that I have never been more so."

She gave a carrot an angry stab with her fork. "If we go to Montvale together, avoiding marriage will become even more difficult." A heavy sigh escaped her and she suddenly slumped back against her chair. "Why run toward something that neither of us wants?"

The stabbing sensation in Griffin's chest deepened. "Because running away isn't the answer. The choices we have made these last few days are not as insignificant as you would like to make them, Miss Howard. We owe it to ourselves and to our families to act accordingly, which means we must face the repercussions with dignity."

"So you would destroy your life, for what? A momentary lapse in judgment?"

He winced and proceeded to eat a few bites of

food before saying, "Rest assured I will do what I can to convince everyone that marriage would be an unnecessary recourse." For reasons he could not explain, her aversion bothered him more than he was comfortable with. Troubled, the only solution was to agree that he was equally opposed to the idea of marriage. After all, they did not know each other particularly well. But the attraction he'd felt toward her the moment they'd met had been steadily growing.

It was the reason he'd followed her out into the garden, the reason he'd stopped her from spending more time alone with Mr. Bale, and the reason he'd so readily kissed her. Only to realize that he was in serious danger of doing a whole lot more.

It was also the reason he'd chased after her to the inn, the reason he'd escorted her all this way, and the reason he could not seem to leave, even though staying did not serve his purpose in any way. If anything, it threatened to disrupt his business and... He took a quick sip of his wine. How foolish he was being when it was clear she wanted him gone.

Her eyes found his from across the table, conveying a depth of gratitude that squeezed at his heart. Her features were a great deal softer now than they had been moments earlier. "Thank you."

A curious tightness worked its way up his throat, so he merely nodded. Fool indeed. If he weren't any wiser, he'd think he was falling for her – a woman who would never care for him in return.

The last thing Emily expected was for her mother to arrive at Clearview only two hours later. But here she was now, standing on the front doorstep with the family coach directly behind her and Patsy, her lady's maid, standing by her side.

Emily stared at the woman who'd raised her, completely befuddled. In her hand, she held the sponge with which she'd been washing the dishes when three loud raps on the front door had caused her stomach to dip with concern.

"Well?" Georgina raised both eyebrows. "Will you keep us standing here all night or do you intend to invite us in?"

Jolted by the firm tone, Emily took a step back and held the door wide. "Forgive me. I was not expecting your arrival." A modicum of composure began to return, allowing Emily to shake off her initial surprise and consider the situation more clearly. "Your letter made no mention of your intention to come here. Nor did the Duke of Camberly's."

"I know." Georgina brushed past her daughter, opened the first door on her left, and peered into the parlor. She shut the door again and moved on to the next, admitting herself to the dining room. "Where is he?"

Emily inhaled deeply. "In the kitchen." When her mother opened the door to Cassandra's study, Emily directed her to the opposite one. Behind them, Patsy arranged the luggage with the help of the coachman.

Emily's mother flung the kitchen door open and stepped into the warm room. "Dear God," she exclaimed, prompting Emily to hurry in after her. Georgina swung back to face her, the outrage she was about to convey reflected in her wide eyes. She pointed to where Lord Griffin stood, wiping a plate with a dish rag. "He's not even fully clothed!"

Emily glanced at her house guest. His appearance hadn't changed in the time it had taken her to go greet her mother, but the lack of a jacket and waistcoat along with his rolled-up shirt sleeves were suddenly far more glaring than they'd been before. Heat rushed to Emily's cheeks, but rather than flee the scene as she felt inclined to do, she cleared her throat and took a step forward.

"We were not expecting company, Mama, so Lord Griffin chose to make himself comfortable. For which I do not believe we should fault him."

Georgina's eyes widened even more. "It is worse than I feared," she said on a breathy exhalation. "You speak of yourself and Lord Griffin as if you are already a couple." When Lord Griffin started to speak, Georgina held up her hand. "Sir. I do not wish to know the extent of your relationship with my daughter, but one thing is clear—you will do the honorable thing or so help me I shall—"

"Mama." Emily bit out the word with a rising sense of indignation. "You have no right to make demands of Lord Griffin. Least of all when I am the one at fault. Indeed, you may rest assured that he has acted honorably toward me from the very beginning."

"If I may," Lord Griffin said.

"Are you telling me that my eyes deceived me when I saw your mouth attached to his at the ball?" Georgina asked, ignoring Lord Griffin completely.

Emily's cheeks grew hotter. She could no longer look at Lord Griffin on account of the fierce embarrassment raking her skin in response to her mother's question. He remained but a blur at the periphery of her vision. And yet, she refused to be put in her place by the woman who ought to have loved her, cared for her, put her first. Instead, Emily's mother had only thought of her own goals and how her daughter might realize them. Coming here was no different than her misguided efforts to fatten Emily up and push her into unflattering gowns years ago.

This realization encouraged Emily to speak with unforgiving candor. "No. Your eyes did not deceive you, Mama. But as I told you at the time, you, Laura, and Aunt Julia were the only witnesses to that incident. No one else knows that it happened." Seeing her mother's mouth set with determination, Emily pressed on, undaunted. "Similarly, no one besides our immediate family knows I left London in Mr. Crawford's company. Unless of course, you have let it slip." She eyed her mother shrewdly before saying, "If that is the case, then you ought to know I shall never forgive you. But in any event, I will not be marrying Lord Griffin. His kindness and consideration toward me deserves more than some backhanded attempt at getting him leg shackled to a woman he barely knows."

"Emily." Georgina's voice was tight.

"And also," Emily said, choosing to ignore her, "I am not a child you can order about. I have lived

happily here these past six years, ever since you..."
She swallowed, the past catching up with her in
a rush that threatened to overwhelm. "You may
stay as my guest, but I will never bow to your will
again. Is that understood?"

Georgina glared back at her for a long, drawn
out moment, but she eventually did as Emily
hoped she would and nodded.

Emily turned to Lord Griffin for the first time
since her mother's arrival. "I will show my mother
and her maid up to their rooms. I trust you can see
yourself back to the cottage?"

He dipped his head in solemn agreement. "Of
course."

Fighting the urge to go to him, to wrap her
arms around his neck and demand the embrace
she so desperately needed, she raised her chin. "In
that case, I shall bid you good night."

His chocolate brown eyes found hers, and it was
as if the strain she'd felt on her heart for the past
six years eased its hold. Because there, in Lord
Griffin's gaze, was something she'd never seen
before – something wonderfully empowering and
rewarding that could only be described as deep
admiration.

The edge of his mouth lifted, curving with a
hint of roguish solidarity that stirred deeper feelings to life. But since allowing herself to dwell on
the secret desires he inspired in her with simply a
smile would lead to nothing but disappointment,
Emily forced herself to turn away.

When she and her mother arrived upstairs after
sending the coachman to lodge at the inn in the
village, Emily showed her to Mary's old room.

Patsy would stay in one of the children's bed-chambers down the hall. "You still have not said why you chose to come here right after sending a letter informing me that you'd see me at Montvale in two weeks from now."

"Does my reason matter?" Georgina asked.

"It might."

Georgina placed her valise on the bed with a snort. "I very much doubt that."

Emily chose to respond with a shrug. "Very well then." She went to the door, eager to escape her mother's company, only to pause there in thought. "Will Laura be all right?"

"Time will tell, I suppose. But I do think my coming here will prevent unfavorable gossip. Your father is going to tell anyone who asks that you and I have decided to come here together."

Emily nodded. "If you need anything, I'm in the next room."

Her mother said nothing until Emily had almost shut the door behind her. And then she murmured, "Thank you."

"You're welcome," Emily replied. The door clicked shut and she blew out a deep breath that seemed to sweep away all the tension she'd harbored inside her veins since her mother's arrival. Drained and exhausted, she walked to her own room and prepared for bed.

CHAPTER EIGHT

A WAKENED BY A BRIGHT BEAM of sunshine falling in through the window and onto her face, Emily blinked and pulled her quilt up over her head with a groan. She'd forgotten to close the curtains last night and was now paying the price, although judging from the color of the light, it was time for her to rise.

With a sigh, she flung her quilt aside and pushed herself into a sitting position. She squinted, rubbed her eyes, and drew her hair back from her face. There were now three guests in her home, and all would have to be fed. She pondered that thought for a moment. Eggs and toast would be the simplest solution.

Satisfied that she knew what to prepare, she swung her legs over the side of the bed, stood, and proceeded with her toilette. The chilly floor nipped at the soles of her feet, causing her toes to curl inward. So she washed quickly, tied her hair in a knot, and put on a long-sleeved day dress cut from faded burgondy cotton. Over her shoulders, she placed a fawn-colored shawl which she crossed over her breasts and tied at her back.

She was just preparing to leave the room when

she looked out the window and spotted Lord Griffin. Dressed in brown breeches and a jacket to match, he was walking away from the house at a brisk pace while carrying something in his arms. But before Emily had a chance to determine what the item might be, he was gone, vanishing behind a large rhododendron bush that stood at the edge of the garden.

Emily turned from the window and went to prepare the breakfast. Her mother was still abed, which was something of a relief since Emily dreaded having to face her after the manner in which she'd addressed her the night before. A daughter did not speak to her mother with such disrespect. It simply wasn't done. And yet, as she stoked the fire in the hearth and lit the oven, Emily reminded herself of Lord Griffin's response. He had not been appalled or outraged by her manner. Quite the contrary. And as flattering as that had felt, it had also been liberating. Not only because she'd had his support, but because she'd had the courage to put the anger and pain her mother had caused into words. Forcing her to hear them had been the most cathartic experience of her life. She finally believed that there was a chance she could put the past behind her and move on, freer than ever before.

Pleased by this awareness, she cooked six eggs and toasted some bread, placed everything on the frying pan and covered the food with a lid to keep it warm. Since Lord Griffin had not yet returned from his walk, she decided to go and see if she could find him and let him know that breakfast was ready.

But when she crossed the grass and passed the rhododendron bush and the lake came into view, the sight that met her, of Lord Griffin's lean body moving elegantly through the water, almost caused her to lose her footing. Discovering him like this was so far removed from what she'd been expecting that she could not have imagined it even if she'd tried.

Caught between doing the right thing, which was to turn away, and the intense curiosity building inside her, Emily drew to a halt. She really ought to go back to the house and give him the privacy he deserved for his morning swim. But in spite of her good intentions, Emily's feet were somehow stuck to the ground. In fact, she was fairly certain that even if a herd of cattle came charging toward her, she would not be able to move.

So she stood, watching one arm sweep slowly up and over his head, muscles bunching briefly in his shoulders, before his hand reached into the water, propelling him fluidly forward. The other arm followed suit and then the pattern repeated with perfect timing as if he was silently pacing himself. Which Emily realized he must be when she noticed that he turned his head to breathe on exactly every fourth stroke. A shallow splashing of water accompanied his movements as he scissored his legs to aid his propulsion.

Emily stared. For a man of his height and build, she would not have imagined him capable of such grace. When he reached the far embankment, he dove beneath the water to turn, coming back up with the agile dexterity of a man accustomed to being in the water. His dark brown hair, almost black now, was pushed back from his forehead by the water. The wetness made it gleam in the early morning light breaking through the branches of a nearby weeping willow. It also made Emily forget time and place. All that existed for her right now in this moment was him, his strength and agility so thoroughly engaging she could not think of anything else.

Until he suddenly stood, rising up under a cascade of water that poured down his neck and over his shoulders. And then his eyes met hers.

With a gasp of awareness, Emily spun to the right, hiding behind the wide trunk of an oak.

"Miss Howard?" She bit her lip and squeezed her eyes shut in a silly attempt to escape reality. "I know you are there." When she stayed out of sight he spoke a bit louder. "You cannot honestly think that I failed to see you?"

"I was hoping you might have." Opening her eyes, she rolled them and muttered a curse, then stepped out from behind the oak.

The problem with this was that Lord Griffin had not remained where he was but had risen further out of the lake, putting his toned chest and well-defined abdomen on very prominent display.

Unwittingly, Emily's gaze dipped lower, to where his body disappeared beneath the surface of the water. A flare of heat rose to her cheeks while hot little embers pricked at her skin, exacerbated by her knowledge that he was probably completely undressed.

She glanced away, unable to look directly at him, until he quietly asked, "Were you spying on me?" Which naturally caused her to meet his gaze directly and with no small amount of chagrin.

For a brief second as she stood there, staring back into his intensely dark eyes, she was tempted to lie. "No," she wanted to say. "Of course not." Perhaps with an added, "How dare you suggest such a thing?"

But then she reminded herself of their agreement and raised her chin instead. Crossing her arms, she told him honestly, "Yes."

His eyebrows rose and his lips parted a fraction – just enough to convey his surprise. And then he laughed, not with humor but with the sort of devilish amusement that Emily imagined must be reserved for only the wickedest scoundrels. It suggested that his thoughts had turned very sinful indeed.

"I cannot help but marvel at your candor," he murmured in a low, seductive tone. "And your curiosity is certainly inspiring."

His eyes darkened as he took a step forward. The water slid away from the lower part of his chest, revealing his navel.

Emily stared even as she took a step back.

"I wonder," Lord Griffin said as another stride offered a view of his hip, "how far this curiosity of yours," his other hip appeared along with a narrow dart of black hair leading down over his pelvis, "will take you."

Emily closed her eyes, her mortification stomping out all of her courage. "I just came to tell you that breakfast is ready. I'm sorry for the intrusion which wasn't..." She swallowed past the dryness in her throat. "I'm sorry," she repeated, before she turned on her heel and hurried back to the house, as she ought to have done when she'd first seen him.

But when she arrived in the kitchen, she was met by chaos. Her mother was busily rummaging through cabinets and drawers while boiling water overflowed from the kettle. The flames beneath it hissed in response, puffing out steam that thickened the air.

Emily grabbed a dishtowel, then snatched the kettle from its spot above the fire. "Mama. What on earth is going on?"

Georgina spun toward her with an expression that bordered between concentration and panic. "I need tea. I've never started a day without it and have no intention of doing so now." Straightening, she placed one hand on her hip and glanced at the hearth as if it were her worst enemy. "Since you weren't anywhere to be found, I was forced to take matters into my own hands."

"I can see that." Emily placed the kettle on the counter and went to retrieve the tin in which tea was kept. She fetched the teapot next and proceeded to make the hot beverage her mother required. "Could Patsy not have helped you?"

"I sent her to post a letter to your father."

"Before breakfast?"

"Of course not, dear. I'm not that awful. She found the eggs and toast and made a sandwich that she could eat on the way."

"Hmm…"

"This is good," Mrs. Howard murmured a few moments later after the tea had steeped and she was able to take her first sip from the cup that

Emily had prepared. She took another and sighed, then set the cup aside and considered her daughter. "I'm sorry I made a mess."

"It's all right." Emily closed the drawers and cabinets her mother had opened, arranged two plates with the eggs and toast she'd made earlier, and went to join her at the table.

Her mother stared at the plate before her while Emily made a cup of tea for herself. "Did you really cook this?"

Picking up her teacup, Emily cradled it between her hands while blowing softly to cool the drink before taking a sip. "I don't have a cook hiding somewhere in a closet, if that's what you're asking."

Her mother raised her gaze slowly and when her eyes met Emily's there was something new there – something far more meaningful than surprise. "I must say that I'm rather impressed."

Emily's chest tightened. "Thank you," she rasped, covering the emotion her voice betrayed with another quick sip of her tea. She set her cup aside and reached for the butter.

"Will Lord Griffin not be joining us?"

Emily paused. "I…um…I do not know."

"I'm only thinking that it would be rude of us to start without him."

"Right." Emily retrieved her hand. She'd hoped to finish breakfast and remove herself from the kitchen before Lord Griffin arrived. Facing him now, after their most recent interaction, would only make her uncomfortable. And besides, if she wasn't busy eating, she would have to face the silence now hanging between herself and her mother.

Too much resentment had built up between them over the years, crushing every chance they might have had of getting along. Emily leaned back in her seat with a sigh. When Langdon had broken things off, she'd known she'd lost her chance of marriage and children forever.

Of course, her mother had disagreed. She'd simply ordered up another bright gown – a lime green horror of a dress – and told Emily to keep on trying. Instead she'd shoved the dress into her dustbin and accepted Cassandra's invitation to join her at Clearview.

The door opened and Lord Griffin stepped in, distracting Emily from her thoughts. His hair was damp and mussed in a way that made him look wonderfully attractive. But unlike earlier, he was now properly dressed. Even his neck was hidden beneath a perfectly knotted cravat.

"Good morning, ladies." He closed the door behind him and approached the table. "I hope you can forgive my delay in joining you."

"Of course," Emily told him as she went to prepare his plate.

He waited for her to place it before him and to resume her seat before claiming his own, his knee brushing hers beneath the table in a manner that made her heart jolt. "Nevertheless, I would ask you not to wait for me in the future." He watched while she poured him a cup of tea, her hand made a little unsteady by his perusal. Thanking her in a low, sensual murmur that caused her belly to shudder with pleasure, he turned his attention on Emily's mother. "I hope you slept well last night."

"Oh, indeed." Georgina took a few bites of food. "The room I've been given is incredibly comfortable, and this breakfast is most delicious." She stuck another piece of egg in her mouth and chewed before saying, "I was not aware that my daughter is so very capable."

"Circumstance forced me to acquire some necessary skills," Emily told her. Even though she'd meant for her words to be a statement of fact, she failed to stop them from sounding bitter.

Her mother pressed her lips together and nodded. "Of course." She lowered her gaze and proceeded to cut her toast into tiny pieces. "I did not mean to sound condescending, Emily, but rather to compliment you on what you have accomplished."

"It is no more than what most women manage to do every day when they can't afford servants."

A gust of uncomfortable silence swept through the kitchen, and Emily bowed her head, regretting the haste with which she'd just spoken. She wished she could simply accept her mother's rare praise with gratitude, but the grievance she felt was too deeply ingrained and not easily overcome.

"True," Lord Griffin said when Emily was sure she would have to endure the rest of the breakfast with no other sound but the scraping of silverware to keep her company, "but you were raised in an upper class household, Miss Howard. So as your mother correctly points out, you have proved you are able to adjust to new ways of life in a manner I'm sure most young ladies of similar backgrounds would balk at."

"Perhaps," Emily agreed, not liking the smallness that filled her conscience on account of his pleasantly spoken reprimand.

"As a matter of fact, I am equally impressed. Especially by your modesty."

"My modesty?" Emily choked, coughing on the end of her words. Did he really have to mock her as well?

"You turned your back on the easy path and chose to scale a mountain instead." His voice was gentle, tender even, and so beguiling it forced her to meet his gaze. And in his eyes she saw only warmth and…something she would have labeled as affection if she hadn't known better. "Your mother knows it wasn't easy, yet you persevered and succeeded, proving that you can do anything you set your mind to." He smiled, causing Emily's heart to expand with pleasure. And then he leaned back, took a sip of his tea, and added, "I believe that is what she was trying to tell you."

"Quite right," Georgina agreed. "Thank you for being more eloquent than I have ever managed. My own parents always taught me to be direct for the sake of efficiency, but that can be a disadvantage sometimes."

Lord Griffin chuckled as if he actually enjoyed Georgina's company. "You should know that your daughter has also inherited that trait— a propensity for directness, that is, though in a slightly different capacity."

"How so?" Georgina asked, her eyes bright with interest.

Emily stared at her and then at Lord Griffin, incredulous at their relaxed manner when she herself felt as though she was strung as tight as a bow.

"She speaks her mind," Lord Griffin said. "Which is not only admirable, but also extremely attractive."

Emily's mouth dropped open. He had not just said that. Had he?

Judging from the gleam now brightening her mother's eyes, it would seem that he had. Emily groaned. Was he deliberately trying to undermine their efforts to avoid getting married?

"Attractive?" Georgina echoed with a slight crease to her brow. "You find opinionated young women attractive?"

Emily smiled. Finally. Lord Griffin had found a topic on which the two would never agree. To her mother's way of thinking, a young lady had only one purpose besides getting married, and that was to show off all her accomplishments while refraining from speaking as much as possible.

"A person's opinion is the best indication of their intelligence," Lord Griffin murmured. "In my experience, foolish people either have no opinion at all, or they tend to babble on endlessly without ever making their point clear. So when making a new acquaintance, I always strive to consider opinion. After all, it is the quickest way to determine compatibility."

"I see." Georgina's satisfaction with Griffin's response was clear in the way she smiled.

Seeing straight through to the plan forming in her head, of Lord Griffin and Emily getting married despite their protestations, Emily chose to change the subject immediately. "We have dinner plans on Friday at a nearby estate." She explained how she and Lord Griffin had met the Partridges in town and that both had appeared to believe he was Caleb.

"So you wish for me to lie?" Georgina asked in dismay. "To a lady and gentleman?"

"You may remain here if you prefer," Emily offered, but her mother quickly dismissed that idea.

"Since this is a matter of protecting our entire family's reputation, I shall find a way to overcome my aversion in order to do what I must. And I do believe my presence will add credibility to your story."

Lord Griffin pushed his empty plate and cup aside so he could lean forward with his folded arms on the table. "I completely agree."

"Do you have something appropriate to wear to this event?" Georgina asked Emily.

Emily stiffened. She hadn't packed before leaving London, so the only evening gown she had at Clearview was the one she'd been wearing when she'd arrived two days earlier. Salvaging that disaster was out of the question. "I've a respectable dress cut from cornflower blue muslin. It will suffice."

"For a dinner party hosted by gentry?" Her mother shook her head. "On no, my dear, that will not do at all. You must wear silk. So if you haven't such a gown, then I suggest we order one today from the local modiste. I shall need one as well, of course. And you mustn't worry about the cost. It shall be my treat." She stood, so Lord Griffin rose as well. "And what of you, sir? Have you the appropriate evening attire required, or will you join us for this excursion so you can visit the tailor?"

"I will happily escort you both."

"Excellent. Then I shall go and ready myself immediately." She looked to Emily whose jaw was starting to ache from gnashing her teeth. "Thank you for breakfast. I found it to be most satisfying."

Emily was tempted to tell her the dishes now had to be washed. Instead she kept quiet, holding back her emotions just like a corked bottle of champagne forced back the pressure bubbling within.

To say that the relationship between Miss Howard and her mother was strained would be an understatement of monumental proportions. Griffin waited quietly until Mrs. Howard had left the kitchen before returning his attention to her daughter with every intention of addressing the issue.

Except she spoke first, reminding him of the point he'd been trying to make about her outspokenness. He still wasn't sure he'd phrased himself correctly. At least not well enough to convey the extent of his admiration for this woman who'd been released into London ballrooms by her over-eager mama. The mission had been the same as it was for all other debutantes, only Emily's chances of success had been greatly reduced by the very same person who'd wanted her to succeed. And as a result, Emily had failed at the one thing she'd been expected to do, which was marry well.

Anyone else in her position would have been

crushed by the adversity, but not Miss Howard. She had the strength and perseverance of a warrior princess.

"What. Are. You. Doing?" Fire burned in her eyes, not the kind brought on by desire, but the kind that warned of impending battle.

Griffin found it equally arousing, his focus momentarily wavering on account of the heat charging through his veins. It was not dissimilar to what he'd felt when he'd found her watching him during his swim. He knew he'd pushed her comfort to the limit when he'd challenged her curiosity, but he hadn't been able to resist the opportunity. Something about her made him want to be reckless.

"I don't know what you mean," he said, forcing his mind back to her question.

She glared at him, which only made his muscles draw tight with anticipation. "My mother is first and foremost a meddler, and you were encouraging her at every opportunity."

"By being nice to her?"

Emily pinched the bridge of her nose and shook her head. "No. By supporting her arguments and speaking too highly of me."

It took some effort not to laugh, but Griffin managed and affected a serious expression instead. "I hope you can forgive the compliment."

A hint of humor tugged at her lips, but rather than surrender to it, she fought it and won. "You do not know her as well as I do. She will consider your praise to be a sign of interest. In me. And once she does so, she will be more determined than ever to see us wed."

"I see," Griffin murmured, pretending that this was indeed the most dire outcome he could possibly imagine. But the truth was slightly different. For some odd reason, he was no longer repelled by the idea of having to make Miss Howard his bride. Not even under duress.

In fact, the biggest problem was not so much having to marry her, were it to come to that, but the responsibilities he'd left behind in Austria. Prolonging his stay in England indefinitely wasn't an option, which meant he would soon have to stick with his plan and depart.

He eyed the stern set of Miss Howard's jaw, the displeased line of her mouth, and the sharp irritation that pushed back the brown in her eyes and turned them a bright shade of green. "Have you ever considered travelling?" he asked, the question springing from his throat and catching him slightly by surprise.

She shook her head. "No. Not really."

"Would you like to?" he pressed.

"I'm not sure," she said with a frown. "Why do you ask?"

"Just curious."

She snorted. "I do not believe that you're being honest with me."

His stomach muscles tightened and his heart beat slightly faster. Not with excitement but with a different kind of sensation – one he had not experienced in years. Griffin swallowed, a little distressed by the realization that he was nervous: nervous that she would discover his true line of thinking and nervous that she'd be appalled by the idea of actually becoming his wife.

"You're trying to distract me by changing the conversation to something else," she said before he could offer an honest explanation.

The breath he'd been holding rushed from his lungs, removing the strain on his nerves. He forced a mischievous smile. "I'm sorry, but I'm not very fond of being told off."

"I wasn't..." She sighed in response to his raised eyebrow. "Very well. Can we simply agree that you should stop providing my mother with reasons to not only like you but to imagine she has a chance of forcing a match?"

"Certainly." He would not reveal that he planned to secretly court her anyway. Not when she was so clearly opposed. He'd been too, until recently. But then he'd realized a few intriguing things, like the fact that she drove him mad with desire, that he loved simply talking to her, and that he was reluctant to leave her company.

And then there was the surge of jealousy he'd felt when he'd seen Mr. Partridge showing an interest in her. Just the idea of Miss Howard so much as touching another man made him want to hit something. Because if there was one truth that rang loud and clear above everything else, it was that he wanted her for himself.

Forever.

CHAPTER NINE

THE OUTING TO TOWN WAS not as terrible as Emily expected it to be. Her mother did not insist on orange or yellow fabric during their visit to the modiste. Not even lime green was suggested. But when Emily gave her attention to a purple silk that slid sensually over her fingers as she touched it, her mother said she believed it a shade too dark for her skin.

Instead, she brought Emily's attention to a crimson silk that begged to be turned into an elegant gown. "I cannot possibly," Emily murmured even as she ran her fingers over the supple surface. "The color is far too bold."

"No more so than the purple one you were just considering."

True. "This one just seems more scandalous somehow."

Her mother made a face that informed Emily she was being ridiculous. "For a debutante perhaps, but you are an older woman, if you'll forgive me for saying so. Your age cannot be debated." She held the fabric up next to Emily's face while they stood before a long mirror. "It's perfect. Truly. The sort of color that is sure to get you noticed."

Emily considered the fabric. Ordering an evening gown made from it was incredibly tempting. And yet, Emily knew that her mother's motive in suggesting the fabric was solely to secure Lord Griffin's attention. And this gave her pause. "It is just a dinner party, Mama. There is no need for me to stand out."

"Of course not." Her mother pulled the fabric away and returned it to the shelf where she'd found it. She then picked up a cream-colored silk and handed it to Emily. "Perhaps this would be better?"

Compared with the crimson, the cream looked impossibly dull and uninteresting. Still, Emily held it up to her face and considered the option. "No," she admitted after a second. "I do not like it." Not now that the bright red fabric was stuck in her head.

"Why not have another look around then. Perhaps a different color will strike your fancy, like green or blue?" When Emily failed to find another color she liked, her mother reached for the purple silk that Emily had initially selected. "I think you ought to ignore my opinion since it has been wrong so often before. If this is the fabric you like, then that is the one you should choose."

Except it no longer held appeal. In fact, as Emily considered it once again, it did look too dark against her skin. She glanced across at the crimson silk neatly resting on a nearby shelf and made her decision. Twenty minutes later, after deciding on a pattern, having measurements taken and offering to pay the dressmaker double for expedited service, Emily excited the dressmaker's together with her mother and went to meet Lord Griffin.

They found him at the tailor where he was just finishing up his order of evening attire. "It ought to be ready by Friday morning," he said, addressing both Emily and her mother.

"Just like our gowns," Emily said.

He smiled. "A convenience to be sure since we shall be able to pick up everything during one trip."

"Speaking of trips," Georgina said, "I want to propose that we offer the cottage at Clearview to my coachman. Having him at the house will make it easier for him to take us wherever we need to go at only a moment's notice."

"But Lord Griffin is staying there, Mama."

"Yes. And that was both correct and necessary when it was just the two of you. But now that I am here, I see no reason why we cannot move Lord Griffin to one of the bedchambers inside the house."

A shiver crept over Emily's skin. "But—"

"He is a duke's brother, Emily. An aristocratic gentleman. We cannot ask him to remain in that tiny cottage, and we certainly can't ask my coachman to stay in the house instead. That would be highly irregular."

"I suppose so," Emily hedged with a quick glance directed at the only man in the world who could make her grow hot with a single look.

His expression gave no indication of what he was thinking, which wasn't very helpful at all. Especially when her own stomach was tying itself into knots at the idea of having him sleep so close to her.

"Then it is settled?" Georgina asked.

"Perhaps the coachman could remain at the inn," Emily suggested.

"You know that would be both impractical and a neglect of the coachman's responsibilities toward me as his employer. So unless Lord Griffin is opposed..?"

"I would happily agree to move out of the cottage and into the house so that you may keep your coachman nearby, Mrs. Howard."

Emily turned her head just enough to catch Lord Griffin's eye as she mouthed the word, "Traitor."

He responded with a roguish smirk, which only increased her discomfort. Especially since she failed to see his motive for bowing to her mother's suggestion without the slightest protest. It made no sense for him to do so. Not when he was supposed to be avoiding an attachment.

"I managed to purchase the tools I require to fix your clock," Lord Griffin told her later when they returned to Clearview.

After taking lunch at the inn while they waited for the coachman to pack his things and ready the carriage, they'd enjoyed riding back to the house instead of walking.

"Thank you," she said as she followed him into the dining room where all the clock parts were now spread out with what appeared to be organized precision. Emily blinked. "Oh dear."

"You must not worry," he told her quickly. "I know what I'm doing and will put everything back together in perfect order."

Emily moved further into the room so she could better study the array of cogs, wheels, springs, and miniscule screws. "That is not my concern." Heavens. Her voice was struggling to form words. The emotion she felt, brought on by gratitude, was almost too much to bear.

"Then what is troubling you?" The question was gently spoken. It also brought him closer to where she stood, spiking her awareness of him. Her entire body tingled in response to the rich scent of sandalwood clinging to his person.

His hand settled softly against her lower back in a manner no doubt meant to offer comfort. Instead, it made Emily catch her breath as heat erupted inside her. "I did not realize how much trouble this would be for you," she said, the words scratching her parched throat while she struggled to stay upright. To not lean into his hand. To not ask for more.

His hand fell away, leaving a chill in its place. But he remained by her side, so close she could feel the air shifting between them as he moved. "Fixing this clock is not an inconvenience." The low voice with which he spoke swept through her like butterflies riding on a breeze. "I am happy to do it. Especially since I know how much it would mean to you."

"My grandmother always understood me. I loved her enormously and wished she'd been there for me to confide in as I grew older." A sting brought moisture to Emily's eyes, and she walked a few paces, adding distance to help hide her tears. "But she died right before my first season and this clock..."

"You need not explain."

"I don't think I can," she told him, her voice a bit shakier than she had hoped.

"I know." She swiped at her eyes and turned more fully toward him. Before she could ask what he meant, he dipped his hand into his waistcoat pocket and pulled out a watch, attached by a golden chain. "This is my most prized possession. A gift from my brother, George, on my tenth birthday." He dropped his gaze to the dial. "He gave Caleb a tool set and Devlin received a compass." A low chuckle wrought by sadness escaped him. "George knew what our paths in life would be before we did."

"I'm so sorry." It was difficult seeing him like this, made vulnerable by grief.

"He should not have died as he did."

Emily swallowed. She knew a fire had killed both George and his father while they'd been attempting to save the horses trapped in one of their stables. It was how Caleb had been made duke and the reason why Lord Griffin had returned to England.

"I was shocked when I learned of it," he added.

Emily nodded, but remained silent, partly because she had trouble finding the right words and partly because she wanted to give Lord Griffin room to speak.

"We were never particularly close, but I always looked up to George." The corner of Lord Griffin's mouth twitched. "He was an exemplary marksman. He could hit a coin hung from a tree branch from a distance of fifty paces."

"I would have loved to see that."

Lord Griffin nodded. He returned his watch to his pocket and with it, the brief display of grief he'd allowed her to witness. "He would have liked you a great deal. Of that I have no doubt."

There was something in his words, a deeper meaning that brought a strange sense of comfort to Emily's soul. Before she had time to study it further, Lord Griffin distracted her by picking up something that looked like a spool of flatly pressed metal. "This is the part that needs fixing."

Moving closer to where he stood, Emily leaned forward for a better look, her shoulder inadvertently brushing his arm in the process. A spark darted through her, the shock of it forcing a low gasp from between her lips.

If he noticed, he made no indication. Instead he turned the metal coil over in his hand. "See the unevenness here? I have to straighten that out before I can balance the mechanism properly."

"I suspect that must have happened when Peter dropped it." The boy had done so by accident. He'd been holding the clock, oblivious to Emily's arrival in the room. When she'd spoken, Peter had jumped, and the clock had tumbled from his hands.

Even though it had been a mishap, it had still been upsetting. Especially when Emily had realized the clock no longer worked.

"He probably wanted to discover how it functioned."

"That is what he told me." It had not made Emily feel any better though. She sighed at the recollection. "I'm afraid I still lost my temper."

"That is perfectly understandable." Lord Griffin

met her gaze with both sympathy and understanding. "This clock is an heirloom, irreplaceable because of your emotional attachment to it. Of course it would upset you to find it broken. But the good news is that it is not beyond repair." He smiled then, the sort of smile that could make a woman forget she was not supposed to fall head over heels in love with him. "I am going to fix it for you, Miss Howard. Of that, you have my word."

It was her turn to speak now, to thank him for his kindness, except she was still slightly dazed by his smile, his nearness, his scent, and his overwhelming charm. All of it came together, like a spell intended to muddle her head and make her feel stupid. She swallowed, retreated a step, away from the potent effect he was having on her.

When she reached the door she paused, not exactly looking at him but not looking away either. "I...um..." She made an effort to put her scrambled thoughts in order. "Yes. That would be nice."

He gave her a quizzical look, his head slightly tilted as if he could not comprehend her response. Which was understandable since she could not comprehend it herself. She pressed her lips together, realizing she ought to say something more – something better and more appropriate. Except she could not think with him standing there staring at her, and she feared now that any effort she made to salvage her feeble attempt at conveying her gratitude would only be made worse by additional words.

So she stepped back further, her stomach now

tight and her skin growing hot from the flush of discomfort spreading over her body. A nod was all she could manage before she turned and fled, removing herself to her bedchamber for the next hour. It was safe there, the tidy room offering her an oasis of reprieve from the man who made her feel so much she could not relax in his presence. Around him, her nerves were on constant alert, her senses struggling to comprehend and catalogue each new experience. And as wonderful as that was, it was also trying.

Tossing herself on her bed, Emily felt the mattress dip and rise beneath her back as she stared up at the white plaster ceiling. How could she possibly have thought that a kiss in a garden at night would be simple? How could she have imagined that she could control such a personal experience and ensure complete detachment? How could she ever have believed that letting Lord Griffin do the honor would not cause emotional turmoil to plague her?

She took a deep breath and expelled it slowly while forcing herself to acknowledge one thing: she was so far out of her depth, she just might drown.

CHAPTER TEN

GRIFFIN SPENT THE NEXT THREE days either painting the parlor or working on Emily's clock. This allowed him the solitude he needed in order to sort out his feelings for her. It also gave her a chance to avoid him, as he believed she wished to do. He pondered this new development while running his paintbrush over a spot he'd missed earlier. Her skittishness around him had been gradually increasing in line with his own awareness of her.

Stepping back, he admired his work for a moment before continuing, his hand moving up and down in smooth, easy strokes, though his mind was on something else entirely. Namely on her. She was so damn lovely, especially when she looked shy and uncertain, which was happening now with increased frequency.

Again, for what had to be the millionth time, he played out the incident at the lake in his head. She'd fled, but not before she'd revealed her curiosity or her desire. Fear had won out that morning, causing her to flee, but her flushed cheeks, the fact that she'd stayed to watch him get out of the water until she'd risked seeing too much, piqued more than his interest. It made him want to do things he ought not to want to do with an innocent young woman.

Try as he might though, he could not quite control his indecent imaginings. Not any longer. Not when he felt their attraction was mutual. For she could tell him that he was just a means to an end, the man who happened to accommodate her wish to learn about kissing when no other option remained. But Griffin knew better. Deep inside he'd always known better. Ever since the first time he'd met her when he'd come here looking for Caleb several months earlier and she'd been the one who opened the door.

She'd been the most beautiful woman he'd ever seen, and the spark he'd felt, though he'd dismissed it at the time on account of more important business, had not been imagined. It had been real and fiery and urgent. And while he'd done his best to ignore it since then, aware that pursuing it further would only result in hurting her while acquiring Caleb's displeasure, he'd started to wonder if things might be different if he wanted them to be.

What if he sold his business in Vienna and moved back to England? What if rather than hurt Miss Howard by leaving, he made an attempt at staying?

Was that even something she might want?

All he knew was that she'd once lost her chance at marriage and that she still seemed to resent this. He stared at the white wall a moment. Had she loved the man who'd courted her and been heartbroken over losing her chance with him? A surge of displeasure raced through him, quickening his pulse. He shook his head. No. She'd only mentioned her suitor in passing, as a missed opportunity of sorts, nothing more.

That reminder, the belief that her heart remained unattached, allowed him to breathe more easily. It also forced him to acknowledge the fact that he wanted to be the object not only of her desire but of her affection. He wanted to be the man who did more than teach her how to kiss. He wanted to be the man who reminded her every day of how wonderful and extraordinary and stunning she was, the man who chased away every doubt she'd ever had about herself, who showed her that she deserved to be loved for her courage and boldness.

The door swung open behind him, causing cool air to sweep over his shoulders. He turned and immediately spotted the object of his contemplations, her hazel eyes curious as they roamed around the room before settling on him. A wave of pleasure rolled through him as he spotted that now familiar curiosity and interest brightening her gaze.

The edge of her mouth twitched, dispelling the awkwardness that had been hanging between them for days now. "When you said you would paint the room, I thought you meant the walls."

He frowned. "What?"

She pressed her lips together and nodded toward a spot behind Griffin. He glanced over his shoulder, his muscles tightening at the sight of the fireplace mantelpiece. "Damnation." It was brilliantly white against an equally white wall and he, simpleton that he was, was cursing in front of

a lady. "Forgive me. I..." He scrambled for a rag.
The paint was still wet so perhaps... A few rough
swipes informed him that it was already too late.
In fact, he was just making it worse now by creat-
ing a streaky mess.

"Stop."

He dropped the rag and stared helplessly at the
piece of carved rosewood now hidden away and
unsalvageable due to his own stupidity. "I'm so
sorry." He'd been thinking of her and not of the
task, his hand moving mindlessly over the wood
instead of the wall.

"It's all right. At least you didn't paint the silk
cushions on the sofa."

Turning slowly toward her, he could only stare
at her, incredulous. "I have ruined your mantelpiece."

"Did you do so deliberately?"

"No. Of course not. But that does not make it
all right."

She nodded. "Perhaps not, but getting upset
over it will not help either." She dropped her gaze
to the floor. "It didn't when Peter broke my clock.
If anything, it will only result in unpleasant emotions that won't resolve anything."

"Miss Howard. I... You..." Words failed him.
He'd been careless and she was accepting it without any reprimand.

"You should probably paint the rest of the fireplace too. It will look more deliberate then. But
before you do, Mama suggested a picnic for lun-
cheon because of the weather, and I thought I
would ask you if you'd like to join us."

He stared at her. "A picnic?"

"Where you eat outside on a blanket spread on the ground?"

An involuntary bit of laughter rose from his throat. "Yes. I know what it is."

She laughed as well. "Good. For a moment there I was starting to wonder if the paint fumes had negatively affected your brain."

"No. I do not believe so. The window is open."

A smile tugged at her lips. "You have paint in your hair and on your cheek."

He reached inside his pocket and retrieved a handkerchief which he promptly used to wipe at his cheek. "Better?"

She chuckled. "It's on the other cheek."

He made a second attempt at removing the stain. "How about now?'

Miss Howard shook her head and stepped toward him. "You're making it worse." She held out her hand and he gave her the handkerchief, his body on sudden alert as the expectation of her touch brought a strain to his muscles. He fought the urge to lean closer and instead remained where he was, perfectly still and immobile, save for the rise and fall of his chest.

The white linen grazed his skin, and although it created a barrier between them, he could feel the pressure of her fingertips moving against him. They did so efficiently, scrubbing at him with determination.

That same determination could be found in her eyes, now fixed upon the spot where she worked. She was still at arm's length, not improperly close or even doing something that could be claimed as anything other than helpful. The parlor door was open behind her, denying them privacy.

But her scent… The sweet smell of lavender and fresh soap that suggested she'd recently bathed wafted over him. Along with something more homely.

"Have you been baking?" he asked when he caught a whiff of flour and milk.

A smile tugged at her lips. "I made scones."

His mouth started to water. "I love scones." Leaning slightly toward her, he breathed her in. The scent of her coaxed his senses until they were brought to an almost painful alertness. And then, as if she felt the touch of his gaze upon her, her eyes found his, and her effort to clean him slowed until it halted completely. She stood now, as still as he, her hand holding the handkerchief to his cheek.

Her throat worked as her awareness aligned with his. Lips parting ever so slightly, she blinked as if either surprised or completely undone in some way. The handkerchief shifted and Griffin realized that she was about to retreat as she always did when these moments arose between them. So he raised his own hand, pressing it to hers and holding it captive against his cheek.

"Don't move," he murmured. "Not yet."

"But…" A tremor teased at the word even as her eyes widened.

Her breaths quickened and the blood running through Griffin's veins thickened in response. "Close your eyes. Shut out the fear."

"I don't think I can."

So there *was* fear then, just as he'd thought. "Close your eyes," he repeated.

"Why?"

"Because you are letting distractions interfere with what you really want." He raised his left hand to her cheek, gently scraping his thumb across the silky softness.

"And what would that be?"

"Close your eyes. Just for a moment. And perhaps you'll find out."

She did not look convinced, but her ever-present curiosity won the battle in her mind and she did as he asked, her eyelids sliding shut so her long black lashes lay prettily against her skin. Griffin took a moment to admire not only how lovely she was but the trust she'd just placed in his hands. It filled his heart with warmth, expanding it in size until it squeezed against his ribs.

Slowly, he ran the pad of his thumb along the edge of her jaw while studying her response. Her lips parted slightly and a soft, almost inaudible sigh, escaped her. "Do you like how this feels?"

She was silent a moment, so long he repeated the motion as a reminder.

"Yes," she whispered, just as honest as she had promised to be from the start.

He moved in closer, not enough to touch her with his body, but enough for them both to feel the temperature rise in the air pressed between them. "And this?" he asked as he trailed his index finger down the side of her neck.

A shiver stole through her, but she kept her eyes closed. "It tickles a little."

"In a good way, I hope."

Her breaths grew shallower as he trailed his finger across her shoulder. "What are you doing?"

He moved closer still, allowing his body to press against hers. "Showing you what you desire but are too afraid to face." He allowed the words to blow over her skin. "You wanted to know what kissing is like because you are curious. And yet, you have run from every chance you've had since I kissed you to learn more."

"Because there can never be more. Not with you."

His hand stilled, right at the edge of her décolletage. The temptation to dip one finger inside and explore her more fully was almost too much to bear. "Why?" he asked her instead.

Her breaths quickened and she suddenly drew away, opening her eyes and pinning him with accusation. "Because it would never work."

It wasn't the response he'd expected, but it did make him laugh, not with pleasure but with astonishment. "You're wrong about that, Miss Howard." He would not pretend disinterest in her now. Nor would he act as though she did not affect him more than any other woman ever had. Not when he wanted her more with each passing second and certainly not when his ability to stir her baser desires had just been confirmed. "It would work splendidly."

"And then what? You would marry me? I would move to Vienna?" He opened his mouth to speak but she interjected. "You don't want that and neither do I, come to think of it. So then where would that leave us? With an affair that would make future get-togethers unbearably awkward?"

Griffin blinked. She didn't want marriage.

"You're Caleb's brother, after all, so avoiding

each other indefinitely would be impossible," she continued. "Which is why I refuse to become more involved with you, however difficult not doing so may be. But it isn't fear that's strengthening my restraint, it's common sense and the keen awareness that I would likely regret a deeper attachment to you."

"Would this be the wrong time to remind you that you asked me to give you another demonstration in kissing?" He was grasping at straws now, desperate to stop the chance he had with her from slipping between his fingers.

"Of course not, but that was before..." She caught herself on a gasp and took another step back, even further away from him.

Griffin latched onto her unspoken words with every hope he'd ever had. "Before what?"

She raised her chin, defiance now firmly in place. "It doesn't matter."

And before he could tell her that he was quite certain it did, she reminded him that her mother was waiting and that he was still quite welcome to join them both for the picnic.

"I would like that," he said, both because he was hungry and felt a need for fresh air, but also because he wanted to keep on studying her. She'd held back something important, of that he was certain. Especially since she'd let slip that resisting him wasn't easy. Which meant he was right. She wanted him just as much as he wanted her. Now all he had to do was convince her that she could have him forever and that he would make her happy.

Sitting on the blanket beside her mother and pretending that Griffin's presense was as unremarkable as it would have been if he'd been anyone else, was difficult. For three days Emily had managed to keep her distance from him. It had helped that he'd hidden himself away in the parlor, but at the same time, his frequent absenses had made her forget how gorgeous, charming, and thoroughly tempting he was.

When she'd foolishly touched him in the parlor and then allowed him to touch her, sparks had erupted inside her, awakening every dream she'd ever had of being wanted, desired, loved.

The last bit was what had slammed the door between them. It was what made her fearful of surrender. The knowledge that if he so much as kissed her again, it might break her heart.

Her mother offered her a slice of apple, and Emily accepted, biting into the crisp tartness while a gust of wind raked the grass. Clearview stood in the background, the familiar façade a reminder of all the happiness she'd ever known. This was where she'd learned there was more to life than being a pawn, where she'd found the understanding and support her parents had failed to give her, where she'd discovered her purpose.

"These are excellent," Griffin said as he bit into his second scone. The clotted cream and jam he'd scooped onto one half of it dripped onto his fingers. "The best I've ever had."

Emily grinned. She'd never seen a man eat with such gusto or with such carefree abandon. It proved that he loved the treat she had made and that piece of knowledge did something funny to her stomach and to her heart.

"Here's a napkin," she said, handing him a square of blue cotton.

He accepted the offering with thanks and held it under the scone in order to catch the crumbs.

A pair of swallows darted across the sky, beneath long, filmy clouds giving way to pale blue. The rustling of leaves drew Emily's attention to a squirrel rummaging for food at the foot of an oak. Emily ate the rest of her apple and stood.

"Stay," she told Griffin when he made to rise as well. She needed distance from him, the chance to come to terms with the truth humming through her.

Naive, inexperienced woman that she was, she hadn't thought to protect her heart properly. And now it was too late to do so, because she was already falling hopelessly, madly, and irrevocably in love with him. How could she not when he'd proven how kind he was? When he chose to do for himself what his status and position demanded he have others do for him instead? When he encouraged her to be herself rather than the fabricated version Society asked for?

Emily glanced over her shoulder at where he sat, now conversing amicably with her mother, a woman most unmarried gentlemen tried to avoid because of her boorish manner. But Griffin managed to calm her somehow. In his presence, Georgina was transformed into a less domineering and more understanding person. Which of course was yet another reason to love him.

A smile tugged at her lips as she watched him laugh in response to something her mother said. Emily glanced away from them and gave her attention to the fields beyond the Clearview property where young, bright green wheat swayed happily to and fro. She could still feel his fingers against her skin, teasingly soft and inviting. There was no mistaking what he'd offered, his voice whispering over her skin as he'd stepped even closer, surrounding her with raw masculinity. It was more than a touch and more than a kiss. It was everything she'd ever dreamed of but was now too afraid to accept. He was giving her the chance of a lifetime, and she was now saying no.

She shook her head. If only Cassandra and Mary were here for her to confide in. She desperately needed their guidance in this. But she wouldn't see either for another week. Not until she arrived at Montvale. A letter from Cassandra informing her of this had arrived yesterday. In it her friend had explained that the children were having a marvelous time in London and that a detour to Clearview on their way to the house party made little sense.

"Your mother suggested I check on you."

Startled by Griffin's voice speaking next to her ear, Emily spun to face him. She had not heard him approach and was now momentarily dazed by how handsome he looked with the sun spilling over his hair. It highlighted deep golden strands that weren't visible when he was indoors.

Expelling her breath slowly, Emily managed to slow the frantic heartbeats he'd caused by catching her off guard. "I'm sure she did," she said, responding to his comment with an edge of dryness that couldn't be helped. "Mama has nothing but matchmaking on her agenda."

"You cannot blame her for that. After all, I am a fine catch."

His comment, accompanied by waggling eyebrows and a wry smile, prompted her to laugh without hesitation. "The finest there is," she grinned, "and not the least bit conceited."

"Is it conceited if it is a fact?"

The twinkle in his eyes eased a knot in her chest that she'd not even realized was there until that exact moment. Bantering with him was one of her favorite activities, not only because it was fun but because she was comfortable with him like this. At least as comfortable as she was with Cassandra and Mary. As long as he wasn't being seductive and causing her nerves to tangle together.

"I don't suppose it is, though there is much to be said for being modest."

"In that case, I should tell you that I would make a terrible match. I'm far too difficult to get along with and not nearly good looking enough for you. People would wonder what on earth you were thinking to marry a man such as me when you can do so much better."

Although there was humor in his voice as he spoke, Emily couldn't quite manage the response she knew he was after. "I actually think it would be the other way around. Your popularity in London was undeniable."

His hand caught her elbow, gripping it tightly as he steered her forward, walking her further away from her mother. "You will not diminish yourself, Emily. Not ever again. Is that clear?"

The fierceness with which he spoke caused her skin to tighten and her chest to contract with surprise. "I thought we agreed to be honest."

His hold on her softened, but he didn't let go. "And you are lying to yourself and to me if you keep on insisting that you're not pretty or worthy of attention."

"I'm not pretty," Emily stated, because it was what she genuinely believed.

"And yet somehow you managed to convince not one man but two to kiss you within only five minutes of each other."

"I did not convince Mr. Bale to do so."

Lord Griffin's chuckle was grim. "There is no other reason why he would have walked into a dark corner of the garden with you, Miss Howard."

She hadn't quite thought of it like that. And yet... "It is a well-known fact that men are willing to let their baser urges guide them. I took advantage of that fact."

An incredulous laugh burst past his lips. He halted his progress, forcing her to stop walking as well. "Is that what you think?"

It was what she had thought at the time, but Emily was no longer sure if this theory of hers had merit. Still, she wasn't quite ready to relent, so she gave him a nod instead.

He stared at her for a long drawn-out moment, then muttered something she failed to hear and walked away. She followed him at a slow pace, stopping again when he spun back toward her, his expression both angry and confused and something else she couldn't place.

His finger rose like that of a chastising parent about to tell off a naughty child. "You…" The words seemed to stick in his throat. He shook his head, stopped pointing at her, and instead shoved both hands in his pockets. When he spoke again, his voice was calmer although it still remained wrapped in emotion. "You're wrong."

Unsatisfied with such a simple remark since it failed to explain or convince her of anything, Emily knit her brow. "I don't think so."

"Then let me elaborate for you." There was a glint in his eyes now, a firmness to his mouth and his jaw that made him look rigid and stern. For some indescribable reason, this caused a frisson to dart down Emily's spine. "Men do not go about kissing every woman who bats their eyelashes at them. By God, if that were the case we would not have been alone in the garden that evening but rather surrounded by other kissing couples. And just to be clear, I would not have done what I did if you had been anyone else."

Emily blinked. Fury had stolen into his gaze as he'd spoken, and her body responded, not with fear or displeasure, but with an elemental need to step into his space and wrap her arms around him. She wanted to feel his body flush against hers, to ease the tension in his muscles and kiss him until he was breathless.

But to do so would seal both their fates. Especially since her mother was seated not too far away. So she forced herself to focus, to put her thoughts in order and form a response that would not reveal the impact his words had just had on her. "I do not believe that."

Perfect.

Now *she* was telling him that *he* was being dishonest.

As expected, his eyes widened. He leaned toward her, crowding her with his indignation and rising temper. "Believe what you will, Miss Howard, but the fact of the matter is that I have wanted you since the first day I saw you. So I took advantage. Yes. *I* kissed you. Not because you were eager to experience the act but because I was desperate to know what your lips would feel like beneath my own, because I was too weak to walk away from the chance you gave me, and because I was not about to let you kiss anyone else."

Emily gaped at him. His confession was like a runaway carriage that had driven right over the firm belief she'd had of him kissing her simply because he'd been trying to distract himself from her comment about his scar. "But..." Lord Griffin looked as stricken as she felt. "The kiss you gave me did not convey any of that. I mean, it was not—"

"Passionate enough?" he prompted when she waved her hands in the air as if trying to conjure the necessary word.

"Exactly."

He inhaled deeply, his nostrils flaring, then scrubbed a hand over his face. "I acted on impulse that evening. It wasn't until my lips met yours that I realized the ramifications of what I had done, but as soon as I did, I froze."

"You worried that I would have expectations?"

"A woman's first kiss is a precious thing. It

would only be natural for you to want a deeper attachment after."

Which was something she'd known he could not offer. "I understand. But now that you've gotten to know me better and you've learned how opposed to marriage I am, you're willing to offer me more? Just as long as we're both free to walk away when we're finished?"

He stared at her mutely, as if she'd just hit him over the head with a block of wood. "You say the damndest things sometimes," he eventually told her.

"I dare say it's one of my finest qualities."

"Without a doubt." He seemed to consider her for a moment, as if something vastly important was plaguing his mind. But rather than voice it, he offered his arm and proceeded to lead her back to her mother, who remained oblivious to the outrageous conversation that had just taken place not far from where she sat.

Emily played the exchange over in her head later on that evening while readying herself for bed. Lord Griffin had made his position clear, but whether or not he would try to seduce her had yet to be determined, though she supposed he'd been at it for a while now already. Ever since he'd decided to come here with her.

The chance that this might be the case caused excitement to rise up inside her, even as she reminded herself of how dangerous such an experience could be. After all, she had just acknowledged her feelings for him, and they would only grow stronger if she chose to go down this path. And yet, what was the chance of another man coming along years from now and offering her the same opportunity? If she refused Lord Griffin's advances, she might never know what truly went on between men and women who desired each other.

But would surrendering to seduction be worth the risk of eventual heartbreak?

She stared at her reflection in the cheval glass. Lord Griffin was attracted to her in a way she'd never believed any man ever would be. Perhaps the question she ought to ask was whether or not she could survive knowing that she'd turned her back on what he offered.

The answer to that was a loud and resounding "No."

CHAPTER ELEVEN

IT HAD NOT BEEN GRIFFIN'S intention to reveal how much he wanted Emily, but damn him if he hadn't been driven to exasperation by the certainty she had about her own undesirability. The fact that she would suppose he'd been driven to kiss her because of some primal instinct and not because he was genuinely drawn to her was galling.

Huffing out a breath, he picked up the ratchet wheel with the tweezers he'd purchased and placed it carefully over the mainspring. The coil had been repaired and all remaining pieces cleaned, so the clock should work perfectly once he finished reassembling it. The clickspring was gently eased into place, and Griffin sat back, admiring his work. Only the winding pinon and wheel remained, and then he'd be finished with no more excuses to avoid Miss Howard's company.

And he *had* been avoiding it if he were honest. For the past three days since the picnic, he'd kept to the parlor in order to complete the paint job or to the dining room where he'd worked on her clock. Now that both tasks had almost been completed, he would have to come up with additional ways to keep his distance from her. The alternative would be to surrender to every temptation she offered.

Of course there was the third option of simply leaving. He could be back in London within three days and on his way to Vienna the next. Mrs. Howard was here now, after all, along with her maid and coachman. Griffin's protection was no longer needed as much as it had been before. But the very idea of leaving Miss Howard behind, of travelling away from her and adding distance between them, squeezed at his heart.

He couldn't do it.

Not yet.

But if not now, then when?

He scrubbed his hand over his jaw and glanced around. What he needed was a drink. A large glass of soothing brandy. Spying a crystal decanter through the china cabinet's glass door, Griffin pushed back his chair and went to retrieve it, relieved to discover that it was full.

He filled a glass, returned the decanter to where it belonged, took a fortifying swallow, and considered his options once more. Miss Howard was being indecisive and distant. Ever since he'd blurted that he'd been mad for her right from the start, she'd put up a wall between them. Hell, she'd done so even before, he reflected. After he'd caught her spying on him during his morning swim.

But her distance toward him had grown more pronounced in the last few days, and he found that he now missed more than just attempting to court her with seduction. He missed talking to her; the simple exchange of opinions, experiences, and recollections that they had begun to enjoy. He took another sip of his drink. Perhaps he was going about this the wrong way. Perhaps he'd been too forward.

This was certainly an angle worth considering. Because they'd agreed to be brutally honest, he'd thought she'd appreciate directness, even when it came to his advances. But he was starting to suspect he might be mistaken about that. Perhaps a more subtle approach would be better, or at least less likely to scare her off.

And she *was* scared, though of what exactly he wasn't quite sure. But he'd seen it in her eyes when she'd stepped away from him in the parlor and again when he'd passionately told her of his desire.

He wasn't sure why this would be the case unless she worried he'd move too fast or expect too much. So then, the way forward would be with increased subtlety and flirtation.

And then?

Griffin returned to his seat, set down his glass, and finished fixing the clock. He wound it with the key and was swiftly rewarded by its soft ticking. Whatever happened would be up to Miss Howard. All her life she'd been steered in one direction and told what to do. If there was one thing he could give her that he believed would mean more to her than anything else, it was being given the chance to choose.

Of course he almost forgot all about this honorable intention of his that evening when it was time for them to leave for the Partridge residence. Griffin was waiting in the foyer when a glimpse of red at the top of the stairs caught his attention. He looked up, mesmerized by the shimmering silk now making its descent, and by the woman it encased.

Dear merciful God, she was stunning and more than capable of bringing ten thousand men to their knees if she put her mind to it. Griffin could only stare as the part of the gown that covered Miss Howard's legs came into view. It was followed by her hips, her waist, her breasts, and finally, when he managed to tear his gaze away from that particularly delectable part, her face.

"You look," he swallowed so she wouldn't catch him drooling, "incredible."

The shy smile with which she responded only added to her allure. Innocence incarnate, even when she pretended sophistication. Griffin could scarcely breathe.

"Thank you," she murmured, the words softly spoken beneath her breath. She cleared her throat. "I must give Mama credit. Scarlett was her suggestion."

Griffin shifted his gaze to Mrs. Howard, who'd somehow materialized next to her daughter without him noticing.

"Good choice." He smiled politely and prayed his expression did not reveal the extent to which Miss Howard stirred his imagination. And other things.

Thankfully, Mrs. Howard's eyes brightened with appreciation, none the wiser. So Griffin opened the front door and escorted both women to the waiting carriage.

"I feared the dress would be too bold," Emily discreetly told Lord Griffin when they arrived at Partridge House. She'd spent the drive fidgeting with her skirt while he'd conversed with her mother from the opposite bench. Apparently, the two shared a fondness for Vermeer, music boxes, and Vivaldi.

By the time they arrived at their destination, the Four Seasons in its entirety had been discussed with several favorite parts hummed in time to the tap of Georgina's slipper.

"In my opinion, it is perfect," Lord Griffin assured her in an equally low whisper as they accompanied Emily's mother up the front steps. His hand settled briefly against her lower back, the heat from it pressing possessively into her skin for the second it lasted.

And then they were at the front door, being welcomed by the Partridge butler and ushered into a grand foyer where shawls were collected before they were led into the parlor to meet their hosts. Mr. David Partidge was the first to step forward and greet them, his attention going first to Emily's mother and then to Emily herself.

His eyes lit up when he stepped toward her, his lips curving with appreciation as he took her in. He reached for her hand and bowed over it, pressing a kiss to her gloved knuckles. "Exquisite," he murmured. Straightening himself, he held her gaze, apparently for a beat too long since Lord Griffin cleared his throat, forcing Mr. Partridge to acknowledge him next.

Mr. Partridge released Emily's hand, though not without her noting the slide of his fingers against her own. She glanced at Lord Griffin and sucked in a breath. His expression was rigid, his jaw clenched tight as he stared at Mr. Partridge with flint in his eyes.

Mr. Partridge did not seem to notice, or if he did, he failed to show it. Instead, he smiled and offered Lord Griffin his hand. "Mr. Crawford. It is such a pleasure to have you join us for dinner. If you please, allow me to introduce you to my parents, who have been very eager to make your acquaintance. You remember my sister of course, Miss Amanda Partridge."

"Indeed," Lord Griffin muttered, his voice a clear indication that he did not like Mr. Partridge in the least.

Emily steeled herself for what she feared might turn into an unpleasant evening and followed him and her mother over to where Mr. Partridge's parents and sister stood waiting.

"This is my father, Mr. George Partridge and my mother, Mrs. Lydia Partridge," Mr. Partridge said with a warm smile.

The older couple greeted Emily's mother first, then Lord Griffin, and finally Emily. Deciding not to aggravate Lord Griffin any further, Emily struck up a conversation with Miss Partridge in an effort to avoid speaking with her brother. But Mr. David Partridge was apparently quite determined to gain her attention, for he extricated himself quite smoothly from the group comprising his parents, Georgina, and Lord Griffin, and came to join her and his sister instead.

"I was wondering if you could give us an update on how the children you care for are doing," he said. "If memory serves, there are five?"

"That is correct," Emily said, a little impressed that he would remember. "Two boys and three girls. They're in London at the moment with Lady Cassandra."

"Clearview must seem empty without them there," Miss Partridge said.

"There's certainly less noise," Emily confessed.

"Of that I have no doubt," Mr. Partridge told her with a chuckle. He studied her a moment before quietly asking, "Do you miss it?"

"I miss *them*," Emily said and for some reason that answer seemed to please him, judging from the increased brightness in his eyes.

"You have a good heart," he said as if thinking out loud.

"The same could be said of you," Emily replied. "There are many who would donate to charitable causes but only a few who would actually get involved. The fact that you visit the orphanages you help in order to ensure that the children there are properly cared for is very impressive."

"You flatter me, Miss Howard."

"I speak the truth," she told him honestly.

"My brother can't bear to see children suffer," Miss Partridge added. "It would seem the two of you have that in common."

Emily dipped her head in silent agreement. When she looked up, her gaze met Lord Griffin's from across the room, the anger she saw there unnerving her more than she cared to admit.

A nerve ticked at the edge of his jaw, and for

a second she feared he might storm across the room, pick her up, and carry her out of the house. But then his attention was broken by something Mr. George Partridge said, and Emily expelled a breath she had not even realized she had been holding.

"May I escort you?" Mr. David Partridge asked her when the butler announced it was time to go in for dinner. He held his arm up and Emily carefully placed her hand upon it. To do otherwise would have been rude. And besides, Lord Griffin did not own her. He had no right to oppose Mr. David Partridge's attentions or to let them bother him.

Bolstered by this knowledge, Emily straightened her spine and decided to enjoy her host's company. After all, Mr. Partridge was not only handsome but very likeable. "When do you plan on returning to Dorset?" she asked him once the first course was underway and she'd grown accustomed to Lord Griffin's glower from across the table.

"The day after tomorrow," Mr. Partridge informed her. "I must get back, loathe as I am to part with this particular area of England." He turned his gaze toward her as he said it, leaving no doubt in Emily's mind that Lord Griffin had been correct. Mr. Partridge did have intentions toward her, and they included the prospect of courtship and marriage.

She glanced at Lord Griffin and caught herself swallowing. His gaze was so intense it seemed to burn straight through her. Her cheeks grew warm and her hands a bit clammy. She reached for her glass, desperate for something with which to distract herself from both of these men. This wasn't what she was used to. She'd been a wallflower all her life and did not have the necessary skill or experience to tackle a territorial fight carried out by two dominant males.

Mr. Partridge smiled and in that smile she saw hope and determination. He shifted it toward Lord Griffin, took a sip of his wine, and asked, "How is your wife faring, Mr. Crawford?"

The emphasis on wife was not lost on Emily. Hands trembling, she set the glass to her lips and took a big gulp. Apparently, the battle had already begun, and with Mr. Partridge reminding Lord Griffin, whom he thought was Caleb, that his aversion to his interest in Emily was inappropriate and misplaced.

Heaven help her.

Lord Griffin's eyes narrowed. "Perfectly well," he clipped and stuck a piece of pheasant in his mouth. When he spoke again, his expression had eased and his voice had become suspiciously pleasant. "I daresay she misses not only myself but Miss Howard as well. The two are, as you well know, longtime friends. Practically sisters, in fact." He picked up his glass and swirled his wine slowly about before saying, "As such, Miss Howard is not only under her parents' protection, but under mine as well."

Dear God.

Emily had to clamp her mouth shut to keep it from falling open. Had Lord Griffin really just told Mr. Partridge that he would have to go through him in order to get to Emily? He might as well have tossed a glove in the man's face for all the difference it made.

Mrs. Lydia Partridge coughed, alleviating only a fraction of the tension now filling the dining room. "I must say, your concern for a family friend's well-being is admirable, Mr. Crawford."

"Unusually so," Mr. Partridge said dryly, his eyes no longer shining with pleasure but rather glaring at Lord Griffin with severe irritation. He frowned even as the conversation was redirected toward the subject of a new play that was due to open in London – one that his sister was very keen to see.

"Perhaps we can go together," Miss Partridge suggested several minutes later when everyone had been informed of the general plot.

"An excellent idea," Emily agreed, the smile she pasted on her face pulling painfully at her cheeks. Whatever Lord Griffin's reaction might have been to her answer, she failed to see it on account of the very deliberate effort she made to ignore him. And because she was irked by his behavior, she even decided to add, "I plan on visiting my parents again at the end of May, and since I have only a few friends in London, your added company along with your brother's would be most welcome indeed."

"I am so very pleased to hear you say that," Mr. Partridge murmured a little too smugly for her liking.

Emily forced a smile and gave her attention to her food. She didn't dare look at Lord Griffin for the remainder of the meal and was happy to avoid him completely when he and the other men went to enjoy their after-dinner drinks in the library.

Meanwhile, she did her best to focus on the conversations taking place in the parlor where she and the ladies were served sherry, but doing so was impossible when her thoughts kept straying to Lord Griffin. He had no right to act like a jealous fiancé, not to mention the fact that he risked revealing the truth. If the Partridges discovered he wasn't really Caleb and they'd been lied to, it was more than her reputation and his that risked being ruined. Her mother's was now at stake as well. So for him to allow whatever irritation he felt to show was completely unacceptable and very much deserving of her ire.

The more she thought on this, the more she believed it, and by the time she said good night to the Partridges, she'd convinced herself that Lord Griffin deserved to be put in his place. She had to remind him of the risk he'd taken by letting himself be ruled by emotion. So she took her seat stiffly in the carriage and waited for it to take off.

But before she got out one word, her mother said, "Well, that went rather well."

Emily spun her head sideways to look at the woman who'd brought her into this world. "If having an unpleasant evening was the aim, then yes, it most certainly did."

Lord Griffin grumbled something from the opposite side of the carriage and stubbornly turned to look out the window, even though there was nothing but darkness to see.

"I fail to see your point," Georgina said with the same degree of cluelessness she'd shown when she'd chosen to plump up her daughter and dress her in orange. "We have all agreed to meet again in London, so whatever you felt went wrong has not deterred the Partridges from wanting to further their acquaintance with us." She patted Emily's hand. "And Mr. David Partridge was so attentive toward you too. There can be no doubt about his interest. So if you and Lord Griffin don't wish to marry, perhaps you could entertain the idea of marrying him instead?"

Emily dropped her gaze to the floor of the carriage. Perhaps she could find an escape hatch there? A low growl reminded her why she was eager to flee, and it was because she would sooner or later have to deal with a man whose desire for her was just as terrifying as her desire for him.

Forgetting himself completely, Griffin muttered a hasty, "Good night," before stalking into the Clearview dining room and shutting the door behind him. It wasn't until he'd poured himself his second glass of brandy that he was levelheaded enough to reflect on the fact that he should have waited for Miss Howard and her mother to head upstairs before quitting their company.

He was just so bloody furious he could scarcely see straight, and he had been so for several hours now. So he'd snatched the first chance he'd gotten to escape the woman who'd caused his blood to run hot through his veins all evening. First, on account of the gown she'd worn and then, by enjoying the attention of Mr. Damnhimtohell David Partridge.

His gaze had lingered on her as if she'd been a

delectable feast he was hoping to one day devour. He had paid particular attention to the swell of her breasts when he'd bowed over her hand, pretending gentlemanly politeness when Griffin had practically been able to see every sordid fantasy he hoped to play out with her painted in the air.

Christ almighty!

Griffin raked his fingers through his hair and squeezed his eyes shut while pinching the bridge of his nose. He'd never experienced jealousy before, certainly not this all-consuming variety and never because of a woman. It had made him almost barbaric, his need to conquer and claim her and put her off limits to all other men so intense, he'd completely lost focus of what truly mattered. Her reputation and her mother's as well.

Damn, if he hadn't made a muck of things, but it couldn't be helped. Not when she'd chosen to bat her eyelashes at the foppish bastard and serve him encouraging smiles. Hell, she'd even issued him a direct invitation to meet with her in London.

Griffin tightened his grip on his glass. Perhaps he should leave her to it. Leave in the morning and go back to Vienna. Put as much distance between himself and Miss Emily Howard as possible. Before he lost his mind completely. Before she reduced him to a fool.

Hell.

She'd already done so. His unacceptable behavior this evening was proof enough. And it had to be stopped.

He took another deep swallow of brandy just as the dining room door eased open. The snick of the handle drew his attention. His head turned sideways, and his eyes settled perfectly on the woman whose presence he'd grown so fond of.

Yes, damn it. He more than wanted and desired her. He needed her in a way that he'd never needed anyone else before. Even though she had the power to turn him into a raving lunatic. She was still wearing the red gown, and the only thing he could think of as she stepped further into the room and closed the door behind her was what it might be like to pull her neckline down over her shoulders. Would she sigh with pleasure or push him away when he pressed his mouth to her skin?

The steel in her eyes suggested that she wasn't looking to be seduced but rather to have some choice words. His muscles tightened with antici-pation. An argument would be equally welcome as a means by which to alleviate some of the ten-sion straining his body.

"You behaved badly tonight," she began.

Her back was straight, her chin slightly raised, and her face a perfect display of severe displeasure.

Griffin set his glass aside and flexed his fingers. The way she said that... Heaven have mercy on his sordid mind but her scolding manner did not have the humbling effect he believed she hoped for. Rather, he found it to be unexpectedly arous-ing.

Oblivious, she moved toward him, closing the distance. "Your attempt to dissuade Mr. David Partridge from giving his attentions to me was not only rude but—"

"Are you interested in him?"

Miss Howard's eyes widened and he realized

belatedly that he had practically barked the question, the name David Partridge igniting a fury inside him that made him wish the man would materialize before him for the sole purpose of being punched in the face. But rather than burst into tears or flee the room, she raised her chin higher. "No. But that is not the point."

Griffin nodded, too relieved to do anything else as his muscles relaxed and his breaths evened out.

"You risked all of our reputations this evening," she went on, "because of some ancient caveman instinct you failed to quell."

His muscles drew tight once again and he moved toward her, deliberately dominating the space between them with his much greater size. As he'd expected, she took a step backward. "Was it misplaced?" he asked gently.

She sucked in a breath and retreated some more, moving right when he cut off her path to the left. Until the dining room table brought her to a halt when her bottom bumped against it. "I…um…" She glanced over her shoulder as if to make sure that there was an obstacle in her way.

Griffin moved in closer, more determined than ever to discover if they had a chance of sharing a future together – if tormenting himself for her would ever be rewarded. So he planted his hands on her waist and lifted her up, seating her on the edge of the table.

"Griffin!" Surprise lent a breathy and thoroughly intoxicating element to her voice. Her hand went straight to his shoulder, gripping it firmly in an instinctive effort to keep her balance.

A surge of heat hit him square in the chest in

response to her use of his given name without the honorific. "Yes?" He pressed his thumbs gently into her waist before letting his hands slide down over her hips until they settled boldly on top of her thighs. Holding her gaze, he eased her legs apart to create a space for him to stand.

Her eyes widened when he stepped in between, then again when he pushed up against her, right there were he knew he'd affect her the most. "This is…" her words turned into a sigh when he pulled her to him for added contact "…not very proper."

He gave a low chuckle and let his hands slide up her arms, over her shoulders, along her neck, and into her hair. "It's nothing compared with what I am thinking."

Half dazed, her eyes met his from beneath lowered lashes. "That cannot be true."

The words reminded him of her innocence, causing him to examine his actions. His hands stilled on the verge of pulling pins from her coiffure. What the hell was he doing? He closed his eyes briefly and took a quick breath, inhaling her fragrance of lavender and soap. Jesus, he ought to be ashamed of himself for taking advantage, which was obviously what he was doing.

"If you want me to go, then I will," he said, forcing the words out with the sort of effort that ought to be rewarded with a medal.

"I'm not sure what I want anymore," she confessed in a voice so low he almost didn't hear her.

He opened his eyes, pulled a pin from her hair, and placed it on the table. "Perhaps it's time to find out." When she nodded, he continued undoing her hair until the locks cascaded over her shoulders. He ran his fingers through it, savoring the silky feel of it sliding against his skin while allowing himself to envision her in his bed, her hair spread loosely upon his pillow.

Moving one hand to her jaw, he cradled her lightly while stroking her cheek with his thumb. She leaned into the touch with a sensual sigh that challenged his finely held control. Griffin dipped his head, almost grazing his lips with hers though not quite. He'd already made his position clear. If she wanted more, she would have to take the next step.

So he waited for what felt like a hundred years, hovering there on the brink of kissing, until finally, blessedly, she raised her mouth to his.

CHAPTER TWELVE

S OFT BUT FIRM.
Emily felt the gentle press of his lips against hers just as keenly as when he'd kissed her at the ball. But unlike then, he did not draw away this time. Instead he stayed, allowing her to adjust to each new sensation: the slow exhale of his breath mingling with hers, a hint of brandy, the scent of sandalwood clinging to his skin, and the slight abrasion of stubble scraping her chin.

Without even thinking, she wound her arms around his neck and drew him closer. A low rumble vibrated through him, like distant thunder warning of an approaching storm. Her fingers raked upward into his hair, and she felt his lips part on a tight inhalation, his hand flex against the curve of her cheek. He was holding himself in check, his body poised, every muscle tightly strung while he let her explore.

Smiling against his mouth, she paused for a second to ponder how best to proceed and involuntarily licked her own lips and Griffin's by proximity. The effect it had on him was almost explosive. He was like a slumbering beast brought awake with a start, pulling her to him as if he was starved and her mouth was the banquet on which he would feast. She gasped in response and he took advantage. He claimed her mouth with his own, tasting, biting, and licking. It was savage and needy, yet expertly done. She could tell he was skilled, so she let him guide her, submitting completely to his advances and loving every wild, uninhibited second of it.

This was what she'd been seeking, this unleashed passion that brought her body alive. It heightened her senses and tuned her awareness until it aligned with his, each nerve ending sparking in response to each touch and wrenching new, unfamiliar sounds from her throat.

When he broke away from her mouth, she whimpered in protest. Her hands tightened their hold on him, desperate to pull him back. Until he began planting soft little kisses along the edge of her jaw. She tilted her head then and loosed her grip, yielding to his expert ministrations. His teeth nipped her earlobe and she sucked in a breath, surprised by the pleasure the playful pinch gave her.

"I could kiss you forever," he murmured, his voice stirring the hair at the nape of her neck, sending lovely shivers racing down her spine.

"This is certainly better than your previous attempt." Where did that sultry voice come from? She didn't even know she could speak like that, as she imaged a courtesan would.

He chuckled against her, sending fluttery heat straight into her belly. "That was no attempt at all, you cheeky minx."

Before she could manage a response, his mouth

captured hers again, more insistent than before, as if he had something to prove. Emily did her best to keep up, copying him in an effort to hone her own skills. His hand roamed over her shoulder, the tips of his fingers playing lightly with the neckline of her gown. His thumb grazed her breast.

Yes.

Please.

She needed more. Needed him. His hands on her. Everywhere.

Intent on encouraging him, she arched her back, pressing herself more firmly against him. He shuddered and he broke the kiss once again to rest his forehead against hers.

"Emily..."

His voice was rough and unsteady, his fingers so close to where she wanted them most. A series of low, labored breaths escaped him. She felt his chest rise and fall, a brief straining of limbs before they relaxed. He let his hand fall, placed a soft kiss at her temple, and took a step back.

No.

Emily stared at him, her body still hungry for something that she was convinced only he could give her. She wanted to grab him, shake him, rail at him for—

"You should go. Before I take additional liberties."

She shook her head while he helped her stand, smoothed out her gown. "But I..." Dear God, she would be both honest and brave even if it killed her. She met his dark gaze. "I want to continue."

A nerve ticked at the edge of his jaw. "No." He

found her hand, raised it to his lips, and met her gaze while pressing a tender kiss to her knuckles. "Not tonight." His voice was firm, unyielding.

So she went, swaying slightly on legs that seemed too weak to hold her. She paused before stepping into the hallway and looked back to find him watching, his body rigid, like he was struggling to stay where he was.

"Go," he urged her, "and make sure you lock your bedchamber door."

The reality of what she risked if she didn't was evident in the strained tone of his voice. And now that a moment had passed since their kiss and she could think clearly again, she appreciated the effort he made to save her from making a terrible mistake. Because kissing was one thing, losing her innocence quite another.

So she did as he told her, acutely aware that her feelings for him had quadrupled during the last ten minutes. Which meant careful consideration was in order, before she did anything further.

When she woke the next morning, Emily stayed in bed for at least an hour. She stared at the ceiling while going over everything that had happened the night before, from the moment she'd put on the scarlet dress to when Griffin had told her to go to bed.

Had he really kissed her as if the world were ending? She pressed her fingertips to her lips and smiled against them. Yes. He most certainly had. And it had been marvelously enlightening.

She rolled onto her side with a grin. No wonder

Mary was eager to sneak off with Caleb at every opportunity. It made sense if this was what they were doing.

She bit her lip and felt her brow tighten with a frown. There was more to discover of course. Cassandra had told her enough to make her aware of that. And she'd also read a book or two in an effort to better understand why copulation appealed to so many people when it seemed like something that would be both awkward and uncomfortable.

But if Griffin kissed her the way he had last night in the process, perhaps then...

She sighed and pulled her pillow over her head. When she'd set out to learn what kissing entailed, she'd meant to leave it at that. Except now, she was apparently considering a whole lot more. With a man she'd fallen in love with. Only he would be leaving soon. Not for London or even Scotland, but for Austria, which might as well be China for all the difference it made.

With a groan of frustration she sat, determined to stop her mind from babbling to itself. One thing was certain and that was that Griffin was interested. In her.

She chuckled at that thought. Would their kiss last night lead to a deeper attachement between them? Would he let it? She had no idea.

A knock sounded at the door. "Come in," she called.

Her mother entered, carrying a cup of tea. "I worried you might not be well." She handed the tea to Emily, who took a grateful sip. "You're usually up much earlier than this."

"What time is it?"

"Almost ten."

Emily placed her cup on the table and went to find a dress. The one from last night was flung over a chair in the corner, reminding her once again of the kiss she'd shared with Griffin. "I'm sorry," she muttered, averting her face so her mother would not see her blush. "You must be starving by now."

"Not really. Lord Griffin made breakfast." When Emily stilled, her hand on the wardrobe door, her mother added, "He's surprisingly capable."

No doubt about that.

Emily's cheeks grew hotter. Had his tongue really licked over hers? Good God. She would now have to face him. Without being sure where they stood with each other and without revealing anything to her mother. Her stomach rolled over on that realization.

When she'd woken, she'd been too distracted by the lovely recollection of Griffin's embrace to ponder the complexities of the situation. She did so now and was suddenly less eager to leave her bedchamber than she had been a moment earlier.

What if he regretted it? After all, he had pushed her away in the end. What if he'd done so after realizing that the kiss had been a spontaneous mistake?

She grabbed a dress, a green one, and turned to her mother. "I will be down in a moment. Thank you for the tea."

Her mother stared at her. "Are you sure you are well?"

"Of course."

"You seem...flustered."

"I'm just surprised by how late I slept," Emily said, a little too brightly. She avoided looking at her mother by going in search of clean undergarments and stockings.

"Very well then," her mother conceded. She paused, then went to the door. "I will see you downstairs."

As soon as she exited the room, closing the door behind her, Emily breathed a sigh of relief. Her shoulders sagged and she leaned the weight of her body against her dresser. If only she could stay up here, hidden away for the rest of the day. And tomorrow. At least until she believed herself capable of having a conversation with Griffin without being affected by the memory of their kiss. Which would likely be never.

With a groan of frustration, she pulled off her nightgown and flung it on top of the scarlet dress. She was a grown woman, for heaven's sake, independent and perfectly free to choose her own destiny. To let a man addle her like this was silly.

So what if they'd kissed each other? It only confirmed that they shared a mutual attraction. That was all. Nothing more to it. And if things progressed and the opportunity for more arose, well then that would be all right with her too. She certainly wouldn't worry over it. No point in that.

Satisfied that she had overcome any doubts or concerns about seeing Griffin again, Emily entered the kitchen, ready to face him with a smile and a pleasant, "Good morning."

Except he wasn't there. Only her mother was seated at the table. Hmm... Emily approached.

Her mother glanced up from the piece of mending she was working on.

"I found the sewing kit in the hallway cupboard. Hope you don't mind me borrowing it."

"No. Of course not." Emily frowned. "That looks like Bridget's dress."

Her mother turned the garment over in her hands. "It was lying on top of the sewing kit together with a few more items, so when I finished repairing the tear in my petticoat, I decided to fix those as well. Do you mind?"

"No. Of course not." Emily pulled out a chair and sat. "But can't Patsy do it?"

"Oh, I have asked her to dust and sweep the downstairs rooms."

"Thank you, Mama."

A faint smile brushed Georgina's lips. "I wish there were more I could do to make up for all my mistakes." She slumped against her chair with a sigh. "You were my oldest daughter. The one who was meant to secure the best match."

Emily stiffened as bitterness rose up her throat. "Instead, I became your biggest disappointment."

"Yes. You did." Emily's mouth dropped open. Her mother's brutal honesty was startling. "I blamed you for not securing a proposal when I ought to have blamed myself for being too pushy."

"And for insisting on hideous gowns."

Mrs. Howard's lips quirked. "I mistakenly believed bright colors would draw attention."

"And they did, though not in the way you probably hoped."

"No." Georgina set her mending aside and hesitantly placed her hand over Emily's. "I know

I frightened Langdon away when I went to see him. All I wanted was to have him propose, and instead I achieved the opposite." She curled her fingers around Emily's and squeezed. "Can you ever forgive me?"

Emily met her mother's gaze and felt the lingering resentment she harbored crack in response to the pain she saw there. She nodded. "Of course."

Her mother smiled and glanced briefly away, her eyes suspiciously shiny. A sniff followed along with a few rapid blinks. And then she jutted her chin toward a covered plate. "You should eat. Lord Griffin will likely be disappointed if you don't."

Emily lifted the upside down bowl that had been used to keep her food warm and found scrambled eggs, sausages, and toast waiting. Her stomach growled in response to the appetizing meal. It looked and smelled delicious.

"Where is he by the way?" Emily casually asked as she picked up her knife and fork.

Her mother poured some tea for her before refilling her own cup. "In the library. He said he had some extra paint and that there were a few peeling spots in there he could patch."

Emily cut a piece of sausage and egg, spearing both with her fork before popping them into her mouth. Her mother picked up her sewing needle again and continued repairing the torn seam on Bridget's dress. They exchanged a few words here and there, but for the first time ever, Emily found the silences in between comfortable.

She left her mother after agreeing that they should start packing in the afternoon so they would be ready to leave for Montvale the next day as planned. In the meantime, it was time for Emily to pluck up her courage and seek out Griffin. She paused outside the library and almost changed her mind when she felt her stomach twist. The door was open, allowing her a glimpse of his back. He was standing near the window, his head bowed over something that she presumed must be a book.

Her heart quickened and her throat went dry. She'd slid her fingers through that hair ruffling over his jacket collar at the nape of his neck, had felt his thighs press into hers. Swallowing, she considered walking away, then chastised herself for her silliness.

Pull yourself together!

She raised her hand and rapped the door frame. Griffin turned, the book in his hands snapping shut as it came into view. Emily gasped. Of all the things he might have been reading. She stared at him and he stared back.

Was that guilt in his eyes?

She crossed her arms. "That's mine." She'd forgotten that she'd neglected to put the book back in her room before leaving for London.

"I…er…I did not mean to pry," he muttered with the same sheepish expression the children wore each time she caught them being naughty.

"Of course not. You just happened to pick it up by accident and then it fell open and you couldn't help letting your eyes roam over the pages."

His lips quirked. "They do have a will of their own."

She chuckled. Ordinarily, it would have embarrassed her to find him reading her notebook, but his visible discomfort managed to distract her.

And besides, there was something enjoyable about unnerving him just a little.

Emily moved further into the room. She glanced at her notebook, now lying face up on the table. "I ought to be angry with you." She met his gaze and deliberately held it. "I ought to remind you that one does not read other people's private notebooks."

"I didn't realize what it was until I opened it, and then..." He blew out a breath. "I was too intrigued to stop."

His admission almost slayed her. It also piqued her curiosity. "How so?" She asked the question without even thinking.

Excitement flickered in his eyes, and he stepped toward her, reminding her of the visceral effect he had on her as her pulse leapt in response to their increased proximity. "You've rewritten the ending of Romeo and Juliet." He said it as if she'd solved the secrets of alchemy.

Emily nodded. His enthusiasm was dazzling. She shrugged one shoulder, pretending indifference. "Hamlet too."

He stared at her. "Really?"

"In a different notebook. I..." She could no longer ward off the self-consciousness that had threatened to swamp her since realizing he'd discovered her hobby. Her cheeks heated, but she didn't look away. "I wanted them all to live happily ever after."

His amazement showed in his abrupt laughter. He shook his head. "With a cocker spaniel, apparently," he said, referring to Romeo and Juliet. "And three children."

"It seemed to fit."

Griffin's grin widened. "I wouldn't have thought so, but I actually agree."

"You do?" She glanced back at her notebook. The idea to rewrite the ending of several tragedies had been a lark. She'd done it for herself, not because she'd ever planned on sharing it with anyone.

"It's not only well written, but funny. I particularly liked the banter between the characters."

"You didn't find it ridiculous?"

"Of course I did, but that's what makes it so great." He knit his brow. "Unless that wasn't your intention."

"No. I..." Words failed her. The connection she felt to him right now was beyond anything she had ever experienced before.

"And how did Hamlet and Ophelia fare?" he asked, eyes gleaming with interest.

A smile tugged at her lips as she thought back on her first attempt at crafting a happy ever after. "They decided to exchange the castle for a modest countryside manor where daffodils bloom in the spring and peonies in early summer."

"Those are your favorite flowers as I recall."

She laughed, too quickly and with too much force. "Of course they are. This is after all a story of my imagination." He gave her an odd look, prompting her to add, "Ophelia also discovers that she's a fine cook. Which reminds me that I have yet to thank you for breakfast. It was excellent, by the way. Especially the sausages. I don't believe I've ever had such a perfectly cooked sausage before." Dear God. She was babbling and she wasn't sure why.

"I'm glad you liked it."

"I—"

"About last night," Griffin murmured before she could compliment him on his well-balanced use of salt and pepper.

Emily glanced at the door. Perhaps she wasn't so brave after all.

"Yes," she rushed to say, stepping back further. "We should certainly discuss it."

His expression grew wary. "I think—"

A knock at the front door came as a welcome interruption. "Excuse me." Emily turned, hurrying from the room and toward whoever it was that had arrived with such perfect timing.

She opened the door and was greeted by a messenger who handed her a letter. "From Partridge House," he said.

Emily glanced at the shiny red seal bearing David Partridge's initials. Her shoulders tensed with a curious sense of unease. The messenger cleared his throat and Emily flinched. She retrieved a couple of pennies and paid the man, who gave his thanks before continuing on his way.

After shutting the door, Emily leaned back against it and stared at the letter. She wasn't sure why it troubled her or why she wasn't tearing it open to discover its contents. Her mother entered from the kitchen while Griffin arrived from the library. Both watched her curiously.

"Well?" Her mother finally asked. "Who was at the door?"

"A messenger." She looked at her because looking at Griffin had suddenly become rather difficult. "He brought a letter for me. From Mr. David Partridge."

"Indeed?" Her mother's voice rose on a wave of excitement. "Well aren't you going to open it?"

"I…" She forced her gaze to Griffin then, meeting a pair of dark eyes that threatened to burn her with their intensity. In his hand, he held her notebook.

"You forgot this," he said, holding it toward her.

She considered the distance she'd have to walk in order to retrieve it. It suddenly seemed so far – as if it would take her forever to travel the ten feet between them. Mouth dry and hands clammy, she started walking, uncomfortably aware of her mother's scrutiny.

Georgina huffed out a breath. "How can retrieving a book be more urgent than learning the contents of a newly arrived letter?"

Emily couldn't explain it, but she knew that going to Griffin now would prove that he mattered more, that Mr. David Partridge wasn't a threat, that last night's kiss was important.

She took the book from him as soon as it was within her reach. "Thank you."

His eyes remained fixed upon her the whole time.

"The letter, Emily," her mother insisted, her voice breaking through the dazed effect Griffin had on her.

Emily blinked. "Yes of course." She tucked the book under her arm and slid her thumb beneath the seal to break it. The crisp paper crackled between her fingers as she unfolded it, her heart fluttering with the awareness that Griffin was watching and waiting.

"He thanks us for a pleasant evening," she said after scanning the first two lines, "and looks forward to seeing us again."

"What else?" Her mother had moved to Emily's side and was now leaning in, attempting to glimpse Mr. Partridge's words herself.

Emily straightened the paper and turned it slightly away from her mother's inquisitive gaze. "He says he plans to visit one of the orphanages he's supporting next month and hopes to find us in London at that time so he can call on us."

"Oh!" Georgina squeaked the word and clapped her hands together. "His interest in you is clear."

"But unreciprocated." Emily folded the letter and tucked it in her pocket. "I'm sorry, Mama."

"He could be your last chance." The words, as kind as Emily knew they were meant to be, stabbed at her heart. She tightened her jaw and bit back the sharp rejoinder that instinctively rose up her throat. "Then that is a chance I am willing to take."

"Lord Griffin. Perhaps you—"

"Don't." Emily glared at her mother, watching as she shrank back with a muttered apology. She would not let her interfere where Griffin was concerned. Not when he and she had agreed that marriage wasn't an option. Not when she knew he would only commit to such a thing out of duty. Not when he didn't love her. "You must stop trying to pawn me off and accept the fact that I will not marry."

"I just want you to be happy," her mother whispered.

Emily reached for her hand and squeezed it. "I already am."

"If that is true, then I am happy for you." Her mother's lips stretched, attempting a smile that didn't quite reach her eyes. Bowing her head as if to hide her real thoughts on the matter, she retreated to the kitchen.

Emily looked at Griffin, still standing there in the library doorway, a silent spectator to her humiliation. "I am sorry."

"Don't be. Your mother is just trying to do what she believes to be best for you." His brow puckered slightly. "You should not be so hard on her, Emily."

"But—"

"I need to get back to the painting if I am to finish before we leave for Montvale."

He turned away and disappeared back into the library. One second later, the door closed behind him, leaving Emily standing alone in the empty hallway. She wasn't sure what had just happened, but she sensed that she'd somehow managed to ruin things between them. Why else would his comment make her feel so small? Why else would watching him walk away leave her empty inside and more lonely than ever before?

There was no mistaking Emily. She'd very clearly pronounced that she had no intention of marrying anyone. Ever. Griffin speared his hair with his fingers and tried to stay calm.

Not an easy task when he wanted to over-turn furniture and punch holes in things. What the hell? He would have bet money that the kiss they'd shared last night would have changed her mind. It had certainly stripped away any doubts he might have had and put everything into very sharp focus. In fact, the more he'd considered it, the more certain he'd been that asking Emily to be his wife was the best way forward. Until she'd snatched away any hope he'd had of her saying yes.

Damn!

A raw ache pulled at his gut—the fear of losing what he now wanted the most. Her.

He wanted her in his bed, as passionate and eager as she'd been last night. His muscles flexed in response to the image forming in his head, of creamy curves sprawled out on satiny sheets and a coy smile inviting him closer.

Reaching out, he steadied himself against a bookcase while trying to catch his breath. What the devil had Emily Howard done to him?

The answer shot through him with simple precision. She'd been unpretentious and bold, courageously honest, principled and...wonderfully different. She spoke her mind without being dismissive, was modest, good natured, and optimistically inclined. And when she met his gaze with a smile, it was as if she wrapped her arms around his soul and gave it warmth.

Which was a perfectly ludicrous notion, of course.

In fact, if he didn't know any better, he'd say he was losing his mind.

He closed his eyes on a sigh, pushing the tension out of his lungs. Two weeks ago his aversion to marriage had been indisputable. He'd deliberately avoided the unmarried ladies, had taken care not to give the wrong impression about his availability. And now, ironically, he was the one who was eager to put a ring on his finger while the woman he'd set his sights on had decided that marrying was no longer something she wished to accomplish.

And yet...

He dropped his gaze to the spot on the table where her notebook had been just a half hour earlier. The writing had been charming and witty, but most especially romantic. It wasn't what one would expect from a woman who'd turned her back on marriage, but rather from one who still dreamed.

The personal touches were further indications of this, like the daffodils and peonies, the country manor and the cooking. Griffin wouldn't be surprised to learn that Emily's ideal life included three children and a cocker spaniel as well.

He smiled, liking that thought. And then he frowned. Because if marriage was something she actually wanted, then why did she keep on insisting it wasn't? Griffin wasn't sure he could answer that question correctly. All he knew was that Emily was free to make her own choices and that he had given her no cause to think that marrying him might be an option. Even though he'd kissed her.

Hell, she believed he had every intention of leaving England at the first available opportunity. Which had been his plan. Until his life had been turned upside down.

He shook his head, befuddled by the depth of emotion she'd managed to awake in him. Joy and anxiety fizzed through his veins. He had to do what he'd meant to do earlier when the messenger's arrival had stopped him from revealing the yearnings of his heart. He had to find the opportunity to tell her how much she'd come to mean to him. It was the only way forward and the best chance they had of forming a permanent attachment.

Through honesty.

CHAPTER THIRTEEN

THEY ARRIVED AT MONTVALE TWO DAYS later. The journey had been uneventful. Emily had tried to sleep most of the way, or had at least pretended to do so for the sake of avoiding Griffin's attention. Since their conversation in the library, he'd been trying to get her alone, insisting that there was something they needed to discuss.

Emily could only imagine. The poor man obviously felt obliged to offer for her hand after the passionate kiss they'd shared. She could see it in his almost pained expression whenever he looked at her. But she would not let him make such an unnecessary sacrifice. Especially not when she feared she might actually accept his proposal. And then where would they be? He would be forced into the very state he wanted to avoid while she'd have a husband who would never reciprocate her love.

It would be an intolerable arrangement.

So each time he tried to pull her aside, she avoided him under the pretext of needing to complete a chore or having to pack. By the time he'd helped her into the carriage yesterday morning, he'd been scowling at her. And of course, for some absurd reason, this had only increased her awareness of him. Even as she'd turned her head into her corner of the carriage and closed her eyes in an effort to sleep, she'd felt his presence all around. His voice, as he conversed with her mother, had slid over every curve of her body like intimate caresses impossible to ignore.

It had been both lovely and irritating at the same time, leaving Emily in something of a bother by the time she alit from the carriage at Montvale. Griffin offered his assistance, his hand closing firmly around hers in a way that caused sparks to ignite in the pit of her belly. Her breath hitched, more so when he moved in closer to her person.

"We must speak, Emily. You cannot avoid me forever." His voice was raspy and strained, like a blade grinding over a whetstone.

"Of course," she said, attempting a breezy tone that sounded a little too squeaky to her ears. "I am ready whenever you are."

The low growl of disagreement with which he responded to that comment tickled her insides and sent little shivers scurrying over her shoulders. She raised her chin and took a step forward, deliberately adding distance so she could gather her scattered thoughts. Having him near was like over-imbibing. It muddled her head and prevented her from simple reasoning.

Thankfully, Mary and Caleb appeared at that moment, both coming down the front steps of the house in order to greet them. They were followed by Cassandra and the children who raced past Mary, whooping until they reached Emily, their arms enfolding her in a hug as they piled around her.

Emily laughed in response. She'd not expected such a boisterous welcome and found herself swept off her feet by it, the joy these children provided bubbling up inside like rich champagne. She hugged them close and kissed the tops of their heads while assuring them that she'd missed them all just as much as they had missed her.

"Goodness, Bridget," Mary chided in a mild tone, "you must release poor Emily so she can move. You too, Edward. One would think you haven't seen her in years."

"We're not used to not having her around," Daphne explained as she caught Emily's hand in a grip surprisingly tight for a girl of her age.

"I wasn't around when we were in London either," Emily reminded them as she gazed into their upturned faces. Peter was almost the same height as she now. Another year and he would most likely surpass her. A curious tightness squeezed at her throat on that thought. She cleared it quickly to add, "If you will recall, you remained with Cassandra at Coventry House while I stayed with my parents."

"Yes. But we saw each other every day," Penelope said.

Bridget nodded in firm agreement of this fact. "So we could accept your absences there."

"But then you left for Clearview without even saying goodbye," Edward said with a hint of accusation in his young voice.

Oh dear.

Emily sought out Mary and Cassandra, hoping they'd step in and offer their help. She'd no idea how they had explained her sudden departure from London to the children.

"If you will recall, Emily had to take care of a few things before coming here," Cassandra said.

"What things?" Peter asked with the deductive alertness of a boy who was not easily fooled by anything.

"Mrs. Howard," Caleb said, directing attention away from Emily and toward her mother instead. "Allow me to introduce you to the children who have been in your daughter's care." His no nonsense voice forced the squabble back into order, and as he called out each name, each child stepped forward with either a bow or a curtsey.

"I am so pleased to make your acquaintances at last," Georgina informed them with a delight that Emily found surprising. In London, her mother had given no indication of wanting to meet them, but she supposed a lot had changed since then. They'd made peace for one thing, forgiving each other for things that should have been put behind them years ago.

Grinning, Caleb gave his attention to Griffin next while Cassandra and Mary ushered Emily toward the front steps of the house. "You will tell us everything, won't you?" Mary whispered as they entered the foyer.

"There's not much to tell," Emily said.

Cassandra snorted. "You're a terrible liar." When Emily raised an eyebrow, her friend said, "Your cheeks have turned scarlet. I can barely see anything else in this dim interior."

Stepping away from them, Emily patted her cheeks in an effort to cool them. They did feel rather hot and grew increasingly so when Griffin stepped through the door, his gaze meeting hers with unnerving swiftness. Emily glanced away and proceeded to take off her bonnet, which she handed to the waiting butler. She caught a suspicious glance from Cassandra, but was thankfully saved from further scrutiny when Bridget and Daphne began asking if it was time to go in to tea yet.

"Cook has made strawberry tarts in preparation for your arrival," Penelope explained. "We're all very eager to enjoy them."

"By all means then," Georgina declared. "Lead the way."

"You wouldn't rather go freshen up a bit after the journey?" Mary asked.

"I'm not sure the children can wait," Georgina said with a grin.

Once again, Emily was struck by how happy and relaxed her mother appeared. The almost stern and opinionated woman she'd always known had been utterly transformed. It was remarkable to see. She shared a smile with Mary and Cassandra before following the crowd into the parlor where the tea and tarts stood ready.

Another hour passed before Emily was able to see her allotted bedchamber. Thankfully, the children were too busy savoring their treats and playing with Bridget's pet cat to ask any more uncomfortable questions. And since Cass and Mary kept Emily occupied with accounts of what they'd been up to recently, she was saved from having to talk about Griffin. Until her bedchamber door closed behind her and she found herself quite alone with her friends.

Both of them smirked with apparent amusement.

Emily narrowed her gaze. "What?"

Mary laughed. "Is that all you have to say for yourself?"

"The simmering air between you and Griffin did not go unnoticed," Cassandra explained.

Emily went to the window and glanced out at the garden below. It was pretty and inviting, with graveled walkways and rosebushes promising a wild display of color and fragrance in the months to come. "I cannot imagine what you are referring to."

"And we are but a pair of blind simpletons," Mary murmured. "Come now. We have always been open and honest with each other."

"And we will get the truth out of you one way or the other," Cassandra said with a grin.

Emily turned to face them. She rolled her eyes. "Oh, very well." She studied their eager expressions for a second before saying, "Griffin kissed me at your ball, Mary. Mama witnessed the whole thing and demanded we marry. So I ran."

"I knew it had to be something like that," Mary said, her voice rising in a squeak of excitement. "Didn't I tell you, Cass?" She returned her attention to Emily while Cassandra nodded. "And Griffin went in pursuit."

"The man is obviously smitten," Cassandra said with a bounce in her voice.

Emily shook her head. "No, he isn't. He was merely trying to do the gentlemanly thing by ensuring the safety of a stubborn woman who was quite determined to quit his company."

A second of silence ensued. It was followed by her friends' explosive laughter. "Is that what you think?" Mary asked. When Emily slowly nodded, she said, "Even Caleb suggested that you and his brother would eventually marry. And that was *before* he kissed you at the ball."

"What?"

"The two of you have been eyeing each other since the moment you first met," Cassandra said. "Except now..." She scrunched her nose and peered at Emily. "You're more flustered around him while he looks like he'd appreciate the chance to get you alone somewhere."

"It's nothing really. It's just—"

"Did anything else happen between you two at Clearview?" Mary asked with a wry smile that hinted at scandal.

"No!" Emily cleared her throat. "My mother was there for the most part. In fact, it's the oddest thing, but I do believe Griffin has somehow helped us overcome our differences."

"That's wonderful," Cassandra said.

Mary nodded. "I quite agree." She was silent a moment before asking, "Are you sure nothing else happened between you and Griffin?"

"Well, I..." Oh, for heaven's sake, lying to her friends was impossible. "He may have kissed me again. Or rather, I may have kissed him. I'm actually not sure which."

Cassandra squealed and Mary laughed. "I knew it!" Mary exclaimed. "The fire in his eyes when he looks at you suggests that there has to be more to your recent interaction than the one kiss you shared with each other at the ball."

"You have to tell us everything," Cassandra said. She took a seat on Emily's bed and patted the spot beside her.

With a sigh, Emily surrendered. She spent the next several minutes giving her friends a quick outline of everything that had occurred since the moment she'd spotted Mr. Bale and had suggested they go for a walk together in the garden.

"And you're certain that Griffin doesn't want marriage?" Mary prodded.

"I have overheard him saying that it is the last thing on his mind," Emily said. "He plans to return to Vienna as soon as possible. Escorting me to Clearview and coming here have delayed him."

"Or," Cassandra said with a brightness that Emily suddenly lacked, "he's increasingly reluctant to go. Because of you."

"I think that's unlikely," Emily said.

Mary frowned. "Why?"

"Well, I'm hardly the sort of woman who turns a man's head," Emily blurted.

Cassandra and Mary both stared at her. "And therein lies the problem," Cassandra whispered. "You still don't think you're good enough, even after he kissed you and followed you all the way to Clearview, installing himself there when he had every excuse not to do so."

"He was being a gentleman," Emily muttered.

"With roguish intentions." Mary chuckled. A smile chased away the laughter, and she took Emily's hand. The mattress bounced a little as she shifted her weight to turn more fully toward her. "As I understand it, returning to Vienna is rather pressing for Griffin. He's already been away too long, so I am quite sure the only reason he's still in England is because he is hoping to secure an attachment with you before he goes."

Emily forced herself not to be swept away by the excitement with which her friends spoke. "I don't want him to do something rash out of duty or obligation."

"I'd say the fact that he keeps on kissing you proves there's a bit more to it than that," Cassandra pointed out.

"But..." Was it possible that Griffin actually wanted to marry her like her friends were suggesting? And if so, could it really be because he truly wanted her? The chance that it might sent a thrill darting through her.

"Would you perhaps consider going with him?" Mary asked. "To Vienna, that is?"

"I...I have no idea. I'd have to think about that." Vienna seemed so incredibly far away, but then again, if she were going with Griffin, it might not be so bad. And yet... She shook her head. "No." When her friends looked puzzled, she said, "Griffin might want me, but he does not love me the way I love him."

"Are you sure?" Mary quietly asked.

Emily nodded, her heart overcome by sadness. "I cannot spend my life waiting for him to feel more for me than he does – hoping he'll one day return my affection when that day might never come. It would simply hurt too much."

Strolling through the stables with his brother,

Griffin savored the whinnying sounds of horses and the earthy smell of muck and hay. He paused to nuzzle one of the mounts. "I look forward to riding with you in the coming days." He glanced at Caleb. "We haven't done so since we were lads." Before they'd gone off to university. Before their lives had been changed by Caleb's sudden departure.

As if sensing an underlying hint of regret, Caleb stepped closer and leaned one shoulder against the stall. "Do you wish things had been different?"

There was no mistaking his meaning.

Griffin shook his head. "No. You did the right thing by going away. Devlin and I saw that, which was why we both left as well." He winced. "Staying behind and following the path Papa had prepared for us wasn't an option."

"It's incredible, isn't it," Caleb murmured, "how poorly a man can know his own sons?"

"I don't believe he ever cared to know us."

"No. I don't believe he did either." Caleb patted the horse's neck and straightened himself with a forced smile. "His loss, since we turned out rather well in my opinion."

"We certainly managed to do alright without him."

"That we did," Caleb agreed. He let his hand drop and proceeded to study Griffin a moment. "What are your plans now?"

Griffin moved away from the stall and recommenced walking. "That depends."

"On a certain Miss Emily Howard, I suspect?"

Seeing the sparkle in his brother's eyes, Griffin could not help but grin. "I must confess she's prompted me to reexamine everything I hope to accomplish."

"Like getting married and starting a family?"

Griffin nodded. He kicked some fallen hay out from under his boot, savoring the scrape of the heel against the flagstones. "You know that neither featured very strongly in my plans for the future. Until now." He smiled, comfortably and openly. "I swear that woman has put some sort of spell on me."

Caleb laughed and slapped his hand on Griffin's shoulder. "She wouldn't be the first one to affect a man so. That I can promise you."

"So you're just as in love with Mary as you were four months ago when you married?"

"More so, if you can believe it." They exited the stables and started back toward the house. "I'm happy for you, Griffin. Let's hope that I'll soon be congratulating you on your engagement."

Griffin savored the warmth of the afternoon sun spilling over his cheeks as they walked. His heart fluttered beneath his ribs both from nervousness and excitement. Pursuing Emily felt right. Instinct told him that they would be good together. Now all he had to do was convince her. It was a feat he looked forward to with growing anticipation.

"The rest of the guests should be arriving tomorrow," Caleb announced during dinner.

"Who else are you expecting?" Emily's father asked before he stuck a piece of veal in his mouth. He and Laura had arrived from London that afternoon.

"Cassandra's brother, Viscount Aldridge and his wife, Vivien, have been invited. Then there are Mary's parents, her sisters and their husbands, of course." Caleb paused to take a sip of his wine. "I've also taken the liberty of inviting Langdon and his wife."

Emily sputtered, the sip of wine she'd just taken going down the wrong way. "Langdon...?"

"He's an old friend," Griffin explained, apparently mistaking Emily's question for ignorance. "I haven't seen him since I left England. Last I heard he was visiting family in Scotland, so it will be great to finally catch up on lost time."

"Fantastic," Emily muttered with a cough that earned her a quizzical look from Cassandra.

"Are you all right, dear?" Georgina asked, leaning in.

Emily nodded. She managed a hoarse, "Of course." Laura gave her a curious glance from across the table.

Georgina lowered her voice. "You're not still in love with him are you?"

Emily forced back a frustrated groan and gave a quick shake of her head. "I never was." When her mother said nothing further, apparently satisfied by this response, Emily turned her attention to her plate while the conversation continued around her. Langdon would arrive tomorrow. She would have to face him again for the first time since she'd been informed that they wouldn't suit.

It had been awful, not because she had loved him as her mother believed, but because he had been her one chance of starting a family of her own. He'd given her hope by encouraging her dream of a countryside manor, three children, and a cocker spaniel for them to play with. But when he'd asked to speak with her father, it had not been to ask for his daughter's hand, but rather to break things off. The coward had not even had the courage to tell Emily himself.

Dreading the upcoming meeting, Emily found it hard to focus on anything else for the rest of the evening. After supper, she remained silent while enjoying a cup of hot tea with the rest of the ladies. Perhaps she could feign illness and remain in her bedchamber for the entire duration of Langdon's stay?

"Is something the matter?" Mary asked, her prodding voice breaking through Emily's troubled thoughts. "You've been very distant all evening."

Emily sighed. She could not be dishonest with her friend, nor did she wish to be. Setting her teacup aside, she stood and beckoned for Mary to take a turn of the room with her. When they were some distance from the others, she said, "I know I have always told you and Cass that I never secured an attachment to any gentleman because I was too…unappealing."

Mary frowned. "You said you were a wallflower with whom no gentleman wished to dance."

"And that is true, although I did have a brief understanding once. Or so I believed. With the Earl of Langdon"

Mary's eyes widened. "Do you mean to say," she asked in a hushed whisper, "that you were hoping to marry him?"

"Yes."

"Oh, good grief."

Emily caught her friend by the arm and steered her toward the window. "My heart never suffered on his account, but my hopes were ruined and... Well, I discovered soon after that Mama was to blame, for she'd gone to speak with him that very same morning. Her visit obviously gave him cause to reconsider his intentions."

"You believe she may have overwhelmed him?"

"I have no doubt of it since the purpose of her visit was to question him about his experience in the bedchamber."

"You cannot be serious!" The exclamation caught Cassandra's attention. She glanced at them briefly before turning back to Caleb's mother with whom she, Laura, and Georgina were conversing.

"Perfectly so," Emily muttered. "Her intention, as she described it at the time, was to ensure that he would be both willing and capable of providing her with sufficient grandchildren." Mary pressed her lips together. Her shoulders started trembling. Emily glared at her. "It isn't funny."

"I know, and I'm sorry. It is just..." A snicker burst past Mary's lips, followed by a small snort. "Imagining that conversation and Langdon's response to it has stirred my imagination."

"Yes. Well. I suppose I can appreciate that now. In retrospect." Emily sighed. "It has taken me years to forgive her, but speaking to Langdon again isn't something I ever imagined having to do. Least of all at a house party where I'll be forced to endure his and his wife's company."

"You mustn't worry," Mary assured her. "Now that you've made me aware of your predicament, I shall do what I can to ensure that your interaction with them is kept to a minimum. I promise you that."

"Thank you." Emily grabbed her hand briefly and gave it a squeeze. "You and Cass are the best of friends. I cannot imagine what I would do without you."

When Griffin returned to the parlor later, Emily was discussing the medicinal benefits of various teas and herbs with the other women.

She liked that he dove right into the conversation, adding that he'd had great success adding cloves, citrus, and honey to tea made from mint leaves and chamomile when treating a cold. "Adding a finger of brandy helps too, not only with the healing effect but with the flavor as well." He winked, causing all the ladies to laugh.

"I have always liked adding port to my tea when taking it in private," the dowager duchess confessed.

Caleb stared at his mother. "Really?" He arched his brows.

The old woman shrugged her slim shoulders. "As you say, it vastly improves the flavor."

Laughter bubbled up Emily's throat, catching her by surprise. She met Griffin's gaze and noted the sparkle of mirth in his eyes. There was something undeniably funny about the idea of his reserved and very proper mother sneaking port into her tea. Noting her own mother's look of disapproval directed her way, Emily struggled to regain her composure. But the comforting warmth of sharing a connection with Griffin lingered long after other subjects were raised for discussion. It eased her into a state of relaxation that helped her forget about Langdon and his imminent arrival so she could enjoy the rest of the evening.

After saying good night to everyone, Emily spent the next half hour preparing for bed. A fire burned low in the grate, heating the spot where she sat combing out her hair. The light from a candle on her dressing table flickered, casting an orange glow over its immediate surroundings. Everything else was muted by shadows, the furniture vaguely outlined in the dark.

Emily set her comb down and picked up the candle. She crossed to the window and looked out at the purple scenery beyond. Stars sparkled overhead like pieces of shattered glass tossed up into the air, the moon a bright orb of gold suspended against the darkness. Recalling a different glance out a different window, at Griffin striding toward the lake, caused a smile to tug at her lips. She would never forget how incredible he'd looked as he'd emerged from the water, or her body's response to the sight. Even now, the mere recollection caused a wave of heat to wash over her skin.

She took a deep breath and closed the curtains, the bed that faced her when she turned a stark reminder of what she so desperately longed for. But would she have the courage or the opportunity? She shook her head with a chastising curse. Her best chance of enjoying such activity would have been at Clearview. *Before* her mother had arrived. Sneaking about now in her friend's home with both of her parents present and other guests ready to catch Griffin ruining her was—

A soft scrape at the door gave Emily pause. It sounded like a cat or a dog clawing to get in. The noise came again, urging her forward. She hesitated, tilted her head, and listened again.

"Emily?"

The hushed whisper, barely audible through the door, almost made her drop the candle. Stupidly, she glanced around the room, as if it would tell her how to respond. The whisper was repeated, slightly louder this time. She reached for the door handle, gulped down a lungful of air, and opened the door, her eyes meeting Griffin's across the threshold.

"I know this is highly irregular," he whispered, "but I need to speak with you in private, only I can't seem to get you alone." He glanced both ways, as if to ensure that no one was coming. "May I come in?"

Emily hesitated briefly. If he entered her bedchamber she would most likely kiss him again, and if she kissed him again, there was a chance she would beg him for more. So if she had any doubts about heading down that particular path, the time to address them was now.

He doesn't love you. He won't offer marriage. All you will ever be to him is a brief distraction.

She stepped back and opened the door wider, her mind completely at ease with whatever might happen between them. This was her chance. Right now. With Griffin. She could not pass it up even if it meant having her heart broken when he eventually left her.

His shoulder nudged hers as he walked past. She

closed the door gently behind him and turned. The light from the candle brought his features into stark relief, sharpening the angles while smoothing out the softer lines. The effect was dramatic, almost theatrical in nature, and utterly captivating. She was transfixed, unable to look away.

"Emily."

Griffin's voice broke through the darkness, the low cadence lulling her body as easily as a hot bath might soothe aching muscles. He dropped his gaze and allowed it to wander, leaving a blazing trail of awareness in its wake.

"Yes?" She had to say something, had to fill the silence now squeezing between them.

He looked up and she sucked in a breath, completely undone by the predatory way in which he watched her, like a wild jungle cat hunting its prey.

She heard him inhale, a ragged sound that raked her nerves and caused her to shiver. "You drive me to distraction," he murmured. She didn't realize he'd moved his hand until she felt it, the sensual brush of his fingers upon her arm.

A shudder went through her, sucking the breath from her lungs. "Really?"

He laughed, like only a rogue would do, with the sort devilish intent that could easily divest a woman of her virtue.

His feather-light touch trailed over her skin, igniting a fire inside her that burned through each limb.

Leaning in, he closed the distance between them to press a soft kiss on her cheek. The effect was dizzying: the scrape of his unshaved jaw, the smell of his sandalwood scent infusing the air, a hint of the chocolate he'd had for dessert. "I want you more than I've ever wanted anything else in my life," he murmured while nuzzling his mouth into the spot where her neck met her shoulder.

Leaning back, Emily clutched the candlestick, careful not to drop it or hold it too close. "More than a freshly baked scone?"

He laughed against her, the vibration sending a charge of delicious shivers straight down to her toes. "Yes. Although I'd be lying if I haven't considered the fact that by marrying you I'll be able to have both."

She slid her hand between them and tried to give him a nudge. Thinking with him so near wasn't possible. "You said you wanted to talk."

He didn't budge. "I thought that was what we were doing." His hand moved to her waist, kneading her flesh beneath the chaste cotton before pulling her closer.

"Griffin." His name was both sigh of pleasure and warning.

"Mmm..."He buried his nose in her hair and inhaled, breathing her in as if she were a fragrant bouquet of flowers. "Marry me, Emily. Be my wife and let us dispense with this madness."

The words curled through the air, teasing and tempting like a sweet, intoxicating aroma, so alluring that Emily almost missed their significance.

She blinked as if jolted awake. "What?"

"I could arrange for a special license. We could—"

"No."

He went utterly still. His breaths rose and fell, heavier than before. "We could be happy together," he said, completing the sentence she'd just interrupted. "I enjoy your company and I get the sense that you enjoy mine."

"And that's enough reason?"

"No." He nudged her with a shake of his head. His hands moved. One slid up her side, the other swept round to her back, holding her steady. "There's also this."

Before she could draw a breath or question his intentions, his mouth captured hers, reminding her of why she'd let him into her room and why doing so might have been a mistake.

CHAPTER FOURTEEN

H E KISSED HER WITH ALL that he was, pouring each moment he'd spent in her absence into each swipe of his lips. God, how he'd missed her—the soft press of her breasts against his harder chest, the flare of her hip right beneath where his palm rested, and the carefree abandon with which she drove her fingers up into his hair.

Their attraction to each other and the passion they shared was sensational. Griffin had never known anything like it before her, and instinct told him he'd never find it again if he let her go. So he held on tight, pulling her closer and reveling in her soft sighs of pleasure.

You came here to talk, you scoundrel, not to seduce.

Just a little bit more.

He just had to feel some skin, had to sate his curiosity and quench the thirst she subjected him to. So he took a liberty he knew he shouldn't, tugging on her nightgown and easing it upward. The fabric bunched in his fist to reveal the supple perfection of her thigh.

Griffin pressed his hand into its softness and allowed imagination to grip him. His body responded with a burst of desire that stoked his arousal until the most urgent thought in his head was getting her naked and into his bed.

"Griffin?" His name brought primal need to a halt. He froze, his thoughtless intention compounded by the sudden awareness that her leg was now bared all the way to her hip.

"Christ." He lowered her nightgown and took a step back. "I'm sorry."

"Really?"

No.

Maybe.

He stepped back further, ran his fingers roughly through his hair. "I got distracted." He sighed. "You…have that effect on me, Emily."

She chuckled. "I must confess you do the same to me."

He stared at her, the tips of his fingers tingling once again with the urge to touch her. Instead, he forced himself to keep some distance between them. He had to in order to gather his thoughts.

"How can I convince you that marriage would be the right thing for us, Emily?" When she shook her head, he pressed stubbornly on, determined to conquer whatever concerns she might have. "Just consider the life we would share, both as friends and as lovers." He didn't need perfect lighting to know she was blushing. He could tell by the way her breath started to quiver. "Based on how well we got on at Clearview and the fierce desire we have for each other, I dare say our marriage would be rewarding."

"It's a huge decision, Griffin. And a permanent one as well."

Concern began nipping at his shoulders. She was

not as easily convinced as he had expected. "We can live in a countryside manor where daffodils bloom in the spring and peonies in the summer. We'll cook together. I'll purchase a cocker spaniel for you, and we'll have the three children you wish for." When she didn't respond, keeping silent so long it unnerved him, he added, "And we can visit Clearview as often as you like." God. He was starting to sound desperate, but he really didn't care. "Cassandra and the children can come visit us as well. I'll do whatever it takes to make you happy."

"Why?"

"Well because…" He wasn't sure how to express it exactly. All he knew was that he wanted Emily by his side and that he would give her the world if that was what it would take. "I've never liked a woman as well as I like you. You're the first one with whom I think marriage could work."

She turned her face away on that statement, concealing her expression in darkness. And then she shifted, sliding away from the wall and moving past him. Griffin followed her movements with his gaze. He wasn't sure why a sudden anxiety pulled at his gut or why it now felt as though a ravine existed between them. Not until she spoke.

"After our last kiss, I made a decision. It's the reason why I opened the door to you this evening, the reason you're standing here now in my bedchamber when you ought to be in your own." She set the candle on her bedside table. "I gave up on marriage long ago when…" Her words trailed off, and then, as if catching herself, she shook her head swiftly. "It doesn't matter. But I am curious to know what I might be missing. And so, I thought that perhaps you might be willing to show me."

Griffin gaped at her. She might be six and twenty with more life experience than a debutante, but she was still an innocent. The last thing he expected her to suggest was an illicit affair. Uncomfortable, he shifted. Was that all she truly wanted? To use him for an experience? Had he misread her so poorly?

He cleared his throat, wary of how to proceed. "As enticing as such an arrangement may be, I could never in good conscience accept." She stared at him, compelling him to add, "You deserve better than that."

A choked sob escaped her. "And you believe that would be for me to tie myself permanently to a man for whom the very idea of marriage was loathsome just a few weeks ago?"

Had he really said that? "A lot has changed since then, Emily."

"Yes, but not enough."

"What do you mean?" Surely she'd realized by now how strongly he felt about her?

"Well, for one thing you do not love me. And I refuse to marry for anything less."

Griffin blinked. "I'm sure that with time I shall—"

"What if you don't? What if you never love me the way I…" With a gulp of pain she gave him her back. A whispered plea followed. "Please go."

Griffin stood as if roots had sprouted from the soles of his feet and driven through the floorboards beneath. "Emily." He wanted to go to her, hold her, force her to understand that she mattered to him, that he cared about her, and that love would grow between them if she'd just allow it.

But the fierce shake of her head denied him. Her rigid posture informed him that she no longer wanted his touch. And as hard as that was for him to accept, he forced himself to do as she asked.

"Very well." Incredibly, he managed to move his feet and direct his body to the door. He paused there. "We will speak again tomorrow when we've both had some time to think. For now, I shall bid you good night."

He opened the door and exited her room. Her whispered words of parting drifted after him like ghosts through the night. How he'd managed to muck this up was beyond him, but one thing was clear and that was that he'd grossly underestimated what Emily wanted.

On that thought, he let himself into his own bedchamber. Her words repeated in his head. *What if you never love me the way I...*

What?

How did that sentence end? With *deserve, hope,* or *need*? He shrugged off his jacket and started undoing his cravat. Then he froze. Could it possibly have been, *the way I love you*? His heart skittered at the very idea, and his chest grew oddly tight. Dare he hope this was what she'd been meaning to say? And what if it was? She'd already said she would only marry for love, which meant he would have to love her in return.

His brow strained in response to his frown, causing an ache that he rather relished, for it was something he could more easily relate to. Everything else, this feeling of loss that had drained all happiness from him when she'd told him no, leaving him hollow inside, the constant desire to be near her, to simply see her smile, was something so foreign he'd not taken time to examine it closely. Or rather, he'd deliberately chosen not to because the intensity of his emotions where Emily was concerned, his inability to think rationally in her presence, and his eagerness to defy propriety for her, terrified him. Even now it had taken remarkable restraint on his part not to claim her. Years of good upbringing must be to blame, the gentleman he'd so often pushed aside when it came to widows and demimondaines stepping forward to show him the way.

A quick tumble was not the way to go. Not when it came to Emily. No matter how much she believed otherwise. He knew her by now, knew that she would regret it because of her romantic nature.

He undid his cravat, tossed the long length of fabric on a nearby chair and removed his waistcoat. His shirt, trousers, unmentionables, and hose followed, leaving his skin susceptible to the cool air in the room.

Padding across the floor, he pulled down the sheets, climbed into bed, and blew out his candle. For long moments after, he stared up into the infinite darkness while going over every interaction he and Emily had shared during the past few weeks. He adored her smile, her easy laughter, the determined purpose with which she went through life, and her willingness to suffer embarrassment in favor of honesty. But did he love her? He wasn't entirely sure, which was why he'd kept silent earlier when she'd brought it up. Because when it came to the contents of his heart, the last thing he wanted was to make a mistake. He had to understand what he felt for her before he let her know.

In the meantime, however, courting her properly wouldn't be amiss. She deserved to be treated with honor and respect. And as challenging as that might prove since she'd probably try to avoid him after his idiocy this evening, he was damn well going to try. Because going back to Vienna without being somehow attached to Emily simply wasn't an option.

She was never leaving her bedchamber again. Not after last night's disastrous conversation with Griffin and certainly not when Langdon and his wife were due to arrive at some point during the day. She'd rather eat rotten food and endure being sick for a week.

Very well.

Maybe that was a bit dramatic.

But the thought of having to face either man today was unbearable. She considered her appearance in the mirror. Shadows darkened the skin beneath her eyes, a testament to how poorly she'd slept.

She pinched her cheeks to add some color, then turned away from her reflection when it didn't provide the desired result. Had she really been one second away from blurting her feelings for Griffin to him? Dropping her face in her hands, she let out a groan.

He'd offered to marry her for heaven's sake, and she, fool that she was, had demanded more. Because loving him when he did not love her in return would be devastating. It would wear on her heart and destroy her soul.

She knew this, but it still didn't soothe the pain or regret slicing through her after she'd refused him. That had lingered, keeping her from the deep, peaceful sleep she was used to. Instead, she'd been restless, her dreams plagued by running and being chased, of flowers wilting, her parents shouting, and then, right before she'd woken, a pistol aimed straight at her forehead.

She glanced at the door. Someone would come and check on her soon, either her friends or her mother. When they did, they would see the state she was in and proceed to ask questions. Questions she'd no desire to answer. Which meant she had to pretend everything was as it should be and that her heart wasn't breaking because of a wish that would never be realized. No matter how much she longed to hide away here in her bedchamber forever and avoid reality, she had to dress and go down to breakfast. It was her only chance at normalcy.

"You look exhausted," Laura observed when Emily stepped into the dining room ten minutes later.

Apparently her attempt at looking well rested by widening her eyes and smiling was unsuccessful. And now everyone was looking at her, though she was grateful to find Griffin absent.

"I started on a new book last night," Emily said, stifling a yawn. "Couldn't put it down." Which wasn't a complete lie. At least not the part about having a new book. She'd found it in the library the previous evening before dinner. She just hadn't opened it yet.

"What's it called?" Georgina asked while Emily slid into a chair next to Mary. Cassandra and Laura sat directly opposite with Emily's father, Caleb, and the dowager duchess a bit further down the table to Emily's right while the children occupied the other end of the table.

"Patisserie Extraordinaire." She poured herself a cup of tea while explaining, "It's a French pastry book."

Cass grinned. "Only you would consider that bedtime reading."

"What I can't comprehend," Georgina said, knitting her brow, "is that you would find it so engrossing that it would keep you awake."

Busying herself with the slice of toast she'd procured and a dollop of jam that needed spreading, Emily shrugged one shoulder. "It stirred my imagination." With the hope of avoiding additional questions, she addressed Mary. "Have you planned any activities for the week ahead?"

"Oh yes." Excitement sparkled around Mary's words. "We'll have a treasure hunt, a picnic, an archery contest. Games on the lawn."

"And a play that the children have been preparing," Cassandra added with pride.

"It's about a group of animals that have been captured in the jungles of Asia and Africa and how they experience being brought to England," Penelope said.

Emily took a bite of her toast.

"I'm to play the zebra," Daphne declared.

"You'll make an excellent one, I'm sure," Emily told her with love expanding her heart. It hadn't occurred to her how much she'd missed her and the rest of the children until they'd welcomed her with hugs and kisses yesterday. "Do you have a good costume?"

Daphne scrunched her nose. "I'm still working on that."

"I've finished mine," Edward said, earning an eye-roll from Bridget.

"You also have the easiest one," she said. "A lion. That's a one color outfit and something to use as a mane."

Emily ate the rest of her toast while following the children's continued discussion on costumes and rehearsal. She discovered that Peter and Penelope had the bigger parts and that both wanted everything to be perfect.

"Perhaps we should go for a walk after breakfast," Mary suggested, pulling Emily's focus back to her. "Before the rest of the guests start arriving."

Emily's gaze went instinctively to the vacant seat adjacent to Caleb's. She wouldn't ask. To do so would be too obvious. "Has Lord Griffin not yet risen?" The words escaped her mouth before she could stop them.

Caleb disengaged from the conversation he was having with Emily's father, no doubt alerted by the mention of his brother's name. "He has gone for a ride. I met him in the foyer before coming in for breakfast."

"Perhaps we ought to prepare a plate for him,"

Emily said, words still flowing from her mouth of their own volition. "He will likely be hungry upon his return."

Caleb held her gaze for a moment. Until Emily felt like squirming. "That is incredibly thoughtful of you."

"Yes," Mary murmured. "Very thoughtful indeed."

Emily broke eye contact with Caleb, which allowed her to notice her mother's secretive smile and the flicker of understanding in Cassandra's gaze. Feeling like a bug beneath a magnifying lens, Emily grabbed a clean plate and proceeded to pile food onto it. "It's easy to do since the food is already out, and it will save the servants the trouble."

It had nothing to do with the fact that she cared about Griffin's wellbeing or that she wanted to do something nice for him. Even if she might have ruined things between them last night by turning him down. She could only hope that she hadn't, but his continued absence as the morning wore on concerned her. He still wasn't back when she and her friends returned from their walk, and while Emily had initially been nervous about seeing him again and not knowing what to say or how to act around him any longer, anxiety started to grow in its place.

By the time she sat down to lunch, an uncomfortable restlessness kept her from enjoying the meal. There could only be one explanation at this point. Griffin was either avoiding her or he'd had an accident with the horse. Her heart thumped loud and fast at both thoughts, and she caught herself glancing at doors and praying for him to walk through one of them soon.

"He's done this many times before," Caleb said, breaking through Emily's worries that afternoon. She was standing on the terrace, staring out across the fields and wringing her hands. Every awful possibility played out in her head, making her sick with dread.

She flinched in response to his words for she'd not heard him approach and was startled to find him standing close to her shoulder. "I beg your pardon?" Caught off guard, she wasn't quite able to make sense of his meaning.

"You've been searching for something all day, and judging from your questions during breakfast, I expect it must be Griffin?"

"I..." She swallowed the lie on the tip of her tongue and gave a small nod. "I must admit that I've gotten used to his presence."

"And now you find his absence unsettling?" He rocked back on his heels while studying the landscape she'd been scanning. Rolling hills lay in the distance, beyond the flat fields bordering the Montvale property. A forest of dense trees sat to the left, and to the right Emily could glimpse a few houses where the nearest village began. "But you don't have to worry. Griffin's just thinking."

"Thinking?" By saying he meant to go for a ride and then not returning? "How do you know that?"

"Because it is what he did when he was a lad and needed to work through a problem." He dropped a glance at her and grinned, his appearance so similar to his brother's and yet so different. Having gotten to know Griffin better, Emily could easily tell them apart now, even without the scar. Each had his own unique expressions. While Caleb smiled broadly, showing off neat rows of teeth, Griffin tended to just lift one corner of his mouth. And then there was the way in which Griffin frowned. His eyebrows would arch in a way Caleb's didn't, his brow puckering mostly above his nose while Caleb's frowns were more evenly spread across his entire forehead.

"Your Grace," a footman announced from behind them, causing them both to turn. "The Earl of Langdon has arrived."

"Thank you." Caleb gave his attention back to Emily. "Stop worrying. You shall see my brother again very soon. If you'll excuse me now, I must go and greet my guest."

Emily waited until he'd disappeared back inside before taking a long fortifying breath. It was time for her to face the man she'd once believed she would marry. And she would do so with her head held high and a smile on her face. After all, she had not loved him. There really wasn't any reason why they could not put the past behind them and try to be friends.

CHAPTER FIFTEEN

GRIFFIN SWUNG OFF HIS HORSE when he reached the edge of the Montvale property, deciding to walk the remaining mile. Or perhaps he was looking for a way to delay his arrival. Being gone most of the day without explanation would likely result in questions. But he'd had to get away in order to gather his thoughts and think clearly. He would not have been able to do so knowing that *she* was nearby.

He kicked a lump of earth with the heel of his boot as he passed over it. His horse, Apollo, puffed out some air. The effort caused his upper lip to flutter in a way that showed off his solid teeth. Griffin breathed in the afternoon air and reached up to slide his hand over Apollo's neck. The horse swung his head and nickered.

Griffin smiled. During his ride, he'd come to one startling conclusion. And that was that he was an absolute fool. What surprised him was the length of time it had taken him to draw this conclusion, which was most of the day. But the fact had become increasingly clear the more he'd thought about Emily and the time they'd spent together at Clearview. He'd looked back on their conversations, on the joy in her eyes when he'd fixed her clock, the pleasure with which she'd cooked for him, and a host of other reasons why his heart felt full when he envisioned her face.

Yes, there was desire. His lust for her had grown into a chained creature that pulled on its manacles, desperate to be freed. But there was more: a yearning for her company, a longing to hear her thoughts and to share his own thoughts with her, a sense of loss creeping under his ribs when she wasn't near. She was bright and happy and beautiful, and he, idiot that he was, was hopelessly in love with her.

Except he'd been too bloody dense to realize it sooner. Worse, he'd failed to tell her last night when the opportunity had arisen. Which meant she might not believe him now. She might just think he was telling her what she needed to hear in order to get what he wanted. So he was back to the idea of courtship. It was the only way he could think of to show her the contents of his heart and convince her that she had become the single most important person in his life.

With this in mind, he'd stopped in the village to buy a few things – gifts with which to surprise her during the coming days. Things he hoped might prove not just how well he knew her, but that he'd been paying attention to her in a way that only an infatuated man would. He smiled at that thought. Everything would be right with the world now that he'd figured out how he felt. It would no longer feel as though it tilted sideways at an uncomfortable angle.

Satisfied with the self-discovery he'd undertaken and the plan he'd made right after, Griffin returned Apollo to the stables, collected the purchases strapped to his saddle, and strode toward the house. He had to force himself not to run up the front steps since coming off overly eager would look too suspicious. So he deliberately paused and took a deep breath before opening the front door and entered just in time to catch the swirling hem of a gown disappearing up the grand staircase.

Griffin frowned and took a step back when Mary arrived from the parlor, her face drawn tight and her mouth set in a firm line. Cassandra and Laura followed on her heals, both halting as soon as they spotted him.

"Is everything all right?" he asked just as Caleb came to join them.

"Not exactly." Mary said with a quick backward glance at her husband.

"You've hurt her," Laura said with sadness.

"How could you?" Cassandra asked, her soft tone affecting him more than if she had yelled.

Griffin frowned. He looked to his brother, hoping to understand what had happened. Clearly they blamed him for something, though what it might be, he could not fathom. But it did have the prompt effect of dimming his spirits and casting a shadow of uncertainty over his happiness.

"I'm not sure what you're accusing me of," Griffin said as calmly as he could manage. He offered a smile in an effort to ease the tension, but it only seemed to irritate them more.

Muttering something that Griffin couldn't hear, Mary shook her head and continued toward the stairs. Cassandra and Laura were right behind her, but when they reached the first step, Cassandra paused to say, "You ruined her chance of happiness. Recovering from that won't be easy."

The words echoed through Griffins mind, over and over without making sense. He looked at Caleb whose expression was growing stonier by the second. "What the devil?"

"You've got some explaining to do." Caleb gestured in the direction of his study. "And then a fair bit of groveling, I expect. If Emily's ever going to forgive you."

Griffin stood where he was for a good five seconds, unable to move. None of this made any sense. Unless someone had seen him entering or leaving Emily's bedchamber last night and she now had no choice but to marry him. That would explain Cassandra accusing him of ruining her chance of happiness, he supposed.

"Griffin?" Caleb's voice jolted him out of his reverie. He blinked and forced his feet to carry his heavy body forward. When he entered the study, Caleb was already pouring brandy into a pair of tumblers. "You're going to need this."

"What I need," Griffin said, rallying, "is for you to tell me what the hell is going on."

Caleb gave him a pensive look, then went to the door, shut it, and handed one of the tumblers to Griffin. "Have a seat."

Bristling, Griffin glanced at one of the two chairs standing opposite his brother's. A wide mahogany desk stood between them. He didn't feel like sitting. What he felt like right now was pacing – a means by which to work through the agitation sparking his nerves.

"We've a lot to discuss, Griffin. Sitting would make that easier."

Taking a sip of his drink, Griffin placed his purchases on the nearest chair and sat down in the other. He leaned back, fingers drumming impatiently on the armrests. "Proceed." He wanted this over with quickly. If he had to apologize for something he didn't even know he had done, then by all means he'd do it. One way or another he would get back to the plan he had of showing Emily that he loved her.

"Langdon arrived an hour ago." Caleb took his own seat, sipped his brandy, and allowed the comment to linger while studying Griffin.

"Can't wait to see him," Griffin said. "It has been too long." And Caleb was now causing further delay. Griffin took another sip of his drink, savoring the sharp, burning flavor as it slid down his throat.

"His wife is extremely talkative. Pleasant lady and perfect for Langdon, but not the sort one can trust with a secret."

Griffin frowned. "What in blazes are you talking about?" If he was suggesting that he had a secret with Langdon's wife whom he doubted he'd ever met, then perhaps a physician should be called to evaluate the sanity of everyone who might believe such rubbish.

"Well," Caleb muttered. "We were having tea and enjoying a pleasantly mundane discussion about what we've all been up to these past ten years, when Lady Langdon let it slip that she ought to be glad her husband did not marry Emily after all." His eyes searched Griffin's face before he quietly added, "She claimed to have you to thank for her matrimonial happiness."

Griffin stared at Caleb. "What?" He tried to think back, to some moment in the past when he might have discussed Emily with Langdon. She would have been too young when he'd left for Vienna, so if Langdon had formed an attachment to her and Griffin had cautioned him against it, it must have happened later.

By correspondence.

An unrelenting chill suffused his body, like a spindly hand reaching inside his chest to clutch at his heart. "Dear God."

"I gather you now recall what Lady Langdon was referring to?"

Griffin gave a tight nod. He then downed the remainder of his drink before going to the sideboard and pouring himself another. Fortification would not be enough to get him through this. What he needed was a bloody miracle.

"Griffin?" His brother's voice prodded him gently.

Griffin turned to stare at him blankly. Every dream he'd allowed himself to have today was crumbling and turning to dust. He would lose her over this. There was no chance in hell that she would ever forgive him.

"Langdon wrote to me roughly six years ago and asked for advice about a woman with whom he was contemplating an attachment. Her name may or may not have been mentioned. I do not recall, for I had no idea who Emily Howard was at the time, so it would not have mattered anyway." He expelled a tortured breath, added more brandy to his glass and went back to his seat. "All I remember is that she was described as a woman from a good family whose dowry would help Langdon pay off a debt his father incurred prior to his passing. Beyond that, she was said to be unremarkable – a wallflower as I understood it. While Langdon wrote that he liked her character and enjoyed her company, he was critical of her appearance and doubted he would ever find her attractive. So he asked me to advise him on whether or not he ought to abandon all hope of a passionate union in favor of one that ensured his financial security."

"Marrying for convenience is common enough."

"Yes, but I knew Langdon wanted more, and he would not have asked my opinion unless he was struggling with some uncertainty. Besides, he was an earl while the woman he contemplated marrying had no title to speak of." Griffin looked away from his brother, unable to meet his gaze any longer. "Since his heart was not invested, I told him to end things with her and keep on looking."

"And thus put an end to Emily's hopes of ever making a match, of escaping her domineering mother, and starting a family of her own."

"She did escape though," Griffin muttered. He hated how defensive he suddenly sounded. "She went to Clearview."

"Yes. She did. But I daresay she'd rather have been a wife and a mother."

Shit.

Caleb was right. "Emily's smart. She'll know I told Langdon that she wasn't good enough for him. She'll know I judged her before I met her.

She'll think the only reason I'm pursuing her now is because she looks different than she did back then."

Caleb tilted his head. "Does she?"

Griffin Shrugged. "She says she's lost weight. That it has altered her appearance."

"Langdon did compliment her excessively on her looks when he arrived. His wife started looking rather displeased."

"Perhaps Lady Langdon dredged up the past on purpose," Griffin said. "She may have been jealous and deliberately sought to wound Emily."

"If that was her motive, then she succeeded. I worried Emily might either fling her teacup at Langdon or burst into tears. Thankfully, she left the room before it came to that."

Griffin scrubbed his hand across his jaw. *Christ, what a mess!* The idea that Emily was upstairs now, suffering because of him, twisted his gut. And the risk that he might have wrecked his chance with her years ago before he'd even met her caused panic to tumble through him. He was disgusted with himself, with his shallow dismissal of her. Although he was forced to consider that if she'd married Langdon, he would never have had a chance of making her his.

Griffin expelled a breath. He was sorry he'd hurt her, but he was glad she was still unattached.

He looked at his brother, seeking comfort in his steady gaze. "What am I going to do?"

Caleb's mouth slanted just enough to convey that whatever the case, he was on Griffin's side. "That depends on how you feel about her."

Griffin spoke without hesitation. "I love her." It

felt good saying it out loud, as if putting his feelings into words made them real.

"Have you told her that?"

"No. Not yet. It only just struck me earlier today while I was out riding."

Caleb grinned. "Love does tend to catch one by surprise, that's for sure." He sobered. "Apologize first. Grovel, if you must. Then tell her how you feel and trust that everything will turn out right."

Griffin snorted. "That is easier said than done." When Caleb said nothing, he explained, "When I asked her to marry me last night, she refused."

Caleb's eyes widened. "You proposed?" Griffin nodded. "And she refused?"

"That is what I just said." Irritation added a bite to Griffin's words.

"It would seem that your problem is far more difficult to tackle than I realized." Caleb's features tightened, straightening his mouth. "You cannot force her to be your wife."

This wasn't helping. "I. Am. Aware." Griffin took another long swallow of his drink. He lowered the glass and stared pensively into the amber liquid. "The thing is I do think she'd marry me if she knew the depth of my affection for her."

"Then I suggest you show her." Leaning back in his chair until the leather squeaked beneath him, Caleb allowed a conspiratorial smile to pull at his lips. "Lay your heart bare, Brother. Women love nothing better than a man who's willing to be vulnerable. But first, apologize for the wrong you have done her. Romancing her will be easier if you've been forgiven."

Emily refused to cry. It wasn't her style. Even though she felt like a good sob would help wash away some of the pain. Still. She didn't like the idea of dissolving in tears because of a man. To do so would give Griffin too much power over her. Power he didn't deserve. So she stared stiffly out of the window, her blurry gaze focused on a tree in the distance.

Silence draped the room in loneliness. Until Cassandra spoke again. "Lady Langdon was wrong to mention her husband's connection to you. It was badly done."

"Deliberately spiteful," Mary said. "I do not like her at all."

"Neither do I," Laura murmured.

Emily glanced at her friends and her sister and turned away from the window so she could better face them. Mary stood next to the dressing table while Cassandra and Laura sat on the bed. They looked every bit as bleak as Emily felt.

"Thank you, but my issue is not with her. It is with Griffin's interference in my affairs." When neither one spoke, Emily said, "Do you not see? These past six years, I have blamed Mama for my inability to secure a proposal from Langdon. I have resented her for something that wasn't her fault at all."

"You should probably apologize to her," Laura said.

"Of course I must, but..." Emily spun away, frustrated with the way things were going and feeling a need to move. Would there always be something in the way of her dreams? "I never would have taken Griffin for such a thoughtless man."

"He probably did what he thought was in his friend's best interest at the time," Cassandra told her soothingly. "His allegiance was to Langdon. Not you."

"Yes, I know. But he judged me and found me lacking. So lacking in fact that he urged Langdon not to marry me."

"Do you believe you and Langdon would have been happy together?" Mary asked.

"That is…" She'd been about to say, 'not the point,' but stopped to consider. "He would have given me children of my own."

"Not necessarily," Cassandra said. "He has no children now, so there's at least a fifty percent chance that he wouldn't have been able to do so."

Emily shook her head. It wasn't really the lost chance with Langdon that she found upsetting. She'd recovered from that a long time ago. It was the fact that Griffin had labeled her unsuitable at a time in her life when she'd struggled to attract attention. Gaining Langdon's had been difficult. The dowry had been an undeniable help. And it pained her to think that even though Griffin had not known her back then, he'd still told his friend that he could do better.

It added a superficial element to his character that she had been certain he lacked. And she'd loved him for his character. But now… "How can I love someone who would be so shallow?"

"I think you've a few different things to keep in mind," Mary said. "For one thing, people change with experience. You ought to consider the man you have gotten to know in recent months, just as he should consider the woman that you are now. To go backward would be a pointless endeavor, for it would only lead to misplaced blame."

"Mary. I—"

"No. Let me finish." Mary held up a hand in defiance of Emily's protest. "You are not the same woman you once were. To punish a man for wanting the one you've become would be not only unfair to him but extraordinarily hypocritical. Do not forget that you have been hoping for Griffin's attention since the moment you met him." She gave Emily a pointed look. "Cass and I would have had to be blind not to notice the way you've been mooning over him like a starved woman in a pastry shop."

Emily sucked in a breath. Her cheeks heated with the embarrassment of having been so transparent. Had Griffin known all along that she was mad about him? If so, she now had yet another reason for never wanting to see him again. "I want to go back to Clearview. I want to return to the life I am used to."

"And abandon your best chance of the happily ever after you have always dreamed of?" Laura asked dubiously. She'd risen and come toward her. Stepping close, she drew Emily into a sisterly hug.

"He does not love me," Emily whispered. "If he did, he would have told me so by now." She pulled away from Laura, afraid the sympathy and affection would bring on the tears she struggled to keep from falling.

Mary snorted. "Men can be thickheaded when

it comes to such things. My advice to you would be to forget the words, for that's all they are, and consider his actions."

Emily frowned and attempted to do so. Her thoughts conjured memories of Griffin insisting that he would protect her, of him fixing her clock, of the pleasure in his eyes when he'd seen her wearing the red evening gown, the jealousy that had followed when Mr. Partridge had shown an interest, and all the kind gestures in between. There was no indication that he loved her, but it did prove that he cared.

"If you leave," Mary added, "you would be running away. And unless he chooses to follow, your issues will remain unresolved."

"I have no idea what to say to him."

"Then let him do the talking," Cassandra advised, "for I am sure there is much he will want to tell you."

CHAPTER SIXTEEN

HIS EAGERNESS TO SEE LANGDON again had abandoned Griffin half an hour ago. He no longer wished to catch up with his friend, and he certainly had no desire to meet his wife when the woman had caused Emily distress. Especially since he had yet to discover if it had been done deliberately or by accident. But since etiquette had to be adhered to, Griffin accompanied his brother into the parlor where tea was still underway.

Griffin greeted those present and then turned to Langdon, who had risen. The earl stepped forward, hand outstretched and with a broad smile upon his face. "When your brother invited me to come here, I could not refuse," Langdon said. "It is so good to see you again, Griffin." He glanced back at the woman who'd been sitting beside him. She too had now risen. "Victoria, may I present Lord Griffin. Griffin, this is my wife, the Countess of Langdon."

Griffin forced a smile and executed a bow. "A pleasure to make your acquaintance," he said while straightening himself to his full height.

Lady Langdon smiled. Her expression was warm and welcoming with no hint of malice. One might even say she was pretty, but what struck Griffin the most was her height, for she was unusually tall for a woman. It was possible then, he considered, that a moment of self-consciousness might have overcome her when she met Emily. Langdon would have been wrong to compliment her on her looks in his wife's presence. Especially when Lady Langdon knew they had once been attached.

"I have heard so many wonderful things about you, my lord," Lady Langdon said. "My husband holds you in the highest regard."

"Thank you, my lady. He and I were once fast friends. It will be interesting to hear how married life is treating him."

Langdon grinned. "Splendidly, I'd say. Victoria and I are extremely well suited."

"I am glad to hear it," Griffin said. He glanced sideways at Mr. and Mrs. Howard, who were busily conversing with his mother. Caleb had now joined in, adding to the noise. Abandoned on the table were four cups belonging to Emily, Mary, Laura and Cassandra. "If you will excuse me," Griffin muttered. He had no desire to socialize further. All he wanted was to make things right with Emily.

"But you only just arrived," Langdon said with a hint of distress.

"True, but I have come straight from the stables. If you would please allow me a chance to freshen up, I would appreciate it."

Langdon inclined his head. "Perhaps we can have a drink later in the library?"

"And a game of cards after supper," Lady Langdon added. "I love playing with friends, but have had little chance to do so recently. We spent the last three months in Scotland, you see, visiting with Langdon's sister and brother-in-law. Neither enjoys games."

"Then you have come to the right place, my lady," Griffin said. "For there are many here who would happily engage you as long as you are willing to lose."

She laughed when he smiled, appreciating the joke, and Griffin decided that as inconsiderate as she had been earlier, she had not meant to cause any harm. He excused himself once again and went in search of his room. Arriving there, he undressed and used the wash basin to remove the sweat and grime from his ride. Once dry, he dabbed a bit of sandalwood on his jaw before pulling a clean shirt over his head. Next he put on a pair of taupe-colored trousers, a waistcoat, cravat, and a navy blue jacket. He then gave his hair a quick comb before putting on his shoes.

With a glance at his dresser, he considered his purchases and wondered which one he should give to Emily first. Making a decision was complicated by the fact that a gentleman was not supposed to offer gifts to an unmarried woman. He had known this, but had not been able to resist. Not when he knew how happy the items he'd bought were sure to make her.

Deciding that he could not carry anything large around with him, Griffin settled on a smaller package that he could fit in his jacket pocket. Excited to see her reaction, and hopeful that it would help her forgive him, Griffin left his bedchamber and went back downstairs.

After ushering her friends out of her bed chamber with the assurance that she would return downstairs shortly, Emily washed her face and patted it dry, savoring the coolness against her skin. Her initial hurt and anger had subsided, allowing her to think more rationally.

Mary was right. To begrudge Griffin for advising his friend as he'd thought best would be wrong. Especially since he hadn't known Emily at the time. They hadn't been friends when this had happened, and his loyalty had been to Langdon, not her. In truth, he had advised his friend well.

Furthermore, feeling slighted by Griffin's dismissal of her six years earlier was childish. She had made a deliberate effort to change in the years since and was proud of the woman she'd become. She had evolved from a shy wallflower into a bold and courageous woman. Should she not then be happy to have caught his attention now rather than hurt by the fact that he hadn't given her younger self a chance?

After all, Griffin *had* asked her to marry him. His proposal might not have happened on bended knee or included words of endearment, but it did mean that he wanted her to be a more permanent part of his life. And after reflecting on his behavior toward her these past few weeks, she now believed that he cared about her a great deal more than she had last night. Yes, he'd yet to figure out how to put what he felt into words, but so did she. For all he knew, she didn't love him either, since she'd not declared the fact.

Finding the downstairs empty, Emily drifted toward the back of the house where a French door was flung open to let in a cool April breeze. Through the beveled glass, she could make out Griffin, his long body slumped in a white wrought iron chair with blue damask cushions. He was keeping company with Caleb and Cassandra, who were leading the conversation with animated gestures and encouraging smiles. By contrast, Griffin wore a tight expression devoid of all humor. He appeared like a man for whom joy had died, causing a tight knot of pain to expand against Emily's breast.

Unbearable guilt was etched in his features, assuring her of the regret he felt over the hurt he'd caused her. She took a deep breath and allowed a brief glance at the lawn where Mary was showing the children how to set up a game of pall mall. The knot eased in response to their happy faces. Peter and Penelope were securing arches to the ground while Bridget and Daphne appeared to be arguing over which colored mallet they would each get to use. Edward's attention was completely swallowed by a pair of squirrels chasing each other up a tree.

Could she really give them up and move away so soon after they'd had to suffer through losing Mary? Even though she and Caleb had visited Clearview once since their marriage and the children had been to see them in London, they'd expressed deep regret over having to let Mary go. Bridget had been especially forlorn, asking Emily how Mary could possibly choose a man over them. And it would be nearly impossible for Cassandra to manage Clearview on her own.

Emily decided right then and there that no matter what happened, she would not leave her friend unless a solution could be found to this problem. Not after everything Cassandra had done for her over the years.

With this in mind, Emily proceeded out onto the terrace. Langdon and his wife were thankfully nowhere nearby. They appeared like colorful flecks in the distance as they strolled toward the lake, the very picture of wedded bliss.

"There you are," Cassandra said, her voice pulling Emily toward the seating arrangement and alerting Griffin to her presence. "Will you join us?"

Before she could manage a response, Griffin was on his feet. His eyes burned into her soul, searing her until the heat flooding her body grew almost unbearable. "If I may," he began, his words uncharacteristically shaky, "I would…" He paused, took a deep breath, but seemed to falter.

It was too uncomfortable for Emily to watch. "Perhaps," she said, but he spoke simultaneously, causing her to swallow her words. She stared at him and he stared back. A nervous laugh pushed its way up her throat as the air thickened.

"Please," Griffin murmured without a hint of humor. "I did not mean to interrupt."

"Oh no, by all means, do go ahead," Emily said. She hadn't really had anything meaningful to say anyway and was far more anxious to hear him out.

"Indeed," Cassandra quipped, "I can barely stand the suspense."

Griffin frowned but chose not to respond.

Instead, he kept his gaze firmly on Emily. And then he spoke, his voice slightly more stable than before and so clear that there was no chance for her not to hear him. "I would be honored if you would walk with me, Emily."

She could see the anxiety building inside him, conveyed by the tension in his posture, the rigidity of his stance, the tight set of his jaw. If she hadn't known better, she might have believed he was furious and eager for a fight. Instead, she noted the truth in his eyes for they reflected the tortured state of his soul.

"Thank you, my lord. The garden does look particularly inviting today. I would be happy to walk with you as long as Cassandra and Camberly have no objection."

"Objection? Oh no. How could we possibly object? By all means do go ahead," the pair spoke in unison, their words overlapping in their eagerness to shoo Griffin and Emily along.

Emily returned Cassandra's seemingly innocent expression with a wry smile that was sure to inform her that she wasn't fooling anyone. It was clear that she wanted Griffin and Emily to resolve their issues as quickly as possible so they could move on. And while Emily appreciated that, she wished her friend wouldn't be quite so obvious. After all, she had yet to hear Griffin out, and then she would have to make some big decisions. Nothing was certain yet. Especially since he would surely have to return to Vienna.

He stepped toward her and offered his arm. "Shall we?"

For some inexplicable reason, the severity of

his voice sent a frisson down her spine. She had no reason to be nervous and yet she was. Perhaps because his demeanor made her feel as though there were insurmountable barriers between them. She could not relate to this somber man he'd turned into, though she had to admit she would not have been pleased if he didn't look slightly remorseful. But the lack of boyishness about his eyes and the absence of his cheeky smiles made her long for the man he'd been before he'd discovered his mistake. For it was as if the light inside him had faded, leaving nothing but darkness behind.

Linking her arm with his, Emily relaxed a little in response to the familiar reaction he inspired in her body. A hum of awareness vibrated through her, and her heart beat faster than it had seconds earlier. "My parents are not outside," she observed when they'd gone a few paces in silence. "Neither is your mother."

"It is my understanding that they have chosen to take an afternoon nap."

"I see." Emily bit her lip and tried to think of something else to say. "Langdon's wife seems nice." She winced when she felt Griffin's arm go rigid. Of all the things to mention.

"Emily, I—"

"A bit tall for a woman, but quite pretty if you take the time to consider her features properly," Emily added. She was suddenly quite unable to keep quiet, the words rushing off the tip of her tongue like water flowing over a fall. "She says she likes playing cards, which is something that I quite enjoy as well, so there is a chance we can find some common ground there. To be sure, she does not appear as approachable as one might wish, but given the fact that we shall be here for a while, rubbing shoulder to shoulder, I cannot imagine us leaving without have formed some sort of friendship. In fact, I—"

"Emily." His voice was louder, firmer, and unquestioningly demanding now. They'd reached the trimmed hedge leading into the rose garden, and he pulled her through the opening and turned her to face him. His breaths were low and labored, his eyes filled with the sort of determination that could convince a woman he would slay every dragon in the kingdom for her. "I have wronged you in the worst possible way and I..." He released her to rake his fingers through his hair. The result afforded him with a wild look of abandon that was rather appealing. "I was wrong to advise Langdon on a matter that I knew nothing about. I should not have said anything. I should have allowed him to make his own decision."

"You were his friend. To answer him when he specifically wrote to you and inquired about your opinion was only natural. Indeed, it would have been thoughtless of you not to."

"Thoughtless?" He scoffed and spun away, the soles of his boots upsetting the neatly raked gravel. "All I have been is thoughtless. Toward you and toward him. For I pretended to know what was best even though I was far away. Even though I had never met you and thus possessed no information on which to base my opinion. And yet I gave it, damning your future and possibly his in the process."

As hurt as Emily had been to discover his

involvement in her broken attachment to Langdon, she hated seeing Griffin as torn up over it as he was. Hesitantly, she approached the spot where he stood, staring down at one of the many flowerbeds filled with thorny stems and green leaves. It would be at least one more month, perhaps two, before buds began appearing.

Stepping up beside him, Emily placed her hand on his arm. The slight tensing of muscle was the only indication that he noticed. "Everyone makes mistakes, Griffin. As it turns out, yours might have been for the best."

He glanced at her, his eyebrows dipping beneath his frown. "You didn't speak to your mother for almost six years because of me."

"You helped us make peace with each other."

"Which wouldn't have been necessary if I hadn't interfered in the first place."

Emily sighed and leaned her head against his shoulder.

"My mother and I had our differences long before I was introduced to Langdon. Eventually, he became a way for me to escape her control, but that is all it would have been since I never fell in love with him." She drew away from him slightly so she could tip her head back and look at his handsome face.

Steeling herself for the cliff over which she intended to leap, she took a quick breath, pushed her fear as deep as it could possibly go, and said, "I fell in love with *you*, Griffin. With your considerate nature, teasing personality, and unpretentious ways."

He stared at her in silence. Oh, how she wished

he would say something so she didn't feel so alone right now. Perhaps she'd misjudged him? Maybe his feelings for her weren't as deep.

"I don't deserve you." He spoke as if what she'd just said made no sense. "You should be angry with me. Indeed, I would prefer it if you would yell or shout or at least give me some sort of set-down for what I did."

She understood. His guilt was eating away at him. "I will admit that I was shocked, angry, and hurt when I first learned of what you had done. But when I forced myself to think calmly about it, to consider the facts using logical reasoning, I determined that I was wrong to feel as though you betrayed me in any way. Because you didn't."

"I still hurt you."

"Yes, you did. At the time. And only because you were being a good friend."

Uncertainty remained etched upon his face. "I don't know. I—"

"For God's sake, Griffin. What must I do to convince you?" Irritation threatened to swamp her fond feelings for him. "If it is forgiveness you want, then by all means, you have it, even though it's completely unnecessary in my opinion." She crossed her arms and pushed back her shoulders with the aim of being completely honest. "Also, if you have any intention of reciprocating my declaration of affection for you, now would be an excellent time to do so."

He reached for her then and drew her roughly against him. Her body collided with his on a startled, "Oof!"

"I love you with all that I am, Emily." His hand

cupped her cheek, fingers stroking tenderly over her skin. "With every beat of my heart and each breath I take. You are everything to me, which is why knowing that I've caused you pain is impossible to accept."

Heart singing with joy, Emily leaned back in his embrace and looped her arms around his neck. "Then I must do what I can to help you forget. And to show you that I am pleased with how things have turned out."

An incredulous smile hinting at mischief pulled at the edge of his lips. "How do you plan to do that?"

"Like this," she whispered with a cheeky playfulness meant to lighten the mood, right before she pulled him closer and captured his mouth with her own.

Griffin's heart beat wildly. She loved him and she was kissing him as if she wanted to do so forever. When he'd thought for certain that he'd lost every chance he'd ever had of spending his future with her, she'd undone him with her understanding.

He'd meant what he said when he told her he didn't deserve her. No woman in the world was as kind as Emily. Whatever he had to do from this day forward to make her happy would be a small price to pay for having her in his life. And her love... It was like sunshine falling on a dreary world; bright and so full of life that he wanted to bask in it forever.

His hand settled firmly against her waist, holding her to him, not wanting to ever let her go. Her lips were rose petal soft and plush like berries, just as tempting as they'd been the two previous times when they'd kissed. But this time was different. This time their hearts were engaged with the sort of unwavering certainty that caused joy to flow through his veins. He wanted to bask in the wonder of Emily Howard; he wanted to watch her eyes light up whenever she spotted him across a crowded room; he wanted to be the man who made her feel safe and cherished.

So he kissed her back with fervor, as if this was the kiss that all other kisses in the world would one day be measured against. It was bold and tender and full of adoration and love. Just like she.

"I think I can get used to your way of helping me forget things," he murmured against the corner of her mouth.

Her lips curved beneath his. "Just as long as you don't forget how much I love you."

"I am the most fortunate man in the world." Except, not quite. But hopefully soon. He drew back, adding some measure of distance between them, and clasped her hands between his.

She smiled, so pure and without pretense that his heart felt like bursting with the shocking awareness that he was the source. He cleared his throat, determined to do the right thing and hoping to God that he wouldn't muck it up.

"I…er…" *Christ*. Why was this so hard? He pushed out a breath in an effort to calm his agitated body. His hands were now trembling, his skin flushed and prickly. He had no ring, but perhaps he had something better. At least for now.

Releasing her, Griffin reached inside his jacket pocket and pulled out the paper packet he'd placed there earlier. He opened it while constantly aware of Emily's curiosity. Yet another thing that he loved about her – this willingness of hers to learn about the world and discover new things. Gingerly, he retrieved the dark spindly stems tied with creamy silk ribbon.

Emily's uncertain frown made him grin. He knew it looked as though he was offering her some dried twigs, when in fact his gift held tremendous value.

Without further hesitation, he lowered himself to one knee and held the odd looking bouquet toward her. "I purchased this earlier today when I rode into town. The fact that it was even available was so unlikely that I knew I had to buy it for you right then and there." He tilted his head and considered her eager expression. "Do you know what it is?"

She shook her head. "I haven't a clue."

"It's vanilla. From vanilla orchids grown in Mexico. They're not at all common in English cuisine."

"So they're used for cooking?"

He nodded. "For desserts. As a substitute for rose water." He considered the small bouquet which had cost him a fortune. "I know it is not a ring, but—"

"It is perfect!" She was suddenly on her knees, her hands on either side of his face as she kissed him again.

He laughed against her mouth. "I haven't even asked you if you'll marry me yet," he managed to say while she smothered him with affection.

"Of course I will, Griffin." She kissed him again and this time he allowed it, even though they were both on their knees in the rose garden and likely to have dirt stains on their clothes. But he didn't care. The only thing that mattered right now was she. Emily. His future wife.

Heaven help him, he could scarcely credit how perfect this day had turned out after all.

"There are some things we must settle however," she said once she'd taken the vanilla bouquet as a token of his affection and he'd helped her rise.

"Yes." He'd considered a few himself. "As you know, I must return to Vienna. That cannot be helped. But where we make our permanent home will be up to you, for I can easily sell my business there and start a new one here in England."

"You are aware that Society would frown on you being in trade, are you not?"

"Your opinion is the only one that matters to me, Emily. As long as you have no objection, I could not care less what Society thinks."

She beamed at him as if he were Apollo himself, blessing her with light and knowledge. "Working on clocks and mechanical toys is your passion, so you should definitely continue, regardless of where we make our home."

He could scarcely believe they were already making such plans. But knowing what they both expected was important. With this in mind, he decided to pose another question. "Will you join me on my upcoming trip? I would like to show you where I have lived these past ten years."

"Yes. I should like that. But there is one request

I must make of you, Griffin. It pertains to a matter that might not be easy to solve."

Apprehension snaked through him. He chose to ignore it by tucking a loose strand of hair behind Emily's ear and savoring the blush that crept over her cheeks "Tell me what it is."

"I cannot leave Cass to care for the children and all of Clearview's responsibilities on her own. It would not be fair, so we'd have to find a solution to that first."

Griffin considered the problem, which was indeed a difficult one. Looking after the manor and raising five children might have been manageable for three women. Emily had once mentioned how much harder it was for just two, so he could only imagine that it would be nearly impossible for one.

"I quite agree," he said, prompting her to kiss him again.

He kissed her back, with all the passion and love that she stirred in his heart. And with the bone deep certainty that everything would work out right, as long as they had each other.

CHAPTER SEVENTEEN

HAPPINESS COULD NOT DESCRIBE WHAT Emily felt, for it was too tame a word to encompass all the emotions Griffin had instilled in her during the past three days. They'd announced their engagement immediately, partly because they'd been anxious to share their joy and partly because the dirt stains on their knees had to be explained somehow. Since then, he'd taken her on romantic walks, kissed her beneath the stars last night and gifted her with a few more items that showed how well he already knew her: a book about Scandinavian cuisine, a brooch crafted to look like a daffodil and a gorgeous leatherbound notebook which he said would be perfect for re-writing *Macbeth* or *King Lear*.

It was perfect and made her heart overflow with the love she felt for him.

As expected, both of their mothers had immediately started planning the wedding, which was due to take place in another three weeks once the bans had been cried. Griffin had suggested a special license, but everyone except Emily had been appalled by that idea, so they'd accepted defeat on that score. But because of the delay, they would have to leave for Vienna immediately after. Doing so wouldn't be a problem however, since Cassandra had apparently met another young woman during her visit to London. Katharine Dunahugh was her name, and she was looking for a means to escape ruination.

"She fell for one of the footmen in her parents' employ," Cassandra had told Emily. "One thing led to another as it so often does, and well, the poor ignorant girl is now carrying his child."

"Her parents must be informed, no matter how much she fears the repercussion."

"Of course they must, that goes without saying, but Katharine has convinced me that it would be better to do so in a letter that she means to write from Clearview."

"Cass…"

Cassandra had thrown up her hands in surrender. "I'm aware it will likely have serious consequences, but I could not refuse her." She'd sighed. "You know I've always had a soft spot for those who must suffer because of Society. And in this case, I rather find myself relating to her, for her situation is not so dissimilar to what mine once was."

"Apart from the fact that Penelope's father was a peer who had every intention of marrying you. There is a difference, you know."

Cassandra's expression had turned melancholy then. "Yes. I suppose that is true."

Emily had quickly turned the discussion to the subject of her upcoming journey, happy when it had appeared to pull Cassandra's thoughts away from the man she still loved and the tragic way in which he had died before they could start their life together.

Tonight, the children would be hosting their play, and after that, she'd agreed to join Griffin for a secret rendezvous in the conservatory. Her skin already tingled with the thought of the kiss they would share. There had been several since he had proposed, each testing their restraint more than the last. And since Emily had been more than ready to throw caution to the wind before, she saw even less cause for them to control their cravings now that they were engaged.

But Griffin insisted, which was frustrating, adorable, and slightly comical since the man could hardly glance at her these days without looking like a caged animal. She grinned as she descended the stairs, certain that if she wished it, she could make him forget all about the sanctity of their wedding night. But that would be badly done of her, all things considered, for he only wanted to do what he believed was best in making the event as romantic and memorable as possible.

So she turned her mind to other things during dinner, like Langdon's account of a fox he'd once thought he'd killed with a slingshot when he was a lad, only to have the beast leap off the ground and growl at him when he'd approached. "I was so startled," Langdon said, "I ran away screaming. Luckily, I was met by my mother instead of my father, for he would likely have given me a thorough thrashing for being so lily-livered."

"How old were you?" Caleb asked.

"Eight, as I recall."

"And your father would have taken the switch

to you for being startled by a wild animal?" Emily asked, appalled.

"He was the sort of man who never showed his emotions, who didn't appear to fear anything, and who expected nothing less from his son. Unfortunately, I was more sensitive and Papa... Well, he believed he could beat that out of me."

"Good God," Mary exclaimed, her eyes wide with horror. She looked at her husband. "Just to be perfectly clear, we are never striking any of our children."

"Of course not," Caleb agreed.

"Nothing good can possibly come of it," Griffin said, the firmness of his voice assuring Emily that this was not a matter they would ever disagree on.

"A letter just arrived," the butler announced. He approached Griffin with the silver salver on which it rested.

Griffin frowned. He tore the letter open and read. His lips flattened and his frown deepened. "It is from my friend, Christoph Unger." His throat worked as if he was struggling to speak. Alarm nipped at the nape of Emily's neck. "There's been an accident," Griffin continued in a detached tone that added to Emily's fear. "Christoph doesn't say how it happened but..." He dropped the letter and stared across at Caleb. "Most of the shop is gone."

"What?" Emily's question of disbelief was barely a whisper.

Griffin blinked. "There was a fire and..." He picked up the letter again and stared at his friend's writing. "Thankfully, Edvard managed to get out."

"Who is Edvard?" Cassandra gently asked.

"My employee." Griffin glanced around the table. "He was badly burned while trying to save the merchandise and has been admitted to the hospital for treatment." He shook his head. "I..." He looked at Emily as if just recalling her presence. "I have to leave for Vienna right away. I can no longer wait."

Logic and reasoning told her that this made sense, that of course he would have to go see just how bad the damage was and if anything could be salvaged. He might even have to manage the tearing down of the structure and a potential rebuild. There would still be clients waiting for orders to be completed, and then of course there was Edvard. Griffin had been his mentor. He cared about him and would want to see him straight away.

And yet, a selfish part of her wanted to beg Griffin not to go. Not right now. Not before the wedding. But of course, he would not be able to wait three weeks, and she would not be able to accompany him. Not as an unmarried woman and not with both of their families ready to stop her from acting so rashly. And they *would* stop her. Especially with Langdon and his wife here to witnesses such a ruinous decision. Covering it up would not be as easy as it had been when she'd left London for Clearview.

So she met his gaze, determined to support the decision she knew he must make. "We will delay the wedding as much as necessary. The most important thing right now is for you to support your friend and take care of your business. I will wait. However long it may take."

Concern was evident in the boldness with which he held her gaze. She could feel his conflict and despair as if they were her own, like a twisting ache in the pit of her stomach.

"Not by much. Just a couple of weeks. That will give me five weeks to go see Edvard, settle my affairs, and come back."

"It's not the way it was meant to be," Emily whispered. She felt terrible for Griffin, for what he had lost, for what his friend had suffered, and for not being able to be there to help him through it. "We were supposed to go to Vienna together."

"I know." Somehow, in spite of how helpless he probably felt at that moment, he managed a smile. For her. "But we'll have the rest of our lives together with plenty of time to travel later. We can go in June if you like, after the wedding."

"You won't mind?"

His smile broadened and Emily felt the love that had caused it spilling through her body like a sparkling rainbow. "Not at all."

"I'll ask Murdoch to make sure the coachman is ready to take you to Cardiff first thing," Caleb said, reminding Emily that she and Griffin were not alone in the room.

Griffin's gaze slid away from hers to focus on his brother. "Thank you."

"This might be for the best," Georgina said, affecting a positive tone that jarred the morose atmosphere. "Not the reason for your departure of course, but the delay of the wedding."

"It will give the modiste more time to work on Emily's gown," Griffin's mother said in a similarly uplifting voice.

"You will be so busy while he's away, Emily, that you will barely have time to notice he is gone," Laura said brightly.

"By then I shall be returned," Griffin said, "and ready for us to begin our lives together."

Emily forced a smile. She appreciated all the attempts at viewing the situation from an optimistic angle, even though she struggled to accept what was happening. Needing closeness, she placed her hand over Griffin's and savored the certainty of his warmth. Five weeks. Hardly any time at all. And yet to Emily, it felt like forever. Especially when she reminded herself that it was longer than the time they had spent at Clearview together.

Blackened walls and empty holes where windows had once been stared back at Griffin in mournful silence. His throat was thick with emotion, his heart weighed down by defeat. Everything he'd worked for these past ten years had been ruined. The vibrant energy of clockwork measuring the progression of time, his mechanical toys, whirring and clicking, and lively tunes played by his music boxes had all been snuffed out forever.

It had taken him years to turn his business into the brilliant success it had become. He'd worked tirelessly, with endless determination, had dedicated vast amounts of time on acquiring affluent customers and on crafting merchandise that was sure to enthrall. But all of that was for nothing. Only a ruin remained, along with the few items Edvard had managed to save.

"I'm sorry," Christoph said. He'd met Griffin at the hospital, which was where he'd made his first stop after arriving in Vienna. "I know how much this place meant to you."

"It was everything." The proof that he could succeed without his family's fortune or his rank. A slap in his father's face and a means by which to survive. He walked forward on heavy feet and stepped through what remained of the charred doorframe. A piece of it broke off in his hand when he gripped it, abrading his skin. "At least Edvard survived."

"And with his eyes and hands intact. All he spoke about whenever I visited him was how life wouldn't be worth living if he ended up unable to keep making clocks."

Griffin understood, for he shared that same passion. But there was more for him to live for now than clocks and mechanical toys alone. There was Emily. Her love was enough to make him smile even as the remains of his business crunched beneath the soles of his boots.

"I had meant to leave everything to him when I decided to marry and live in England. But now..." He bent to retrieve an object that stood out amidst the soot covered rubble because of its rounded edges. Even though it must have rained a few times since the fire, the water had failed to wash away the grime that lay thick on the ground. Above, where Griffin had once made his home, was nothing but a view of the clear blue sky.

He turned the item over in his hands and considered the chipped enamel which had once depicted a colorful garden where a lady walked arm in arm with a gentleman. Now, only hints of the image peeked out from beneath shades of gray. Inhaling deeply, Griffin turned the key that protruded from the back of what had once been a music box. It had been made with the added purpose of hiding jewelry, the inside lined with a vibrant red velvet that appeared to be oddly intact when Griffin tipped open the lid. The tune the pins were designed to play filled the air with a lyrical sound as the metal comb inside the mechanism slid over each individual one.

"I can fix this," he said, more to himself than to Christoph. When he'd left England, it had been with every intention of selling whatever remained of the property, even if it was nothing more than a plot of land. But now, being here and seeing it for himself, having visited Edvard and been reminded of his loyalty, Griffin felt the need to stick with his initial plan. The plan he'd had before he'd learned of the fire.

He turned to Christoph. "I want to rebuild the shop and leave it for Edvard to manage."

Christoph tilted his head and studied Griffin with the assessing gaze of a man who was not the least bit surprised by such an idea. "How can I help?"

Griffin blew out a breath. Helping his friend pay off a gambling debt years ago when they'd first met by teaching him how to improve his card play was now paying off. "I must return to England, so if you can oversee the project, I would be eternally grateful."

Christoph grinned. "I've waited a long time for this moment, Griffin. You've always refused my help before, but I finally have a chance to repay my debt."

"You've done so repeatedly throughout the years by giving me your friendship and your advice." Griffin pondered the logistics for a moment, then added, "I'll give you ten percent of the business in return."

"That's really not necessary."

"Yes, it is." When Christoph prepared to speak once again, Griffin said, "I insist."

Emily had remained at Montvale for the duration of the house party, but her mood had not been the best for keeping company with others. She'd missed Griffin terribly and continued to suffer from the void created by his absence. Not even Mary's suggestion that Emily help with some of the baking had lifted her spirits. Only the children managed to do so a little as they reenacted parts of their play with loud animal sounds and ridiculous gestures.

She'd regretted her lack of enthusiasm during their first performance, but the news of Griffin's departure had been so fresh on her mind, she'd found it impossible to focus. Hence, she'd encouraged the children to remind her of what a lion sounded like or how zebras whinnied until everyone else was exhausted by the noise. Even Cassandra, who never minded the children's antics, had started looking put out.

But Emily was now back in London with her parents and sister. Her mother had barely removed her bonnet upon their arrival before she'd proceeded to plan the coming weeks. Besides visits to the modiste where not only a wedding gown but an entire trousseau would be ordered, Emily was going to have to decide on a menu for the wedding breakfast, create a guest list, and send out invitations. None of these chores appealed, but she knew they mattered to her mother and to the dowager duchess, so Emily pushed herself to participate with as much enthusiasm as she could muster.

"You are so incredibly lucky," Laura informed her during the second evening of their stay in London. She'd found Emily hiding in the library which was one room in the house where their mother rarely set foot.

Emily put down the engineering book she'd been reading. It had been her grandfather's and was therefore slightly outdated, but the section on cogs and gears provided her with some information that would hopefully give her a better understanding of Griffin's interests. She regarded her sister as she approached and sat down across from her on the sofa.

"I know," Emily murmured.

"Do you? Really?"

The urgency with which she posed the question gave Emily pause. She tilted her head. "I believe so, but I get the feeling that you do not think that I do."

Laura flopped back against the seat cushion with a sigh. "Griffin is everything a woman might dream of in a husband. He will be yours, Emily, albeit with some delay, but yours nonetheless. Yet you have been moping about since the day he left as if the world might be ending." She frowned while giving Emily the most direct perusal she'd ever been subjected to by her sister. "It's not fair to those of us who are struggling to make even a half decent match."

Emily blinked. "What?"

"You and I have not been in touch much these past six years. Granted, you are four years older than I, but we are still sisters. And although I will agree that Mama made life much more difficult for you, it has not been so easy for me either. Especially since I have very few friends and invariably end up without a dance partner when I attend balls."

Emily sucked in a breath. Laura was a wallflower too and she, self-obsessed woman that she was, had failed to realize it. She'd been so caught up in her own wants and needs, she'd neglected to notice that her sister might not be coping with Society as well as she'd thought.

"But you're so beautiful," Emily murmured. She shook her head, incredulous. "I cannot believe there are gentlemen in England who aren't vying for your attention."

"Only fortune hunters."

"But why?" It made little sense.

"I think," Laura said, her voice low and hesitant, "that you might have something to do with it."

Emily's mouth dropped open. She straightened in her seat. "You mean to tell me that after all these years my decision to move to Clearview still hangs over your head?"

"There are those who believe you've been living in sin." This last bit was said so quietly, Emily had to strain in order to hear her.

Georgina had alluded to this, but Emily had thought it an exaggeration and a means by which to secure her marriage to Griffin at the time. Had she known…what would she have done? What *could* she have done? She wasn't quite sure. The repercussions of the hasty decision she'd once made had left a mark that she'd been unaware of.

"When I marry Griffin," Emily told Laura carefully, "this family will be related to the Duke and Duchess of Camberly. I can only promise you when that happens, I will use whatever influence I have to make sure you're accepted by the *ton* and that you are given every chance you need to meet the gentleman of your dreams." Because one thing was certain, Laura deserved to be happy.

CHAPTER EIGHTEEN

THE DAYS WERE LONGER NOW than when Griffin had left for Austria, the late afternoon sunlight casting an almost magical glow upon the English countryside. He'd arrived in Cardiff just two hours ago and was now on his way to London by post chaise. The letter he'd mailed to Emily a week earlier had said to expect him on June tenth, but he'd settled things with Christoph and Edvard sooner than he'd expected and had not felt compelled to linger in Vienna longer than necessary.

By the time he reached London, it was past six o' clock. Excitement bubbled inside him, both at the prospect of seeing Emily again, but also because he could hardly wait to give her the gift he'd made for her. So he decided to make a quick stop at Camberly House to inform his brother that he had returned, only to learn that he, their mother, and Mary were all out for the evening.

"They are dining with the Howards at Vauxhall Garden," Murdoch, Caleb's butler, informed him.

Griffin put his hat back on. "Then I shall find them there. Thank you, Murdoch"

He hailed a new hackney and asked the driver to make haste. Vauxhall wasn't far. He'd be there within fifteen minutes at most. And then he would finally see Emily again.

A smile tugged at his lips. He'd bloody well kiss her too, regardless of who might be watching. The mere memory of her rosy lips was like an invigorating tonic. It banished the exhaustion of travel from his body and nearly made him leap from the carriage when it reached the pleasure garden.

Collecting himself, he managed to slow his pace a little. At least enough not to look as though reaching his destination with haste was a matter of life and death.

A group of laughing young men stumbled into his path, forcing Griffin to halt his progress for a moment. "He just got engaged," one of them grinned.

"Congratulations," Griffin said, trying not to sound irritated.

The young men bowed flamboyantly, all clearly in their cups. Nothing would ruin their good cheer this evening and nothing would ruin his either. So he went around them and headed for the pavilion where the supper boxes overlooked a crowded dance floor. Griffin scanned the tables and immediately spotted Caleb, whose head was bowed in Mary's direction while he spoke.

Shifting his gaze, Griffin considered the rest of the group while continuing forward. There was his mother, Mr. and Mrs. Howard, Laura, Miss Amanda Partridge...

He frowned. What was she doing here and where the hell was Emily? Disappointment threatened to crush his elation. She was supposed to be here.

Mary said something to Laura and pointed toward the dance floor. Griffin instinctively turned and as he did so, as he took in the scene before him, time seemed to slow to a halt. The music played by four violinists stabbed at his soul until it started to bleed, his chest strained against his heart, stifling the beat. Because there she was, dancing with Mr. Damnhimtohell Partridge.

There had been moments in his life when it had felt like the world as he knew it had been flipped upside down. Like the day he'd discovered that Clara was married or later, when he'd learned George had died. That same feeling of complete loss overwhelmed him for a second before anger set in and a rage, unlike any he'd ever known, caused fire to burn through his veins. Griffin clenched his jaw so hard his teeth hurt. How dare he? And how dare *she*? Griffin made a deliberate effort to breathe. The air flowing into his lungs felt heavy and uncomfortable, like there was more than there was room for and it was suffocating him. To think that he had hastened back to her, driven by love! He almost laughed at his own stupidity. Loyalty was a rare quality to find in a woman. He'd known this and yet he'd allowed himself to be caught in Emily's snare.

She knew how he felt about Partridge and yet, here she was, dancing with him as if Griffin didn't exist, as if her attachment to him didn't matter. And the bastard was grinning down into her upturned face as if he'd just conquered the world.

Griffin flexed his fingers.

Christ, how he'd love to punch him in the face.

But having his mother witness such poor conduct – subjecting her to scenes of violence – gave him pause. He winced, hating the helplessness he was being forced to endure on account of propriety. Perhaps a visit to Gentleman Jackson's would help him alleviate some of his anger.

He prepared to turn, but just then Emily looked his way, her eyes widening with surprise as her steps faltered in the middle of a turn. Griffin smirked. Just as well that she should know that he'd seen her. When she twisted back to look in his direction again, he executed a mocking bow before turning away. With clipped footsteps and a renewed purpose, he strode toward the garden's exit. A carriage was what he needed now, followed by a sound exchange of fisticuffs and a bottle of brandy with which to drown his pain.

Emily stared after Griffin's retreating back. He'd returned, his handsome face causing a burst of euphoria to spread through her veins. Until she'd noticed his expression. And now he was walking away, intent on leaving her because...because he didn't know what had happened during his absence and because seeing her with David had caused him to think the worst.

"I have to go," she said, causing David to knit his brow in confusion. "You must excuse me."

She didn't even wait for him to lead her off the dance floor, but left him there in her desperation to reach the man she loved so she could explain. Her gown tangled around her legs, slowing her movement. Had he not seen his family sitting in the supper box? Surely he would know that they would not sanction her throwing Griffin over for another man? But no, logical reasoning had likely abandoned him because of who that man was. And because of how deeply Clara had once hurt him so long ago.

Heart racing, Emily wound her way between people enjoying an evening stroll. She quickened her pace to a near run when she spotted the top of Griffin's head near the exit.

"Watch it," an older man told her when she accidentally bumped against him.

Emily muttered a quick, "Excuse me," and hurried on her way. When she stepped out onto the pavement, she looked both ways, studying both pedestrians and carriages.

There!

She only just managed to catch a quick glimpse of Griffin's broad back before he disappeared into a hackney. "Stop!" Sprinting forward as fast as her feet would carry her, Emily called again for the coachman to wait while passersby stopped to stare at her like she was some sort of lunatic making her escape from Bedlam.

The carriage started rolling forward, heedless of her commands, and without even thinking, she launched herself at the door and yanked it wide open. One foot found the step, allowing her to climb up into the dim interior just as the carriage rolled into the street. Panting, she pulled the door shut behind her and collapsed on the bench.

Her gaze met Griffin's and a shudder went through her. He was closer now, allowing her to better see the extent of his anger.

"Pursuing me isn't helping my effort to escape you," he snapped.

"It is good to see you as well," she told him in her most soothing tone. "You cannot know how much I have missed you."

A muscle ticked at the edge of his mouth, and his eyes darkened like thunderclouds ready to unleash lightning. "Not enough, it would seem, or I would not have returned to find you in Mr. Partridge's arms."

The fact that he was almost shouting at her alerted Emily to the depth of the anguish she'd caused him. Aware of his past experience, she sympathized, even as his temper riled her. "I am not Clara," she told him bluntly. "Deceit is not in my nature, Griffin, and you," she pointed a finger straight at his chest, "you have to be able to trust me. Because if you can't do that, then what hope do we have of being happy together?"

He snorted with displeasure. "Trust you?" He crossed his arms and shook his head. "I returned to London as quickly as possible because I was eager to see you. Instead I find you gazing adoringly up at another man, and you want me to trust you?" He leaned forward, his expression hard and unyielding. "Do not make the error of thinking me a fool, Emily." He leaned back again and averted his gaze, giving his attention to the window.

Chilling dread drove its way through Emily's bones like nails being hammered through wood. "You...you have it all wrong." Her throat was starting to close, making it hard for her to get the words out. Pain spliced her heart and her eyes now burned with an awful hint of oncoming tears.

A scoff was Griffin's only response.

Emily clutched her hands in her lap. "We were celebrating Laura's engagement."

"Then I must ask you to wish her well, for I bear no ill will toward her."

Emily swallowed. She started reaching for him but stopped. "You don't understand."

"On the contrary, I think I understand everything perfectly. You enjoyed the attention I gave you, and when I was gone you missed that. This caused you to seek it elsewhere, to fill the void my absence had cause and to—"

"Laura and David are to be married, Griffin." Emily blurted the words without finesse, throwing them at him in the hope they would stick. She blinked in response to his frozen expression. "Mr. Partridge proposed this morning and Laura accepted. I was dancing with him as his future sister-in-law. Nothing more."

The truth slammed Griffin hard against the ground as the words Emily had spoken sank in.

Gripping the seat, he allowed his body to accept that there was no need for a fight, that he had been wrong and that he had misjudged the situation entirely. The tension in his muscles eased and his jaw relaxed. The haze of anger that had clouded his brain like a thick, blinding fog faded away. He stared across at Emily, at her pained expression and shimmering eyes. She was close to tears though she forced them back. He had done that, fool that he was. He'd let jealousy lead him down an irrational road and as a result, he'd hurt her again.

Christ!

"Emily, I—"

"You believed the worst of me, Griffin. You..." Her voice dropped and she closed her eyes. "You didn't trust me."

"I'm sorry." God help him, he was an ass. Advising Langdon not to marry her had been done before he'd gotten to know her. She'd forgiven him for that reason. Because he hadn't owed her anything at the time. But he did owe her now, and rather than believe in her as he ought to have done, he'd chosen to think that she'd cast him aside for Partridge. "I promised never to hurt you again and I failed, Emily. What happened with Clara still haunts me. I keep fearing I'll be deceived once more and...there's also the scar."

"You know I don't care about that." Her voice was small and weak.

Griffin reached for her hand, so cold he wanted to breathe heat into her skin. "God, Emily, I'm so sorry. Please...please look at me, darling."

She shook her head and his heart crumpled.

"The truth is that the scar does matter. To me." Even though her eyes remained closed, her fingers wove between his, causing hope to stir in his soul. "It has ruined my face and made me feel lacking. Overcoming that feeling of insecurity has been a difficult struggle. In instances like tonight it prompts me to wonder why you would ever choose me over someone who's perfect."

She opened her eyes then and gazed up into his face. A lone tear spilled from her lashes and trickled slowly down her cheek. "No man is more perfect than you, Griffin." She reached up to trail the tip of her finger over his scar. "And if you'll allow me, I'll spend the rest of my life trying to convince you of that fact."

Undone by the honesty in her voice and her fierce determination in spite of the pain he'd caused her, Griffin pulled her from the opposite bench and straight onto his lap.

She didn't resist, for which he thanked his lucky stars. After everything he'd put her through, he knew he would be the luckiest man in England when she eventually spoke her vows.

If she still wanted to do so.

To think she might not made his chest crack open in fear. His arms closed around her with a fierceness that almost surprised him. The need to hold her, to feel her warmth, and to somehow communicate the depth of his feelings for her was so necessary to his peace of mind that he worried he'd never be able to let her go again.

Inhaling deeply, he breathed her in, allowing her sweet aroma to awaken his senses. Christ, how he'd missed her; the way her flesh dipped beneath his fingertips and how a loose lock of her hair brushed against his cheek when he drew her more firmly against him.

"What can I do to earn your forgiveness?" he asked against the delicate curve of her jaw.

"Trust me." Her fingers found their way into his hair, raking a path that caused vibrating sparks to erupt all over his scalp. "Believe me when I say that *you* are the only man I want. The only man I will ever want. Not only because you're my perfect match, but because I love you, Griffin. Because I shall always love you."

"And I shall always love you, Emily. But there may be moments like this when the past interferes. When my insecurities and the mistrust I've been taught to harbor threaten to ruin everything. And I'll need you more than ever then, to remind me that it's an illusion and that what we have together is real."

She kissed him then, her mouth settling perfectly over his in the dark interior of the carriage. The press of her lips was soft and gentle and sweet, but also incredibly direct. It was as if she was silently saying, "I will always be here for you, Griffin. I understand you and I forgive you."

He answered her by deepening the kiss, by drawing her breath into his mouth so her soul could merge with his. One palm settled firmly against her back to hold her steady while the other grasped hold of her waist.

No longer a novice at kissing, she nipped his lip with her teeth. The sharp little pinch caused desire to shoot through his body. More so when she gave a low chuckle, suggesting she knew precisely what she was doing.

Abandoning her mouth, Griffin pressed a series of kisses to her jaw and smiled against her skin. This was the reason for his hasty return, this fervor with which she responded to him, the way she seemed to crave his touch as much as he craved hers.

The carriage bumped, jostling her against him in a way that made it damned hard for him to hide his physical response. Not that he wanted to do so, but considering her innocence, there was a good chance it would frighten her away.

But rather than scramble off his lap and return to the opposite bench as he'd half expected her to, she pushed herself closer, as if seeking the same relief he so desperately needed.

"Emily…" His hand moved to her thigh, holding her steady while he wished…oh, how he wished they were anywhere else but in a hackney carriage headed for Camberly House.

Swallowing, he bowed his head against the curve of her neck and breathed her in. She deserved to be cherished and adored, and he, by God, needed to show her how much he loved her.

"The wedding is next Saturday, is it not?"

A sharp inhale was her first response, as if her brain was forced to adjust to the idea of speaking. "Yes." Her voice was breathy, her body moving in a quiet plea for him to respond to her more fully.

Griffin tamped down the elementary urge to rip her gown from her body and ravish her right then and there. Instead, he forced himself to say, "I won't ruin our wedding night, Emily." A statement that served as both a promise to her and a stern reminder to himself. "But I can give you this." And with that pronouncement he swept his hand under the hem of her skirt, skimming past her ankle, her calf, and her thigh.

A small gasp was followed by, "Dear God, Griffin," and then, a soft moan of approval as she relaxed against his touch and surrendered to the pleasure he so desperately wanted to give her.

CHAPTER NINETEEN

EMILY'S STOMACH STARTED TO FLUT-
TER like a giant butterfly when her mother
came to inform her that Griffin had come to call
the next day. He'd said he would last night when
he'd bid her goodnight. After arriving at Camberly
House, he'd alit and instructed the coachman to
return her to Vauxhall, leaving her to ponder the
extraordinary sensations he'd evoked in her while
she made the journey back.

She'd continued to do so when she'd crawled
into bed later. The powerful sensations he'd
evoked in her body had been like water being
brought to a slow simmer before rolling into a
forceful boil.

And God help her, she wanted more.

A fact she was quite certain showed on her face
for her cheeks felt unbearably flushed. But if her
mother noticed, she said nothing as she showed
Emily into the parlor where Griffin waited. He
stood as soon as they entered, his gaze locking on
Emily with an intensity that caused a flare of heat
to charge through her. The edge of his mouth
lifted, producing that mischievous smile she loved
so much. And then he bowed while holding her

gaze.

"It is such a *pleasure* to see you again, Emily. Indeed, it has been far too long."

No one else had seen him at Vauxhall, so when she'd returned after being absent for forty minutes, she'd concocted a story about a friend whom she'd not encountered in years. She'd apologized to David for leaving him on the dance floor, but had claimed it was necessary since her 'friend' had been heading for the exit. Which was partly true. The biggest fib had been saying that she'd also gotten distracted by the fireworks and lost her way when she'd tried to locate everyone again. Mary had not looked convinced, but at least the rest of the party had seemed to believe her. Most importantly, her parents had.

"I've asked one of the maids to bring up some tea and cake," Georgina announced in a bright tone of voice that instantly snuffed out the embers Griffin had ignited in Emily with his heated gaze.

She moved to the sofa on which he'd been sitting and lowered herself to the spot next to his. Her mother claimed one of the armchairs. "I trust you are well," Emily forced herself to say. After all, was that not an appropriate question if one had not seen one's fiancé for a month? A quick glance at her mother assured her that there was nothing wrong with it, so Emily straightened her shoulders and forced herself to look at the man who'd shown her the stars last night in a carriage.

"Indeed," he murmured, the low timbre of his voice a reminder of searing kisses and scandalous caresses.

She shifted in her seat. "How did you find your

friend?"

"Better than I had feared." He smiled then, a different kind of smile than the mischievous variety he favored, but rather one filled with warmth and appreciation. "I've arranged for my business to be rebuilt and have offered Edvard the position of manager." The tea and cake arrived, and as they partook of it, he went on to explain how he meant for his plans to be accomplished and described his intention to create a similar shop in London. "We can hire someone else to run it, so we're not tied to the city ourselves," he quickly added.

"You're the clockmaker though, so would it not be necessary for you to be where the shop is?" Emily asked. She wasn't particularly eager to live in London, but she also recognized that it might be essential to Griffin's work.

"Not really. I see no reason why I cannot make the merchandise anywhere I choose and simply have it brought to the shop. All I'll really need is a talented salesman." He waited for Emily to put down her teacup, then reached for her hand and gave it a squeeze. "I meant what I said when I told you I'd give you the house in the country. The last thing I want is for you to abandon your dream."

Emotionally undone by his thoughtfulness, Emily could only manage a smile and a nod. She feared that any attempt to speak would lead to tears. Especially when he retrieved a package wrapped in creamy silk and tied with lace ribbons. A pink rose had been tucked beneath the bow.

"Open it," he urged her after placing the package in her lap.

Emily hesitated only the second it took her to admire the pretty wrapping. He'd put thought into this, and that idea alone made her heart swell with joy. Taking care, she gave the ends of the ribbon a tug, undoing the bow and releasing the rose. She pressed it to her nose and inhaled its sweet fragrance, then handed it to her mother and proceeded to pull back the fabric.

A gorgeous metal case crafted from gold came into view, the lid a dazzling display of bright colors painted on porcelain to depict a lady and gentleman strolling along a riverbank. Tipping it open, Emily was greeted by a deep red velvet interior, so plush and inviting to the touch that she could not stop from brushing her fingers against it.

"It's a music box," Griffin told her, his voice soft and intimate, as if it were just the two of them in the parlor without her mother present. "I found it in the rubble when I went to inspect the damage caused by the fire. It was blackened and tarnished by soot, but the works were intact and so was the interior, which reminded me of you and how lovely you looked that evening we went for dinner at Partridge House." He didn't need to say that it brought to mind their first real kiss. This was implied in the way his knee pressed into hers as he spoke. "Restoring it was painstaking work, but it's a piece of my past and…" his voice grew rougher "…a testament to my undying love for you."

"It's incredibly stunning," Georgina said, reminding Emily of her presence. "I don't believe I've ever seen such fine craftsmanship before."

"Griffin's work is exemplary, Mama. He is the best at what he does and this box..." She slid her thumb over the smooth, cool surface, loving how glassy it felt to her touch. Looking up, she met his light brown eyes, now swirling with a blend of eager anticipation and fierce emotion. "I shall cherish it forever."

His nostrils flared and his jaw tightened just enough to suggest that the restraint he was forced to endure right now while in company was starting to test his discipline.

Expelling what sounded like a tortured breath, he inclined his head. "It pleases me greatly to hear you say that."

Taking pity on him and wishing she was able to express herself more openly, Emily turned to her mother. "Considering the fine weather today, I thought I might show Lord Griffin the garden."

Georgina stared back at her for a long, unbearable moment, then slowly nodded. "Yes. It will give you a chance to apprise him of the wedding preparations you have made in his absence."

"Of course," Emily agreed, even though wedding preparations was the last thing on her mind at the moment. Instead, she meant to show him the bench behind the rhododendron bushes – the only place where they could be properly hidden from view and where she would have the liberty to show him precisely how grateful she was for his gift.

Emily woke on her wedding day with hope in her heart, a hope that expanded and grew in response to the sunshine spilling through her bedroom window. It created a golden haze of surreal light that brought floating dust motes into focus and bathed the space in happiness.

A smile pulled at her lips as she stretched her arms over her head. In a few short hours, she would be Lady Griffin and nothing in the world sounded better to her than that. It infused her languid body with energy and prompted her to jump out of bed. She could not wait to see Griffin again and to be reassured that he truly would be her husband and that the life she was currently living wasn't a dream.

It had felt like one this past week since his return from Vienna. Following his visit to her home, he'd arranged for additional ways in which to see her. Including a night out at the opera, a couple of walks in the park, and lunch at Mivart's Hotel where everyone, including David, had been present. Griffin was in fact making an effort to put his innate dislike of David behind him and had even gone so far as inviting David to join him for billiards at White's one evening. When Caleb had mentioned this to Emily in passing, her love for Griffin had grown tenfold, for she knew he was doing it for her and Laura so a rift would not arise between them.

Pouring water into her washbasin, Emily proceeded to clean her face. She'd taken a hot bath last night before bed, so she wouldn't have to spend time on that in the morning. A soft knock sounded at the door, and Emily called for whoever it was to enter. As she expected, it was her mother, coming to make sure she was awake.

"I've brought Patsy to help you dress and some breakfast for you to eat while she sets your hair."

"Thank you, Mama. I'm actually really hungry, now that I think of it."

"That's a good thing," Patsy said as she laid out the undergarments the modiste had sworn would ensure a sizzling start to the marriage. Emily blushed as she looked at the creamy silk stays. Embroidered with deep red roses and climbing green vines, they matched the design on the garters and stockings. "It will be several hours before you're able to eat again, and the last thing you want is for your stomach to grumble while you're saying your vows."

There was no denying that, Emily thought with a grin. She took her seat at her dressing table where her mother had placed the tea and plate filled with slices of toast. She picked the one topped with raspberry jam and took a big bite, savoring the syrupy sweetness.

"Now, I realize we've had our differences over the years," Georgina said while Patsy proceeded to undo Emily's plaited hair so it could be combed, "but I am still your mother and as such, it is my duty to advise you on what you might expect once you are married."

Oh. They were about to have *that* discussion.

Emily took a sip of her tea. If only a few drops of brandy could have been added for extra fortification. A pause followed, during which she imagined her mother's brain working on how to address this delicate subject as efficiently and satisfactorily as possible. Emily took another bite of her toast and winced when Patsy's comb caught a knot in her hair.

"Sorry, Miss," Patsy said. "It's a little bit tangled here."

"Considering you have been living with a… deflowered woman these past six years," Georgina continued, "I would imagine that you're not completely ignorant of what can happen between a man and a woman when they…er…like each other a lot."

Emily hid a smile behind her teacup. Was it wrong of her to be slightly amused by her mother's increasingly flustered state? Probably. But she just couldn't help it. Nor could she stop herself from saying, "What do you mean?"

"Well. I…er… Hmm." Georgina dropped onto the bed with a huff. Another pause followed, during which Patsy swept locks of hair up at the back of Emily's head before pinning them in place. "When I married your father," *Oh dear God*, "I was led to believe that he would want to take certain liberties with me that—"

"You need not explain any further," Emily managed to choke out past a crumb that had lodged itself in her throat. She coughed. "I am perfectly aware of what to expect."

"Are you sure?"

"Yes." She sighed. In the mirror, she could see that Patsy was making a valiant effort to refrain from laughing. "Cass did tell me a thing or two over the years, and I've also read a couple of book on the subject."

"Oh." A sigh of relief followed. "Well then. That is good to know. And Griffin does look as though he's more than capable of—"

"Mama!"

"What? I may be over forty, but that doesn't mean I can't spot a prime example of masculine excellence when I see it." She gave a small snort as she went to the door. "You might want to consider that when you ask yourself why it took me so long to reach you at Clearview."

Emily whipped round to face her only to find the door closing behind her retreating figure.

Patsy muttered something beneath her breath before saying, "You must sit still or I'll have to start over."

Blinking, Emily surrendered herself to Patsy's ministrations, but her mind remained elsewhere. Like on the sudden realization that Georgina had wanted her to end up with Griffin right from the start, and that she'd deliberately delayed going in pursuit so they'd have more time to form a closer attachment.

It was a startling revelation, not to mention a plan that could have ended in disaster, had Griffin not been the considerate man she'd discovered him to be. Instinct told her to feel affronted by such deliberate meddling, but would that really be just? After all, she had been the one to run off with Griffin in the first place, and the situation had ended happily with them falling in love. They were about to embark on the most exciting journey of their lives together as husband and wife, so what was the point in asking, what if?

Deciding not to examine it further and simply enjoy what was destined to be the most perfect day ever, Emily ate the rest of her breakfast while Patsy finished her hair.

Griffin waited anxiously for Emily to arrive. The small church where the ceremony would take place was filled with London society, many of them people he believed his mother must have invited. He didn't really care. All that mattered to him was the woman who was going to walk through the door any moment now.

"Relax," Caleb murmured close to his ear. "You'll want to save your rigidity for later."

Griffin dealt his brother a quelling look, even as he did his best not to laugh in response to the bawdy double entendre. But the words did help ease the tension that gripped Griffin's body, even though he knew it would not be completely gone until the priest pronounced him and Emily, hus- band and wife.

The door creaked open, just a fraction. An exchange of voices took place and the choir boys started to sing. Griffin's heart gave a hard beat. And then the door open more fully, allowing him his first view of his bride.

Air rushed from his lungs as awe took its place. She was stunning, all dressed in creamy layers of silk and lace and with what he believed must be diamond-tipped pins sparkling in her hair. He swallowed as she started toward him, her eyes reflecting everything he was feeling right now, from pure elation to the soul deep connection that had blossomed between them.

"Breathe," Caleb whispered.

Griffin blinked and inhaled. His lungs expanded and his heart settled into a calmer rhythm that allowed him to smile with every bit of love coursing through him.

"Emily." She was before him now, and by God she was perfect. A bit of moisture touched his cheek, and he realized it was a tear. "You look stunning," he told her even though the words felt inadequate.

Her eyes appeared to be watering as well. "And you are the handsomest man in the world. I can scarcely believe you're about to be mine."

His heart swelled with pleasure, and although it was not really protocol, he took her by the hand, the sudden need to touch her dictating his movements.

"Then let us proceed with haste," he told her. "I've a sudden desire for all of this to be over so I can kiss you as you deserve."

She blushed, a delightful pink hue that complimented her appearance. Her fingers tightened around his, and together they turned to face the priest.

He was a young man who worked his way quickly through the scripture. He didn't linger on any of the parts like some of the older men of the cloth liked to do. And when he pronounced that Emily and Griffin were husband and wife, Griffin didn't hesitate one second longer. He swept Emily into his arms and pressed his mouth firmly to hers, conveying not only that he loved her but that he needed her more than anything else in his life.

CHAPTERTWENTY

THE WEDDING BREAKFAST DRAGGED ON longer than the ceremony itself. By the time the fifth course was announced, Griffin wondered if it would be terribly rude of him to whisk Emily away before cake was served.

"Please tell me there isn't a sixth course," he said while leaning in close to his wife. She smelled enticingly sweet, like a summer bouquet made from roses and peonies.

"I'm sorry." She bit her lip. "When I had to pick out a menu, I couldn't choose just three or four."

"This is your doing?" He should have known that her interest in food was to blame. "I was starting to think our mothers were trying to torture us."

"If it's any consolation, the cake is next and after that, we can make our excuses."

Griffin tamped down the urge to grumble and reached for his glass instead. "They do say the best things in life are worth waiting for, so I suppose I can manage another hour of this." Rising, he held his glass high in the air. "A toast, to Emily, the kindest, bravest, and most incredible woman I have ever known." He dropped his gaze to hers and smiled in response to the pure adoration he saw in her eyes. "You are the sun that brightens my world, the light that guides me, and the steady certainty that soothes my tumultuous spirit. I would be lost without you, Emily, and I am both blessed and honored to be your husband."

Her eyes shimmered and her smile trembled just enough to inform him that his words affected her deeply.

Rising, she raised one hand to his cheek as if needing to make sure that this was real. "I love you so much, my heart can scarcely contain it," she whispered.

And as she rose up onto her toes to kiss him, their families and friends clapped and shouted encouragement. There was even a whistle, which Griffin was sure had come from Caleb. It infused the mood with a celebratory lightness that caused Griffin to laugh against Emily's mouth as he kissed her.

"Hurrah for the newlyweds," Bethany's tiny voice shouted through the noise.

Emily turned her face in the girl's direction, allowing Griffin to kiss her on the cheek this time while three loud hurrahs followed.

In that moment, Griffin had no regrets over the number of dishes he had to consume or how long it would take. Being here, surrounded by love and seeing the joy on his mother's face when he glanced her way, made it all worthwhile. Because this was as much for her and Mrs. Howard as it was for him and Emily.

Even so, he was glad to leave when it was time to do so. He could scarcely wait to have Emily all to himself and to truly make her his.

As if sensing the direction his thoughts had taken, Caleb caught him by the elbow as they headed toward the foyer and quietly said in a mischievous tone, "If you need any pointers, I'm happy to offer advice."

Griffin coughed. He glanced at Emily, who was busy chatting with Mary and Cassandra, just to make sure she hadn't overheard. "I'm glad to know you've figured out the mechanics of things after all these years, Caleb, but I do believe I can manage."

Caleb barked with laughter, causing the women to look in their direction. "You truly are a rogue, brother."

"I love you too," Griffin said with a smirk before moving closer to where his wife stood. He waited for Mary to finish speaking before asking Emily, "Are you ready to go?"

Emily shifted her body so she leaned into his. "Yes," she said, the soft sensuality of her voice flooding his veins with liquid heat.

Trying not to look too eager by picking her up and running outside to the waiting carriage, Griffin took the appropriate time to bid his brother, Mary, and Cassandra farewell. He then linked his arm with Emily's and led her toward the door. He'd almost managed to step through it when his progress was halted by the sound of Laura's voice calling to her sister.

With a sigh, Griffin braced himself for another delay and released Emily so she could turn back.

"I just wanted to wish you well one more time," Laura said in a rush. She wrapped her arms around her sister in a tight embrace before letting go.

"It will be your turn to walk down the aisle next," Emily said.

"And all because of you." Emotion caught hold of Laura's voice and caused it to crack. "Thank you." Her smile wobbled a little before managing to regain its balance. She looked at Griffin. "Promise me you'll take good care of her."

"Of course." He took a step forward and dropped a kiss on his sister-in-law's cheek. "I will do everything I can to make her happy."

Laura nodded and stepped away, allowing Griffin to finally escort Emily down the front steps of Camberly House. They would spend the next week at Mivart's Hotel, after which they'd return to his brother's home until they purchased a house of their own.

A surge of excitement raced through Emily's body as Griffin handed her up into the carriage, for as lovely as the wedding had been, she looked forward to what came next. He slid in beside her a second later, and then the door closed with a click, blocking out everything else but *him*, the man she'd married. A sudden shyness assailed her now that they were completely alone. Hoping to quash it by busying herself with something, she leaned past Griffin and waved to her friends and family until the carriage rolled forward and they vanished from sight.

Before Emily could lean back against the squabs, Griffin looped one arm around her and pulled her against his side. She tipped her head back and gazed up into his gorgeous brown eyes.

"Happy?" he asked with an adorable hint of uncertainty.

"Extraordinarily so," she whispered, earning herself a slow kiss so perfect and precious it made her toes curl.

"I plan on making you even happier once we reach the hotel," he whispered against her ear, the brush of his breath causing frissons to sweep down her spine. "Happier than you've ever been before in your life."

Her breath caught in response to his low husky tone and the wicked suggestiveness of his words. "I can hardly wait."

"Me neither." His teeth scraped her skin and she helplessly arched toward him. A chuckle rose from his throat and vibrated through her. "You and I are about to have a very long night, Emily." He sat back, eyes darker than before and filled with the sort of intensity that threatened to make her catch fire. Raising her hand to his lips, he placed a tender kiss upon her knuckles, then pulled her close once more and simply held her until they reached their destination.

By the time they arrived in the bedchamber where they would be staying, Emily's anticipation was such that she could scarcely stand still. So she paced around the space, studying everything from the en suite dressing room complete with a tin bathing tub, to the view of the street from the window. Hands trembling, she began removing her gloves, then turned and sucked in a breath when she saw Griffin leaning against the closed door. He was watching her closely, with the sort of predatory interest that made her pulse flutter rapidly.

The edge of his lips drew upward into a knowing smile, as if perfectly aware of how viscerally he affected her. Pushing away from the door, he crossed to a small table where a pair of glasses and a bottle of something she believed might be champagne stood waiting.

"You seem nervous," he said while filling one glass with the bubbly liquid.

Emily's heart raced faster. More so when he locked his eyes on hers and began walking toward her. Tall, handsome, and incredibly elegant for a man his size, Emily could only stare since she'd apparently lost her ability to speak.

"This will help." He held the glass to her lips and tipped it slightly so she could drink.

A burst of fruitiness fizzed on her tongue and flowed down her throat like sparkles falling from the stars. Griffin eased the glass away from her lips and took a sip too while holding her gaze. He then set the glass aside and lowered his mouth to hers in a deep, impassioned kiss that allowed her to taste him.

Every nerve in her body relaxed in response to his skillful distraction. She forgot to worry about what he expected from her or how he'd react when he saw her undressed or if she would make a mistake that he wouldn't approve of. Instead, she allowed sensation to sweep her away and let instinct guide her. So she didn't even notice that he'd unbuttoned her gown until it slipped from her shoulders and by then she did not care. By then she just wanted more – more kissing, more touching, more Griffin.

"So pretty," he murmured against the edge of her stays while running a finger across the embroidery. "You're like a present for me to unwrap." He went to work on the laces until he was able to free her from the restraining garment. His breaths deepened as he stepped back enough to admire his work. "The most tempting present I've ever seen."

The gleam of desire in his eyes made Emily's mouth go dry. So she swallowed and licked her lips, prompting him to release a low growl that produced a thrill in the pit of her belly.

"I need to see you," he murmured. "Take off your chemise."

The command in his voice added heat to the already burning fire inside her. She drew a shuddering breath and slowly pulled the delicate fabric up and over her head, leaving her utterly bare for his perusal, save for the stockings, garters, and shoes she still wore.

He stared at her as if she were an angel descended from heaven. "Christ, Emily." His gaze slid over her body, from her face to the tips of her toes and back up again. Contrary to what she'd expected, she didn't feel shy or inadequate, but rather empowered. Especially when she caught the look of pleasure in his eyes. "You're even more stunning than I imagined."

"You make me feel beautiful," she told him sincerely. Because it was true. Standing before him right now, she felt like a goddess about to be worshiped.

He reached for her, dragged her against him and

grasped her firmly so he could kiss her again. The abrasion of his clothes against her skin, the juxtaposition of him still dressed while she wore almost nothing at all, made her want in a way she'd never wanted before. And she knew that he wanted too, for she could feel him pressing against her with greater insistence the more they kissed.

Without warning, he lifted her off her feet and carried her to the bed. Swallowing her gasp of surprise, he laid her down carefully, then straightened himself. His hair was ruffled from where her fingers had disturbed it, adding an untamed look to his appearance that only made her crave him more.

Panting slightly as if he'd just run up a long flight of stairs, he began untying his cravat. Emily stared, enthralled by his every movement, by the veins pulsing slightly in his neck when he drew the long piece of fabric away, by the smoothness of his shoulders and abdomen once his waistcoat and shirt had been tossed aside, and by the dusting of hair on his legs when he'd finishing shucking his trousers, smalls, and hose.

Mostly, however, she was captivated by the part of him that made him so different from her. Though she realized she probably ought to, she simply couldn't look away. "That is…" She wasn't sure what to say or if saying anything would even be proper but—

"What?" he asked with a note of curiosity. When she didn't reply immediately, he lowered himself to the bed and proceeded to kiss his way up her leg. "Don't stop being honest and bold with me now, Emily. I want to know your thoughts."

He licked her and she responded with a groan. "I also want to know what you like. So..." He lifted his head so he could look her in the eye. "I believe you were going to tell me something about my manhood. That it is..."

"Bigger than I expected." She knit her brow in thought and then added, "Very impressive and rather daunting, to be perfectly frank."

He grinned and pressed a kiss to her hip. "You cannot imagine how pleased I am to hear you say that." He slid between her thighs and settled more firmly against her. "We're going to fit together perfectly, you and I."

"You're sure?" Now that the moment of truth was upon her, she was starting to live in her head again rather than in the moment.

"There may be a little discomfort at first, but after that, it will be like it was in the carriage." Heat rose to the surface once more as she thought back on that incredible experience. "Except this time, we'll leap off the cliff together."

The love she saw in his eyes allowed her to relax, as did the kisses and caresses that followed. So by the time Griffin joined his body with hers, she hardly noticed the brief discomfort it caused. Especially since her husband was quite determined to distract her from it in every way possible. And just as he'd promised, they flew toward the horizon together, until they collapsed side by side with exhaustion.

"I love you, Lady Griffin," Griffin told her after rolling to his side and pulling her against him.

"And I love you, my lord."

He kissed the side of her neck. "How do you

feel?"

"Like I've just had the best experience of my life," she said with a sigh as his hand trailed over her waist.

"I see." He sounded immensely satisfied. "So then I take it you may want to do it again sometime?"

Turning more fully toward him, she moved her mouth closer to his. "Most assuredly," she whispered, upon which she kissed him, conveying without words, the love and devotion that was in her heart.

EPILOGUE

THE TEMPERATURE WAS FINALLY RISING and with the sun shining today from a clear blue sky, it was possible to enjoy the outdoors as long as one was properly dressed. Making her way along a flagstone path lined by bright yellow daffodils, Emily carried a tea tray toward the garden table where Griffin sat. Bird song filled the air and a breeze stirred a nearby birch, rustling its leaves.

Griffin raised his gaze when he heard her approach and smiled as he always did whenever he saw her. His hair might be grey now instead of brown, there might be more creases around his eyes, and his scar might be more pronounced than it had once been, but to Emily, he was still the handsomest man she had ever known. During their marriage, he'd given her the three children she'd dreamed of having. Two sons (Finnegan and Douglas), and a daughter named Lara.

"Is that what I think it is?" he asked as he cleared a spot for her on the table. He'd been working on a mechanical butterfly for Lara's daughter, Rose. It was to be a gift for her tenth birthday, and Griffin was determined to finish it on time, even though the precision required was more challenging now on account of his trembling fingers.

Emily set down the tray. "Scones. Just as you like them."

He helped her arrange the plates and teacups. "You spoil me more than I deserve."

"Not nearly enough," she argued with a deliberate smirk.

Grinning, he patted his lap. "Come sit with me, Lady Griffin."

She accepted his invitation with a chuckle. Her figure was plumper now than it had been when they'd met, but that hadn't changed anything. The love she saw in Griffin's eyes had only deepened over the years. And although there had been moments where doubt had gripped him, where she'd had to remind him that nothing would ever tempt her to leave him, their life together had been filled with joy and happiness.

Emily leaned her head against his shoulder and sighed with contentment. Close to her feet lay Rupert, the fourth cocker spaniel Griffin had given her. She closed her eyes and breathed in the man who meant everything to her and savored the scent of sandalwood clinging to his clothes.

"We ought to respond to Douglas and Lillian," Griffin murmured against her forehead. His breath was warm on her skin and a comfort to her soul.

"Then you have made a decision?" At only sixteen, Douglas had travelled to Vienna with the intention of becoming Edvard's apprentice. Griffin had told him that there was no need to go all that way – that he could learn everything he needed to know by working at the London branch, Crawford and Sons, where Finnegan had been employed. But Douglas had been determined to make his own way, and in the end he'd fallen in love with Vienna and with Christoph's daughter Lillian, so he'd chosen to stay. It was already twenty-three years since they'd had their first child – a son named Jack, whose wife was now expecting.

"If we leave England on May first, we'll be able to celebrate Rose's birthday and Finnegan's wedding anniversary." Finnegan had married a glass manufacturer's daughter and had consequently accepted that he would be snubbed by the *ton* thereafter. But Finnegan hadn't cared, and Emily could not have been prouder of her son's decision. "The weather in Vienna is also excellent that time of year."

Emily's heart swelled with happiness. "They'll be thrilled to know we'll be there in time for their grandchild's birth."

"And you, my lady?"

Leaning back so she could look her husband in the eye, Emily smiled at him and said, "I am thrilled as well."

The edge of his mouth lifted with a hint of mischief. "That is all I need to know." Closing the distance between them, he kissed her with as much certainty, passion, and love as he had done for the last forty-five years, reminding Emily of the beautiful life they had built together and the wonderful memories they were fortunate to have shared. And as his arms tightened around her, keeping her safe, she looked forward to every second that remained of this happy ever after with Griffin by her side.

Thank you so much for reading
MORE THAN A ROGUE.

If you enjoyed this story and would like to know more about the first book in the series, you can do so by reading *NO ORDINARY DUKE*! This story features broken-hearted Mary who hates the aristocracy and Caleb, who wants nothing more than to escape his newly acquired title. Disguised as a laborer, he falls for Mary, but will she still want him when she learns the truth about his identity?

Or if you're looking for a longer read with a rags to riches trope, you might consider trying my Diamonds In The Rough series, starting with *A MOST UNLIKELY DUKE.*

You can find out more about my new releases, backlist deals and giveaways by signing up for my newsletter here: *www.sophiebarnes.com*

Once again, I thank you for your interest in my books. Please take a moment to leave a review since this can help other readers discover my books.

And please continue reading for an excerpt from *NO ORDINARY DUKE.*

NO ORDINARY DUKE

CHAPTER ONE

RAIN STREAKED DOWN THE CARRIAGE windows while Caleb Maxwell Crawford traveled from the London docks to his family home on Grosvenor Square. Dusk had turned to night since he'd stepped off the ship on which he'd sailed from Calais yesterday afternoon. Jaw set, he tightened his grip on the leather satchel beside him on the bench. It held all the evidence he needed to prove how wrong his father had been when they'd parted ways ten years earlier. Filled with letters of praise and articles heralding Caleb's architectural abilities, it would show the old bastard he'd made a success of himself. It would prove that refusing to join the clergy and being cut off financially had not led to his downfall, as his father had claimed it would when he'd railed about Caleb's ungratefulness.

Peering out past the heavy rivulets of cascading water, Caleb narrowed his gaze on the murky darkness. He couldn't wait to gloat and see the astonished look on his father's face when he showed him the lithographs printed in the Paris Gazette. They illustrated in fine detail the mansion he'd designed for the Duke of Orléons.

Building had commenced six years earlier and had just been completed last month. Inhaling deeply, Caleb tightened his hold on his satchel. The carriage drew to a jarring halt moments later, throwing him slightly off balance. Muttering a curse, he opened the door and climbed out into the unpleasant downpour, satchel in hand. The driver helped him retrieve his valise from the boot.

"Here you go sir," the man said while water streamed over the brim of his hat.

"Thank you." Caleb paid him and walked toward the imposing Mayfair mansion that loomed before him. The heavy front door with its massive brass knocker was less than inviting.

Rain gushed down the curved slope of the roof and pelted against the ground. Pulling his hat down over his forehead, Caleb drew the collar of his greatcoat up to protect the back of his neck and climbed the slick stone steps.

He still owned a key and withdrew it now from his pocket to unlock the door. It swung open and gave way to a dim interior. Entering the foyer, Caleb paused to listen. All was silent. Not even the longcase clock ticked away the progression of time.

Shivering, Caleb nudged the door shut behind him. It closed with a resounding thud. Where the devil was everyone?

He sighed and muttered another oath. He didn't like the idea of having to hunt down his family at one of the country estates. But even if they'd left town, there ought to be servants about. His parents had never left a house completely empty.

A soft snick caught his ears, and then the sharp click of approaching footsteps filled the air. The sound accompanied a man whom Caleb instantly recognized, even though his features were far more drawn now than when he'd last seen him.

"Murdoch," he said, addressing the butler. "It has been a while."

The old man drew a sharp breath. The candelabra he carried displaced the darkness. "I thought I heard something, so I came to investigate." Moving closer, he peered up at Caleb. Light from four guttering candles flickered across his face, accentuating the creases there. "Is it really you, my lord?"

Caleb drew his hat from his head and swiped back the wet strands of hair that clung to his forehead. "Yes. I have returned." He set his valise and satchel on the floor and proceeded to take off his gloves. "Where are my parents?"

Murdoch stared at him as if he could still not believe he was actually there. "Your mother is upstairs in her rooms." Breaking eye contact, he proceeded to help Caleb off with his coat.

"And my father, the duke?" When Murdoch failed to reply, Caleb knit his brow. "Is he not at home?"

"No, he is not." The butler busied himself with hanging the coat and setting Caleb's hat and gloves aside. "But your mother will be pleased to see you, I'm sure. Please, follow me." He led the way up the stairs while Caleb followed behind, his curiosity piqued by the servant's unwillingness to supply him with details. Perhaps his parents had quarreled during his absence and were now living apart?

They reached the top of the landing and turned left toward the duchess's apartment. Caleb knew the way well enough, but was glad the butler would be there to announce his arrival. After all, he doubted his mother would be as pleased to see him as Murdoch believed, considering he'd left without saying farewell. But he'd been too angry to do so at the time, and his decision to leave had been made in haste without consideration for anything besides getting away.

Arriving in front of the door leading into his mother's sitting room, Murdoch paused to knock. A maid answered seconds later, her eyes widening when she noticed Caleb.

"Please inform Her Grace that her son, Lord Caleb, is here to see her," Murdoch said.

The maid nodded and the door closed, only to be opened again moments later by the duchess herself. "Thank God you are here!" She stared up at him with shimmering eyes, and then, in the next second, her arms were around him, and she was holding him to her as if he offered necessary support.

Unaccustomed to such a display of affection from his mother, Caleb hesitated briefly before wrapping his arms around her as well. He hadn't expected such a warm welcome and was slightly thrown by the effect it was having on the resentment he'd harbored for the past ten years.

Placing a kiss on his mother's cheek, he listened to her uneasy breaths until she was ready for him to release her.

"Shall I have some tea sent up?" Murdoch asked,

reminding Caleb of his presence.

"Please do," his mother said. She opened the door to her sitting room wider and invited Caleb in. Unlike his mother, whose youth had departed during his absence, the space looked unchanged. "Come sit with me, Caleb. There is much for us to discuss."

He wasn't even sure where to begin. This reunion wasn't going at all the way he'd imagined it would. Since leaving Paris five days earlier, he'd pictured himself storming into his father's study and shoving the evidence of his success under the man's haughty nose. Now, inhaling deeply, he approached the sofa and lowered himself to the vacant spot beside his mother. There was so much to say. Too much, in a way.

Perhaps the best place to start was with an apology. "I am sorry," he told her and reached for her hand. "I should have written to you, but the more time passed, the more difficult it became."

"I know."

He looked at her and was swiftly accosted by guilt at the sight of her watery eyes. Christ, he'd been awful to her. She hadn't deserved it, but his pride had been wounded, and he'd only been able to think of himself and of getting away from the life he'd come to despise.

"At least I am not your only son," he murmured. She had three besides his older brother, George, the heir who'd received all their father's affection.

"You haven't been in touch with Griffin or Devlin?" she asked in reference to the brothers who'd been born only minutes after himself. He shook his head. "They left shortly after you, for similar reasons, I suspect. Now, after everything that has happened, I am hoping they will return as well. I've sent out letters, but it will take time for them to reach your brothers." She met his gaze. Her brow puckered ever so slightly. "I'm surprised you are already here since I had no idea of your actual location. I suppose the agent I hired to find you was good at doing his job."

Unease traversed Caleb's spine. He tightened his hold on his mother's hand. "No one came to find me, Mama. I returned of my own accord."

"But then..." She swallowed and closed her eyes. Her lips trembled and it became suddenly clear to Caleb that she was making a stoic effort to maintain her composure. "You do not know." The words were only a whisper.

"Know what?" he asked even though he sensed he had no wish to hear whatever it was she would say in response.

"Your father is dead, Caleb. A fire broke out at the Everly stables last week," she said, referring to one of the dukedom's larger properties. "He and George went to inspect some repairs. They were supposed to be gone only for a few short days but now..." A sob cut off her words, and her free hand rose to smother the sound.

Caleb's heart thudded against his chest. "And George?" he asked, already dreading her answer.

"When your father didn't come out, George went in after him." Tears streamed down her cheeks. "They're both gone, Caleb. I buried them at St. George's this morning."

It was as if time slowed to a halt. A distinct feeling of disappointment and deep regret trickled through him, numbing his veins. Slumping back, he tried to make sense of it, to accept what his mother told him as fact, only to find that he couldn't.

The door opened after a quick knock, and Murdoch returned carrying a tray. He placed it on the table, exchanged a few words with the duchess, and departed once more. Caleb's mother withdrew her hand from Caleb's and dabbed at her eyes. She then busied herself with pouring tea while he watched with a strange sense of detachment.

He shook his head. "No. It cannot be true."

She sniffed and took a sip of her tea. "You know what this means," she said, as if he'd not spoken. She waited for him to meet her gaze before saying, "You are the Duke of Camberly now."

Caleb stared at her in dismay. "I don't want to be." It was the first thing that came to mind. He liked his uncomplicated life, free from all the responsibilities his father and older brother had faced. He'd never envied either of them. But he had cursed the way his father's sense of duty and obligation had affected his life.

"Unfortunately, that hardly matters. With your father and brother gone, the title falls to you."

He instinctively shuddered and bit back the comment that threatened. To say that he ought to have stayed away would only cause his mother pain. She was happy to have him home and probably quite relieved with the prospect of him taking over the day-to-day running of things. And for her he would do it, or at least he would try.

He drew a deep breath and felt his chest tighten.

"Very well. But if I am going to do this, I will need something stronger than tea. Please tell me you still keep a bottle of sherry in that cabinet over there."

Her wobbly smile tilted as if trying to find its balance. "Yes. I dare say I could do with a glass myself."

Raising her hand to his lips, Caleb pressed a tender kiss to her knuckles before going in search of their fortification. He was conscious of his heart beating a dull tattoo, like a drummer marching him off to the gallows. Recalling the satchel he'd left downstairs, he closed his eyes briefly and muttered a curse. Everything he'd worked for these past ten years had been for nothing. His father would never know of his success. How ironic that the son he'd named his greatest disappointment would now be continuing his legacy.

As had become his habit in recent weeks, Caleb arrived at White's shortly after nine in the evening to enjoy a drink and possibly a game of cards with his friend, Robert Moor, Viscount Aldridge. The two had known each other since childhood and had been sent off to Eton together as lads. The moment Caleb's return to London had been announced six months ago, Robert had immediately come to call, and the two had spent an hour washing away the years wedged between them with a few glasses of brandy.

Since then, Robert had offered invaluable advice and support. He'd invited Caleb out for rides and to Gentleman Jackson's boxing saloon whenever he'd needed to lose himself in something besides accounts, ledgers, investments, and his mother's most recent obsession – his need to think about marriage.

He'd cut her off and walked away the first time she'd made the suggestion and every time since. But when the Season had been well underway and she'd produced a list of potential candidates she considered appropriate for courtship, he'd had no choice but to listen, even though he detested the extra pressure it placed on his shoulders.

"You look more somber than usual," Robert said when Caleb found him. "Trouble with the dukedom?"

Dropping into a vacant chair, Caleb frowned at his friend, who poured a large drink and handed it to him. Caleb took a long sip, enjoying the powerful flavor and the heat it exuded as it slid down his throat. "I cannot stand it any longer." Leaning back, he cradled the glass between his hands and stared at his friend as if he had the power to save him. "It is awful, Robert. I just..." He sighed and scrubbed one hand across his jaw. "I hate being a duke."

Robert had the decency not to argue. Instead, he watched, his eyes increasingly somber until he finally said, "Then don't be."

Startled by the comment, Caleb grinned, the expression so foreign to him now it actually hurt his jaw. "As if it's that simple, but you know as well as I that it is not."

His friend inclined his head, paused for a moment as if on the verge of divulging some piece of information, but then set his own glass to his lips and drank. "Is it not getting any easier?"

Caleb thought back on the endless hours of work that held him hostage in his study. There had been little reprieve and no time at all to consider his own wants and needs since his return. Even now, the satchel holding his architectural designs remained unopened. He'd had no opportunity to share them with anyone or to dream up new ones.

"No," he told Robert with unwavering honesty. "If anything, it is getting worse. The demands on me are increasing with each passing day. Women I've never met are showing up at my home, intent on praising their daughters' charms. Meanwhile, every business in Town is paying me court, and every hostess wishes to make me her guest of honor. And that's not considering repairs I am asked to fund and approve at my various estates and the tenants who all have concerns they've decided to air in a steady stream of letters I receive daily."

Robert's lips twitched as if struggling to contain his laughter. He cleared his throat. "I see."

"Do you really?" Caleb wasn't certain. "You were groomed for this sort of life from the day you were born, while I was largely ignored until I was dropped in the middle of it."

"I also have the added benefit of being happily married to a woman who helps me endure the burden of the responsibility I carry." Robert considered Caleb for a long moment before saying, "Maybe your mother has the right of it. Perhaps marriage is precisely what you need."

Caleb groaned. "Don't be daft. The last thing I

need at the moment is another female to coddle." He winced, aware he'd just referred to his mother in rather disparaging terms, but the truth of it was that as much as he loved her, her constant weeping and insistence he fill a mold he didn't quite fit had driven him to the point of madness.

"Then what do you need?" Robert stared him straight in the eye. "Do you even know?"

It took a moment for Caleb to turn the question over in his head and find the right answer. "Yes," he finally said. "I believe getting away for a while would help."

Robert studied him with increased interest. "Where would you go?"

Caleb snorted. "I have no idea. If I head to one of my country estates, all the problems I'm trying to escape will surely follow."

"So you want to go somewhere where you won't be bothered."

"Just long enough for me to find my bearings again." Because he could not believe this was all there would be to his life— now until he drew his last breath. There had to be more to it than sitting in a study, going over numbers. Somehow, he had to rediscover himself, recover from the shock of losing his father and brother, and find the means to stay true to himself while being a duke.

"Is your secretary capable of running things without you during this absence?"

"I believe so," Caleb said with conviction. The man had worked with his father for the past two decades. He knew everything he needed to know to handle things efficiently, which made Caleb warm to the idea of taking a break. Perhaps it would be more possible than he'd dared to believe.

"In that case, I have a proposal I'd like for you to consider." A smirk made Robert's mouth tilt with a hint of mischief. "I have a modest property in Cornwall. Clearview is its name. It's a decent place, but the money I've sent for repairs has, as I understand it, been spent on other things."

Caleb frowned. "If you think your servants are stealing from you, it might be prudent to go and investigate the matter."

"And so I would if I had the time, but with Vivien's pregnancy, I am reluctant to leave her side at the moment, so I thought perhaps…"

Understanding dawned. "You want me to go in your stead?"

Leaning forward, Robert rested his elbows on his knees and pierced Caleb with a direct stare. "I believe a man like you who enjoys working with his hands might take pleasure in seeing to some of the repairs himself."

"You could be right," Caleb said. The prospect of mending a leaking roof or a crumbling wall held a lot of appeal. "I can also hire new servants for you, if you think that might be helpful."

A flicker of amusement brightened Robert's eyes. "There are no servants there, Caleb. Just my sister, her friends, and the orphaned children they offer sanctuary to."

Caleb blinked. "Your sister?" Robert had several, some younger, some older.

"Cassandra, to be exact. She's five years younger than us, so you might not recall her. She debuted after you left England." His expression cooled a fraction as he added, "She made the scandalous choice of bedding her fiancée before they were married. Poor devil died on his way to the church, struck down by an oncoming carriage."

"Jesus!"

Robert nodded. "Cassandra sought my help shortly after. Apparently, that one indiscretion had gotten her pregnant. When she refused to pass her child off as another's, which was what our parents advised, they threatened to turn her out of the house. So I secretly bought a place for her to live. When two other girls encountered similar hardships, Cassandra invited them to come with her. During the last five years, they have taken in several children, who cost more to keep than they can afford with the measly donations they receive from friends and family."

"In other words," Caleb said slowly, "these three spinsters are mismanaging funds in an effort to run a make-shift orphanage?"

"More or less," Robert said with a shrug.

"And you have allowed this to continue for five years?" Caleb could scarcely believe it. It wasn't that he didn't approve of the kindness these women were showing toward the less fortunate, but if they let the house fall into complete dis-repair, the day would come when they wouldn't even have that. And then what?

"She's my sister," Robert said. "I have tried to help her as much as I can while keeping her scan-dalous circumstances at bay. She and her friends have been hidden away and mostly forgotten, but they are constantly in need of assistance, and I simply don't have the time or the resources to keep ensuring they're well looked after. I have my own family to consider, estates to tend to as well as investments and parliamentary responsibilities. You know how it is."

Wasn't that the truth of it? Caleb flattened his mouth and considered his choices: stay in London, tied to a desk and with endless demands placed before him, or ride off to Cornwall for a breath of fresh air and the physical activity awaiting him there.

He knew which he preferred, but there was still one problem. "It would be unseemly for me to live in a house with three unmarried women."

"Spinsters, Caleb, not debutantes. Makes all the difference, you know. But I actually agree, which is why I suggest you stay in the caretaker's cottage."

"There's a caretaker's cottage?" How big was this place?

"It's nothing to get excited over since it's only one room, but if you want to stop being a duke for a while and pretend you're a..." he waved his hand between them before settling on, "laborer instead, then you're welcome to it."

Uncertainty settled between Caleb's shoulder blades. "How come no one's living in this cottage right now?"

"Because the caretaker I hired to keep things in order had a massive row with my sister's friend, Mary Clemens."

"About?"

Robert sighed. "Using the funds I sent for repairing the roof."

Caleb gaped at his friend. "So this...Miss Clemens, is the real problem I take it?"

"She's part of it," Robert agreed. "She's certainly not afraid of speaking her mind. This is the third caretaker she's frightened off in just over a year."

Raising an eyebrow, Caleb stared at his friend. He was no longer entirely sure he was up to the sort of change he offered. "I will have to think about it." Long and hard and then a few times more to be absolutely certain.

But when he arrived home and found three Society matrons waiting for him with their very eligible daughters, Caleb quickly retreated to his study. He spent the next three hours discussing matters with his secretary and ensuring that the man was indeed capable and willing to handle all his affairs if Caleb chose to remove himself to the countryside for a while.

That settled, he went in search of his mother, who was not the least bit pleased with his decision. He understood her of course and promised he'd soon return, assuring her that when he did, he'd be ready to focus on finding a wife.

Grab your copy of
A MOST UNLIKELY DUKE
today and continue reading!

ACKNOWLEDGMENTS

I would like to thank the Killion Group for their incredible help with the editing and formatting of this book. My thanks also go to Chris Cocozza for providing the stunning artwork. And to my friends and family, thank you for your constant support. I would be lost without you!

ABOUT THE AUTHOR

Born in Denmark, Sophie has spent her youth traveling with her parents to wonderful places around the world. She's lived in five different countries, on three different continents, has studied design in Paris and New York, and has a bachelor's degree from Parson's School of design. But most impressive of all – she's been married to the same man three times, in three different countries and in three different dresses.

While living in Africa, Sophie turned to her lifelong passion – writing. When she's not busy, dreaming up her next romance novel, Sophie enjoys spending time with her family, swimming, cooking, gardening, watching romantic comedies and, of course, reading. She currently lives on the East Coast.

You can contact her through her website at
www.sophiebarnes.com

And Please consider leaving
a review for this book.
Every review is greatly appreciated!

Made in the USA
Coppell, TX
30 December 2019